Chloe Seager gr... ....st London with her Mum and much-loved cat, Katie. She studied English Literature and Drama at the University of East Anglia, where she sadly realised she couldn't act, but did rediscover her love of children's books.

lren's Literature was one of her favourite modules, and it e her wonder why grown-ups ever stopped reading them. now works with YA and kids' books full-time. Chloe lives in East London with her boyfriend and pet fish.

Friendship Fails of Emma Nash

Chloe Seager

ONE PLACE. MANY STORIES

HQ
An imprint of HarperCollins*Publishers* Ltd
1 London Bridge Street
London SE1 9GF

This paperback edition 2018

1
First published in Great Britain by
HQ, an imprint of HarperCollins*Publishers* Ltd 2018

Chloe Seager asserts the moral right to be
identified as the author of this work.
A catalogue record for this book is
available from the British Library.

ISBN: 978-0-00822-117-1

MIX
Paper from
responsible sources
FSC™ C007454

This book is produced from independently certified FSC™ paper
to ensure responsible forest management.

For more information visit: www.harpercollins.co.uk/green

Printed and bound in Great Britain by
CPI Group, Croydon CR0 4YY

Monday, 3 November

posted by EditingEmma 15.00

Not to be dramatic, but Everything's. Going. WRONG.

These were supposed to be the 'best holidays ever'. And yet...
I'm bored.

I'm so bored, I'm boring myself by talking about being bored.
Even my own blog is bored of me. I can hear it sighing as I type.

I wish I had something more interesting to write about, but
what do you do when your best friend (Steph) is off making her
new and exciting relationship official, and your other best friend
(Faith) is sunning herself in Madeira? I've run out of clothes
to design, too. I cannot possibly make any more clothes!! I've
designed ALL THE CLOTHES.

posted by EditingEmma 15.19

'Andrew Morton is in a relationship with Stephanie Brent'.
11 mins

They did it, then. Huh. It's funny... I knew it was coming,
but somehow it's still a bit strange seeing it. I sort of feel like
my name should be up there.

posted by EditingEmma 15.32
'Andrew Morton is in a relationship with Stephanie Brent and Emma Nash'.
24 mins

That's better.
Steph messaged me:

Hahah! How did you do that?! Sx 15.29
Logged on and changed your name to 'Brent and Emma
Nash'. 15.29
Very good. 15.30

Now I'm bored again. Ughhhhh. I bet Steph and Andy are making out right now. I bet Faith is lying on the beach getting an amazing tan. This was supposed to be *my* new and shiny life!!! Where's my new, super attractive lover? Where's my exotic holiday?!?! How can all my friends be off doing cool and interesting things, whilst I'm just sitting here twiddling my thumbs?!??

Still, I suppose it's an improvement on last term…

Welcome To My New Life
So, last term I was basically the most miserable, mopey human being on the planet after being ghosted by my ex-boyfriend Leon. I spent a lot of time moping on social media, THEN a lot of time trying to fill the Leon-shaped hole with other boys who just wouldn't fit using social media, which turned out to be the worst idea anyone's had since Garlic Coca-Cola.

BUT, as a result of all the drama that ensued, good things actually came out of it. I decided to stop stalking Leon (and his super-perfect girlfriend, Anna) and other boys and focus on myself, my interests and friends, and since doing that I have felt *so much* better about myself. It's official. For the first time in a long time, I feel like a real, passable human being and am actually excited about things other than a new update from Leon. I've quit Biology, which I only ever really took because Leon was taking it (probably one of the worst and most pathetic decisions I ever made in my life). I've designed enough new clothes to dress a fleet of penguins (I'm not actually suggesting dressing penguins, but you get my point) and I'm having so much fun with my new fashion blog... (Even if Steph does roll her eyes every time I spend more than five minutes hashtagging.)

In terms of my friendships, I've created an ingenious new chat group for me and my pals called 'Strengthening our Womanly Bonds'. It's where we can post pictures of ourselves doing everyday things to keep each other in the loop. The more mundane the better. These things may *seem* pointless and uninteresting, to the untrained eye, but actually over time will bring us closer together and give new and fresh perspectives on each other's lives... Like...before, I could always conceptualize Steph running a bath, or comb-straightening her hair, but now I actually get to *experience it with her*.

Faith actually left the group three times, but eventually I wore her down.

All in all, things are technically going OK, I suppose...

So why am I feeling so *miserable*?!

posted by EditingEmma 16.34

The Best Pal's New Loved One

Thought about ringing Steph but managed to resist. Sigh. This time last week, believe it or not, me, Steph and Andy were INSEPARABLE.

OK, maybe not inseparable... I mean, I tried. I really did. I thought, if my BFF is going to be with this guy then surely *we* must be BFFs as well, right?! I guess I assumed that because we both love Steph, and Steph loves us, there'd be some sort of chain there. Like, by proxy, that must mean that I'd love Andy and he'd love me. But it seems as if maybe that's *not* the case.

First, I organized this early Halloween celebration (on actual Halloween Mum made me go to a pumpkin-carving class to 'check out the fit pumpkin carver') so that we could start bonding ASAP. I dressed as Gandalf, because who wouldn't want to be friends with Gandalf?

I was mega excited. Hanging out with Steph and her *first proper boyfriend* was to be a monumental landmark in the history of our lives. I documented it throughout the evening in 'Strengthening our Womanly Bonds'. (This was actually the third time Faith attempted to leave the group; screenshot below.)

Faith Connelly

Why did you just send me a picture of your hallway? 18.31
And your street? 18.32
And your mum's car? 18.35

And Steph's street? 18.43
And Steph's hallway? 18.45
PLEASE LET ME LEAVE THIS GODDAMN GROUP. 18.46

But weirdly, me and Andy didn't slide as seamlessly into being BFFs as I thought we might... Here are some things I learned that evening, about hanging out with your best pal's new loved one:

1) Watching Them Bond With Your Friend's Family Will Feel A Bit Weird

I walked into the kitchen, where Andy was standing with Steph's sister Jess, putting different flavours of popcorn into bowls. They were laughing together about something, and for a moment I felt this weird rage... Almost as if I was being invaded. Like...hey...that's *my* Steph's sister, not *your* Steph's sister. What if the Brents like him better than me?!

It also felt kind of *mature*. Suddenly mine and Steph's lives were flashing before my eyes, and we were ancient old women knitting each other spotted nose warmers. It made me feel like running around the room waving my arms in the air...and also a little bit like mooning them.

Anyway, eventually they stopped their freakish bonding. I think they were distracted by my beard.

2) They Might Not Appreciate Your Costume Genius

In stereotypical boyish fashion, Andy had a plastic mask on top of his head and otherwise looked completely normal.

9

'Oh hey,' he said. 'Nice…beard.'

'Why thank you.'

'I thought you were into fashion?' he asked, genuinely.

3) They Might Not Appreciate Your Comedy Genius, Either

As I was trying to get to the bathroom, Andy was standing blocking the door. We did that awkward little bobbing-from-side-to-side thing trying to get past each other, until eventually I said, 'You shall not pass!'

He smiled, but it didn't really reach his eyes.

The evening wasn't terrible or anything, but I guess we just didn't totally…integrate? A lot of the time it was just me and Steph laughing together, like how we normally hang out, but, er… With someone else in the room.

I spoke to Mum about it, and she said it sounded as if Andy might feel like a bit of a third wheel, because me and Steph are…well, me and Steph. So then I thought, all right, obviously I need to try *even harder* to make this work. The next day I ditched the Gandalf outfit as, clearly, he's not for everyone. I organized bowling, shopping, a trip to the zoo… Hell, I even suggested horseback riding. I photobombed all their selfies. I made little matching bracelets. I bought t-shirts that said 'The Three Musketeers!' on them…

… But alas, when I accidentally bowled in the wrong alley-way, knocking down some kid's pins (who then started crying), Steph creased up, but Andy seemed a little embarrassed. Steph wore her bracelet with pride, but Andy covered his with his sleeve. When they discovered me lurking in the background of at least 75 per cent of their pictures, Steph rolled around on the floor with laughter screaming, 'It looks like you're about to KILL us!!', but Andy seemed somewhat puzzled and afraid.

Though our special t-shirts proclaimed a deep and meaningful camaraderie, it seemed as if neither of us were really feeling it.

Evidence: Making friends with your friend's partner isn't as easy as you might think.

I don't want this to sound as if I don't like him or anything. I do. He's perfectly nice. But I just don't want to spend all my time with him, and he definitely doesn't want to spend all his time with me.

Eventually, Mum suggested that whilst 'focusing on my friendships' was a noble effort, perhaps it doesn't always mean being together every waking moment, perhaps it sometimes means giving them some space. And whilst getting to know your best friend's boyfriend is a necessary and worthwhile thing to do, perhaps we both needed some alone time with Steph too. I had to agree that this three-way relationship wasn't working out, and we've since split Steph 50/50…which is totally fair.

I know now that Mum was right. Really, it was ridiculous that I thought we were going to be able to spend as much time together as we did before. Obviously they need alone time and given we spent a hundred per cent of our free time together, something was logistically just going to have to change (because despite what Mr Crispin said in my latest report, I *can* do basic maths).

The only thing is, when you're used to spending all of your free time with someone and then you get left with half of it, no matter how fair it is…you are still left with a giant, gaping hole to fill, and a general sense of loss, misplacement and confusion.

I'm so lonely.

posted by EditingEmma 16.20
I never thought it would come to this, but…I'm even, dare I say it, a *little bit* tired of masturbating.

Hum diddly dum.

posted by EditingEmma 17.54
Yes! Found a brilliant distraction from my pathetic wretchedness. I was just walking past Mum's laptop, completely innocently, on my way to get a banana from the kitchen and…it was open on a dating website. I couldn't resist taking a look. (If she *really* wants me to 'respect her privacy', she's going to have to at least close her tabs. I mean, come on.) It's clearly a new site she's joined as she hadn't answered any of the questions. I decided to help her out:

How do you feel about meeting someone new?
- **I'm ready for a new relationship**
  Too keen. Also she's blatantly still hung up on her stripper ex-boyfriend Olly.

- **I'm not looking for a relationship**
  Then why would you be on here? Go on Adult Friend Finder.
- **I'd rather not say**
  That's very cagey.
- **Let's see what happens**
  I've gone with this because it is the only response that is halfway normal.

Relationship status:
- Never married
- Separated
- Divorced
- Widowed
- I'd rather not say

What is it with this 'I'd rather not say' business? If anyone is actually ticking the 'I'd rather not say' option under 'relationship status', they should really just make a box for 'married'. Because that's what it means, isn't it.

Children:
- Yes
- No
- I'd rather not say

Genius. I've clicked 'I'd rather not say'.

Personality type:
- **Adventurous**
- **Confident**
- **Easy-going**
- **Funny**
- **Generous**
- **Reserved**
- **Sensitive**
- **Sociable**
- **Spontaneous**
- **Other**

Hmm… I suppose I could put 'easy-going' just to be ironic.

Now picking out hobbies. 'Going to the doctor about various illnesses you don't have' isn't on here so that's pretty much half her life out. I checked salsa and t'ai chi. I was actually really proud writing about her business and her interior designing stuff, she's done so well to start her own company… And to raise a child ALONE at the same time… I should probably be nicer to her. Probably.

The thought crossed my mind, thank God I've got fashion designing, now, because 'internet stalking' and 'masturbating' apparently don't count as proper hobbies.

posted by EditingEmma 17.38
WE HAVE A MESSAGE. FROM 'JOHN247'.

It says: 'If beauty were a time, you'd be an eternity ;)'

To think, just thirty seconds ago I was so eager to read this message from this strange man. I feel dirty.

posted by EditingEmma 18.36

Mum stomped upstairs yelling, 'EMMA! EMMA!' as if I wouldn't hear her.

'WHY am I getting email notifications from strange men saying they'd be happy to give me a full body work-up? Or that I've clearly got a case of beautiful womanitis?'

'It's better your potential future partner knows about your hypochondria now, Mum.'

Then she launched into a lecture, 'You've got no respect for me, blah blah'. Rather ungrateful, if I do say so myself.

'I was just trying to help!!' I defended.

'I don't need your *help*.'

'I think you do, Mum.'

'I think you're the one who can play full episodes of *Pretty Little Liars* in her head, without even turning on the TV.'

She had me there. Anyway, then she stormed off. Woops.

Evidence: Just because you've stopped looking for love yourself, don't interfere in other people's love lives. Lesson learned.

posted by EditingEmma 23.26

Nagging Thoughts

I'm trying to sleep, but I keep thinking about things. I know it's completely, *completely* irrational, but… I feel kind of afraid. Steph's beginning this whole new thing without me. This feels different to anyone else she's dated (e.g. Jonno and his fascinatingly small head). It seems…more important somehow. Older. And in all honesty, I'm completely, selfishly terrified. I've put all my eggs in one basket and suddenly I'm being expected to share them. Andy's *eating* my eggs.

The second thing is that damned, unrelenting thorn in my side: my horniness. I'm usually fine with masturbating but… I don't know… Ever since being with my ex-boyfriend Greg (who I misguidedly dated to get over Leon, which, even though I did like Greg a lot, was an awful idea) I guess I've realized that even if boys can be a little bit…um…inexpert at aiding you with your horniness, they still, somehow, manage it just by being there, in a way that is somehow a bit more fulfilling than masturbation.

I know. More fulfilling than masturbation. Who knew?

So now, all I keep imagining is being with someone who *is* good at aiding you with your horniness, who is not you, and well…it's a nice thought.

And a little bit incompatible with being alone.

I've *tried* to quiet my horniness by ignoring it. I really have. Sort of like how leaving a baby alone wailing in a room instead of holding it is meant to be character-building. But thus far my horn hasn't shut up and developed a good, strong personality, it just keeps persisting louder and LOUDER.

The third thing is…UGH. I hate admitting this. The third thing is that even though I have stopped stalking Leon online, I have occasionally stalked him in my mind. Sometimes his name just comes into my brain. Or his face. Or a moment we had together. Just like one of those stupid montage videos they make of you and another person…but IN MY HEAD.

It's not all the time or anything, but…it happens.

Anyway, this is most likely because I've been on my own a bit these holidays. Everything's probably fine. I've got too much time to think, that's all. Stupid thoughts!!!

Steph's coming over tomorrow, thank God. I can stop thinking about myself for a bit and just listen to her talk.

Tuesday, 4 November

posted by EditingEmma 16.08
Steph's Growing Up

Steph just left. I feel a bit emotional.

'So how did it go with Gracie??' I started, as she settled down on my bed. Given that Andy is not just any first-proper-boyfriend, he's also our friend Gracie's brother, it makes the whole thing slightly more complicated.

'It was actually really nice,' said Steph.

I nearly fell off the bed in shock. '*Really nice*?' I repeated. 'With Gracie?'

Gracie, My Ex-Frenemy

In amongst a lot of other antics last term, another massive thing to happen was my fight with Gracie. She did something which hurt at the time (i.e. posted my secret blog online and kind of ruined me getting back together with Leon...) but actually, her doing that made me realize just how not worth it Leon was and also that in focusing so much on my terrible love life, I'd failed to notice how terrible our friendship had become. We're on much better terms now. The other day we all went out together and we didn't snipe at each other *once*. (Apart from when she said mozzarella is the best kind of cheese, which is clearly wrong.)

Still, I must admit I'm surprised by her being OK with this. I wasn't expecting Steph to make it out alive. But apparently, after Steph admitted that she really likes Andy, but said it didn't have to go any further if Gracie had an issue with it, Gracie apologized to Steph for making her feel like she couldn't say anything about it!

'*Sacre bleu*!' I said. 'Really?! That's...so...unexpectedly simple.'

'Yep...it was...'

'*Was?*'

Steph went silent and buried her head in her hands. Then started rocking backwards and forwards on my bed. 'Oh Emma. Then I RUINED it.'

'What?! How? What did you do?!'

Steph took a breath and looked up. 'So after we chatted, we hung out for a bit, and it was all really nice...'

'Yes...?'

'Then Gracie wanted to do some work and I said, cool, I'll go. But then Andy messaged me to see what I was up to.'

'Right...?'

'So I said, well actually, I'm in the room next door. And he said...come see me. But by the time we'd agreed this, Gracie was already taking me downstairs to say goodbye and she'd been so nice about the whole thing and I didn't want to make her feel awkward...so...'

'So?'

'So, um, I just sort of…panicked and left. And, um, walked down the street.'

I started laughing.

'And then Andy was all, *where are you?* And I turned around and walked back up the street.'

I laughed harder.

'And rang the doorbell. I thought Andy would answer, but, um…'

'Oh NO.'

'Yep. Gracie answered. She looked so puzzled. She asked me if I'd left something.'

'Oh, Steph.'

'I knowwwww *I knowwwww*. It would have been so much better to just tell her the first time. And I said, um, hi Gracie, I'm here to see Andy. Oh God, you should have seen her face.'

I wiped a tear from my eye. 'Oh, Steph. You idiot.'

'*I know I know I knowww*.'

'I thought you were so much cooler than that.'

'So did I.'

After that, Steph marched into Andy's room, told him she liked him and asked him out. He admitted that since the accidental kiss at Gracie's birthday party she's all he's been thinking about, and then they kissed again. Non-accidentally.

1.) I still cannot believe Gracie is all right with this. It's a miracle. I'm sort of expecting it to be a big ruse and tomorrow Steph will wake up with meat in her bed spelling 'Judas'.

2.) I can't believe Steph just asked Andy out. Just like that. How does a person develop that sort of confidence? I'm still developing the confidence to believe I might one day send a wink emoji in a 'flirty manner'.

After a few hours Steph got up to leave.

'Andy's coming over to listen to some music, wanna join?'

I smiled. 'Oh, no, I'll leave you to it,' I said. 'Lots of pictures to edit and all that.'

Steph rolled her eyes. (She will never understand the work it takes to get lighting, filtering and captioning just right.)

I would have liked to go with her. But I got Steph all day. I know I should leave them alone for a bit, and go along next time.

posted by EditingEmma 18.31
I Will Never Be Insta-Famous
After Steph left, I tried to rally and focus a bit on my fashion blog/social media. Unfortunately, much like Steph, my mother does not seem to understand the work it takes to achieve quality posts either.

I came into my room and she had put laundry *everywhere*.

'Mum!' I called out. '*Mum!*'

'What?' She huffed into the room.

'What is *this*?' I asked, pointing at the laundry rack.

'Those are your ridiculous sloth slippers, which you insist on keeping.'

'No, not the sloth slippers. Which, by the way, are *not* ridiculous. Why are they drying in here?'

Mum blinked. 'What do you want me to do with them?'

'I don't know. Put them in your room.'

'My room has my laundry in it.'

I clenched my teeth. 'Well, I'm afraid I don't have space for this in here. It's ruining my canvas.'

'Your *canvas*?'

'Yes.' I pointed at the bit of white wall behind the drying rack. 'Unfortunately, because my room is so pathetically small, *that* bit of wall is the only wall that isn't covered in furniture, or an embarrassing poster from my misguided pre-teen years, i.e. the only wall remotely suitable for taking pictures of my designs against. And my laundry is now in the way.'

Mum nodded. Finally, I seemed to have got through.

'Yes, I think I've got a solution,' she said.

And she THREW MY SLOTH SLIPPERS OUT THE WINDOW.

I repeat. MY SLOTH SLIPPERS.

OUT. THE. WINDOW.

'From now on you can do your own laundry,' she said, leaving the room.

Great, so now not only am I still miles away from Insta-fame, I'm also sloth-slipperless and I have to do laundry. Sometimes the divide between the life I'm leading and the life I should be leading only seems to get wider and wider.

posted by EditingEmma 19.19

Took loads of pictures, posted them, got some likes. Standard. I was at a loss for what to do again, so I lay on the floor. It was then I realized that I'd never seen the ceiling from this angle before. And there was a crack in it I'd never noticed. Amazing. *Fascinating*, when you really think about it. I've lived in this room for what, sixteen years, and *never* seen it? How many other secrets does my old, familiar bedroom hold?

posted by EditingEmma 20.35

Mum came back into my room. I was still picking up various objects and looking at them from different angles.

'...Why are you staring at that coat hanger?' she asked.

'Ah.' I held up a hand. 'To the untrained eye it may *seem* as if I am merely staring at a coat hanger. But really, I'm unearthing all manner of astonishing hidden truths about the universe.'

'All right, well, sorry to disturb your enlightenment, but have you read this?' she asked, holding up some mail from college.

'Uh, what do you think?' I said, not looking away from my coat hanger.

'It says they're doing a fashion show this year.'

'OK,' I replied.

Silence. She kept standing there.

'Well?' She tapped her foot. 'Don't you care? I thought you were focusing on your interests?'

'I am.'

'And I thought your interest was fashion?'

'It is,' I said. 'But that doesn't extend to giving up my free time to school. I've not had a brain transplant.'

Mum sighed. 'Look, love, I know you're feeling a bit lost...'

'I'm coping,' I said.

'Yes, so it would seem.' She glanced at the coat hanger. 'All I'm saying is, this might help.' She waved the fashion show leaflet at me.

I looked at it.

'All right, I'll think about it... Thanks.'

She left and I put my coat hanger down. For some reason I felt like I might cry.

posted by EditingEmma 22.37
Quite Predictably, Watching *PLL*

What's *wrong* with me?! I usually love lying around re-watching *Pretty Little Liars*, but I just can't get into it. I'm feeling really strange and unanchored. Mum's right... I'm supposed to be focusing on my interests, but going through the same cycle of making clothes, photographing them and getting likes just doesn't seem to be fulfilling me like it used to. I'm supposed to be focusing on my friendships, and all I've managed to do this holiday is photobomb Steph and her boyfriend, and spam my friends with pictures of me brushing my teeth.

And I guess...I guess I have to admit to myself...what I've really been trying to avoid thinking about...is that maybe... just maaaaaybe... it's because I don't have very many friends?

Aghhh. I don't know... I've never been in this situation before, so it's never really occurred. But it's suddenly dawning on me just how few people I actually have in my life that I can call up and hang out with. How is it possible that just because Steph's busy and Faith's away, I have no one left?! Literally *no one*. How pathetic is that?! How do I only have *two friends* in the entire globe?! The entire globe of nearly eight billion people? TWO? Out of EIGHT BILLION?

Is that normal??!!

I'm Robinson Crusoe, sitting out on a tiny island all by myself. And no one's coming to rescue me.

Wednesday, 5 November

posted by EditingEmma 12.07

PLL Inspiration

This morning continued in much the same way as yesterday. I got up, designed some novelty socks, posted a picture, got bored, put on more *PLL*. All the while feeling pretty sorry for myself.

It was then, watching a show I've seen so often I can genuinely mouth along with certain scenes, that I was hit with sudden inspiration. Right in the middle of watching the same suspects go round and round in and out of suspicion, I had a real, honest to God light-bulb moment. I felt like Thomas Edison himself, on the brink of a massive, life-changing discovery.

I sat up. It suddenly dawned on me... Yes, my entire life is the same TV shows. The same few people. The same activities. But it doesn't *have* to be.

Obviously, I'm not going to stop watching *PLL*. But what I mean is, it suddenly occurred to me that focusing on my friendships doesn't have to mean only pre-existing friendships. And focusing on my hobbies doesn't have to mean just designing clothes when I feel like it.

All that I've been doing...it's not enough. If I'm really going to change my life then I need to go *even further*. Drastic times call for drastic measures.

I know, I know, it's not my first rodeo... But just because last term was a total disaster, doesn't mean all my missions will go awry, right? Ladies and gentlemen... I think it's officially time to begin work on some Brand. New. Resolutions.

posted by EditingEmma 12.29
New Resolutions
ARE. YOU. READY.

So, after A LOT of reflection on all the disasters from last term, I think I figured out partially where I went wrong. Stopping using the internet to torture/alienate myself and actually use it to connect was, in theory, a well-intentioned and worthy mission. However, I think limiting this only to 'romantic' connections was my main error... There are all kinds of connections a mere click away from me that are just waiting to be discovered!

This term, I am eschewing love with a firm hand, but I will continue to use the internet to connect, and to improve my life and me as a person. Behold, my new resolutions:

RESOLUTIONS
Spend even more time purely on myself and my own social media profiles.

I will do this by:

1) Not only stopping stalking Leon, but going one step further and actually never referring to him directly. Ever.

2) Not only by keeping on designing and posting on my

new fashion blog, but also posting about…wait for it…
THE UPCOMING SCHOOL FASHION SHOW.

Now that I'm done finding boys online, spread the platonic love.
I will do this by:
A) Devoting time and attention to my pre-existing pals, but also…
B) Using the internet to SEEK OUT A NEW ONE.

In conclusion, those hobbies and those friends aren't gonna know what's hit 'em!!!

posted by EditingEmma 13.09
Phoned Steph to tell her about my resolutions. At first she didn't say anything. There was just silence.

'Steph?' I called. 'Earth to Steph?'

She took a deep breath. '… I don't even know where to start.'

'Am I to understand you see flaws in my brilliant plan?'

'Just a few.' She sighed. 'OK. First of all, I thought you were going to stop stalking?'

'Ah,' I said. 'Well, I was going to stop stalking *Leon*… But I never said anything about new buddies! I mean, is stalking for a good cause even stalking at all?!'

'OK.' I could practically hear her eyes rolling. 'Next question. Never mentioning Leon. Like, ever?'

'Who?' I asked.

'Aren't you sort of giving him *more* power? Like Voldemort?'

'No,' I said.

'You are. It makes him like this big, scary, lurking thing.'

'Voldemort was eventually defeated.'

'Only because Hogwarts faced him head on.'

'Yeah, well, some wizards got through it by cowering under a bit of rubble. That can be me.'

Steph sighed again. 'OK. Fine. Leon shall remain nameless from now on.'

I coughed.

'I mean, You Know Who shall remain nameless from now on.'

'Thank you.'

'Last question. A school event?'

I paused. 'Yes?'

'A *school event*, Emma? *You*?'

'All right, so it's a *little* out of character... '

Steph snorted.

'... but I have sometimes gone to school events.'

So what if a large part of my attendance at *My Fair Lady* involved hypocritically mocking others for their lack of musical ability? I was still *there*.

'I give it three weeks,' Steph said.

I'll show her! I've already emailed Ms Parker to sign up, and I'm about to get started on...

NEW PALS.

So the concept is a little alien to me and I can't actually remember the last time I made a new friend... Or, er, how... But how hard can it be, right?! I mean, I *have* friends. I must have 'made friends' with each of them somewhere along the line.

Right…a new friend. A. New. Friend. Hmm.

Maybe for now, I should focus not on the how, but on the who…

And I know exactly where to start…

Hello, laptop, my old friend.

posted by EditingEmma 16.08
Emma's List of New Bezzies

I've spent the last hour drawing up a list of potential new best friends for life, based solely on the Instagram/Twitter profiles of other girls at my college. I have to say…it's a little bit weird being back here. Internet stalking, I mean. Although obviously it's completely different this time. In many ways the threat of embarrassment has been completely removed, because there's so much less that can go wrong. Having said that, it's sort of harder in a way than when I was looking for a new boyfriend… At least with dating you can look at someone's picture and know roughly whether or not you find them attractive. But that doesn't matter with friends. With friends it is literally *entirely* about personality, which makes this challenging in a different way.

The pool of super-cool ladies seems almost impossibly big. Plus, whilst people put a bit about themselves online, I know from experience it can be a limited view. I mean, Faith posts all those pictures of rocks and twigs and stuff for her art class and we're still friends. It's hard to tell sometimes isn't it?

Still, I've done the best I can, based on the somewhat patchy evidence, and drawn up a Top Three.

Kayleigh Spencer

Pros: She won some Maths trophy thing for our school, so she's obviously very clever. She shares mainly pictures of cats, which indicates she's warm and unpretentious.

Cons: Although I dig that she's into Maths and cats, I struggle with even the most basic of mathematical concepts and I'm not really an animal person. Cats always seem to hiss at me. Will she sense that?

Anika Khatri

Pros: She seems fun. I can always hear her across the sixth form centre. Judging from her profiles she's also an excellent dancer.

Cons: If she's *too* fun, will she get annoyed by the amount of hours I spend on Netflix? Will she want to make up dance routines together? Because if so, I can say with absolute confidence this relationship won't work.

Hannah Condom

Pros: Hannah is actually on the list purely on the basis that her last name is Condom. From this I figure that she must, surely, have had to develop a sense of humour.

Cons: I'm not sure I could resist constantly pointing out that her last name is Condom.

Having assessed the list, I've decided that Anika Khatri is the place to start. I can just picture it...us having a good old laugh together in the sixth form centre, engaging in constant chatter... People will be able to hear us from all corners of the school. *Oh, what good friends they are*, they'll say. What japes we'll have! What mischief we'll cause! If I'm very quiet, I can almost hear our future bonding ringing in my ears.

Also, at parties if I stand near her whilst she dances and don't move, people might assume I'm also good at dancing just by being near her.

My plan is to go through all of Anika's profiles and collect as much information as possible, and see what I can use as a 'conversation starter'.

posted by EditingEmma 16.58
Research on Anika
She has a big family. (Can I ask her about this? Compare to my tiny one?)

She recently went to Bali. (I've always wanted to go?)

She had a tooth out. (Ask if was painful?)

Hmm. I don't know if I should use the tooth thing. That was six months ago and might give away that I've essentially been revising her life.

posted by EditingEmma 17.15
Something Awful Has Happened
No. No nonono nonononoooo. NOOOOOOOO.

Oh God.

NO.

How can my plan have gone awry already?!?! I only started this afternoon! And I haven't even spoken to Anika yet!!!

I'd just completed my research. I was still on her Twitter, about three years back, when I had a sudden urge for a Jammy Dodger. As I was grasping for the Dodger, which was *just* out of reach, I slipped a little bit...and my other hand was still on the trackpad...

I accidentally clicked.

AGHHHHHHHHHHHHH.

For a moment, I thought, *it will be OK.* You just liked one of her old tweets. Standard. A bit embarrassing but I'll just pretend it never happened, she'll just pretend she never saw the notification and we'll all move on. Maybe we'll laugh about it in years to come when we're bezzies.

But no. I didn't just 'like' one of her tweets from the end of last year.

I RETWEETED IT.

Oh God. And it's possibly one of the *weirdest* things I could have retweeted. It's a photo of her ninety-year-old granddad, saying, '90 today, wow!! Happy Birthday, love you so much.'

Now Anika's very old relative is just sitting there on my own profile. Baring his missing teeth in a grim smile, birthday hat tipped jauntily to one side, a glassy look in his eye, about to tuck into his little piece of cake.

I tried to delete it, but, *of course*, because the Gods of Sod's Law love to taunt me...at that very moment my computer froze up.

'Ctrl Alt Delete!!' I screamed. 'Ctrl Alt Delete!!!'

I waited for the computer to restart and raced back on, only to see that Anika had already been online. My heart sank. She'd already seen it.

What do I do now??!

posted by EditingEmma 17.18

He's still there. It's starting to feel distinctly creepy. Mum came in and said, 'Why are you staring at a picture of an old man?'

His glassy eyes are boring into my soul.

posted by EditingEmma 17.25

Gave in and rang Steph again. I know she's out with Andy today, but desperate times and all that.

'STEPH,' I said.

'What's up?'

'I retweeted a picture of Anika Khatri's grandfather.'

'I…you what?!'

'I retweeted a picture of her grandfather. Help! What do I do?'

I heard Andy's voice in the background.

'It's Emma,' Steph said. 'She retweeted a picture of some girl's grandfather.'

'Oh great, let's involve more people in this,' I said.

'Why?' I heard him say.

'Yeah, why?' repeated Steph.

'It was an accident, OBVIOUSLY.'

'Why were you on Anika's profile?' Steph sounded baffled.

'She's number one on the New Friend List.'

'Hang on, I'm just having a look…'

There was a silence.

'Oh my GOD.' Steph burst out laughing again. 'You total WEIRDO.'

'Steph, this is not helpful. Any advice on where to go from here would be much appreciated.'

I heard mumbling.

'Andy says un-retweet immediately.'

'What about you?'

She thought for a second. 'I say…style it out.'

'Style it out?'

'Yeah. I mean, she's already seen it. There's nothing you can do now. Maybe if you just act like it's totally normal, she'll think it's totally normal.'

'Really?'

'Yeah. Ooh ooh, I know, you should retweet some more random stuff. Make her think you're one of those people who just retweets EVERYTHING. You know, like Desperate Paul?'

'You think that will work?'

'Definitely.'

posted by EditingEmma 19.01

Right, I've just retweeted eleven other things on Anika's account and I've been COMPLETELY indiscriminate. I've retweeted everything from old relatives to dance school stuff to how we should all be using Tesco bags for life.

Should I keep on going? 15.59
The more the better I think. S x 15.59

Feeling a bit calmer now. Hopefully, by the end of the day, I will have salvaged this potential relationship.

posted by EditingEmma 19.45
Emma's New Friend, Part 1: Mission Failed
I don't believe this!!!! Anika's blocked me!! She BLOCKED me!!!

Rang Steph again.

'Steph, she BLOCKED me!'

'What?!'

'She's actually blocked me!'

'How do you know?!'

'It says to follow her, and I never unfollowed! That's a textbook blocking!'

Steph started laughing again.

'Steph! This is no laughing matter! Does she not know we've got a lifelong, rock-solid friendship ahead of us?!'

'I guess not.'

'I feel so deflated. I thought she was fun!'

'Maybe you mistook loud for fun,' Steph answered.

'Or *maybe* I should never have followed *your* terrible advice,' I scoffed.

'Hey, you're the one who RTed a picture of her granddad. I was trying to be supportive earlier but...there was really nowhere to go from there.'

She has zero regard for my humiliation. Oh my God, I don't believe this. This is so embarrassing. *Blocked* by my new best friend. I thought this was going to be a breeze!

Evidence: Meeting new friends online is not necessarily easier than online dating.

Thursday, 6 November

posted by EditingEmma 11.09

New Friend Making: On Hiatus

I've decided that, today, maybe I should give 'making a new friend' a rest. Clearly I was unprepared for the potential threats that come with any kind of human interactions, not just the ones with kissing involved. I'm also trying not to bother Steph again today, because in 'giving her space' yesterday by not physically being with her, all I did was keep on ringing her instead.

Mum came into the kitchen.

'Why have you got a face like a slapped arse?' she asked.

'I'm bored,' I said. 'Because I'm giving Steph space.'

I refrained from adding it was also because I got blocked for hounding some random girl at school with a well-intentioned but ultimately scary amount of notifications.

'What about your other friends?' asked Mum.

'Faith's on holiday.' I shrugged.

'Anyone else?' she nudged. 'Beginning with a G...?'

'Gracie?'

Interesting...

'I don't know.' I frowned.

Me and Gracie are definitely getting along better now, but still, I don't remember the last time I hung out with her on my own...

'If you're really going to focus on your friendships,' said Mum, all *knowing*, 'wouldn't that be the best place to start?'

I suppose I *could* message Gracie... In theory. Although, there are a lot of things one could do in theory. *In theory* I could climb a mountain. *In theory* I could watch something new, instead of starting *Gilmore Girls* yet again from the beginning. And we all know that's never going to happen.

posted by EditingEmma 16.09
I Can Do This
Gave in when I started considering tidying my room as an actual possibility. Right... I can do this. I mean, last term I started conversations with boys I'd only ever seen around school. This term I plan on making friends with people I've never said a word to before (bar Anika Khatri, who we'll put down as the inevitable 'first pancake'). Phoning Gracie, who I already speak to every day, should be a piece of cake... right?!

Right?!

Ughhh. Why am I so nervous?! This is ridiculous. I CAN DO THIS.

posted by EditingEmma 16.15

I Can't Do This

When Gracie picked up the phone she sounded really, really baffled.

'*Emma?*' she asked as if recalling a distant memory, like when the old woman at the end of *Titanic* is looking at her belongings from the wreckage.

'Yes, hello.'

Then I heard her dad say 'Who is it?' in the background.

'It's Emma,' she said.

'Emma?' he replied.

'Emma,' she said again.

'Yes, for God's sake, it's me, EMMA,' I shouted. 'It's not like Willie Thomas is calling you.'

(Willie Thomas is a boy who stands really close to girls at school so he can loom over their breasts. He also mouth breathes.)

'Ew, why would he?'

'Well, that's exactly my point.'

'You rang to tell me that you're not Willie Thomas?'

'I... Forget it. What are you doing?'

'Nothing much,' she said. '*Why?*'

'No reason. God! Why are you so suspicious?'

'... I'm playing a board game with my dad,' she said.

'Cool. Can I come over?'

'You want to play a board game? With my dad?'

'Yes.'

'*Why?*'

'FOR GOD'S SAKE. I'M NOT WILLIE THOMAS.'

We got there eventually, but that was *painful*. We've arranged to hang out later... Oh God. What if it's awful?! What if we have absolutely nothing to say to each other without Steph and Faith?! I must keep reminding myself... it can't be any worse than some of the awful dates I went on last term. Right?!

RIGHT?!

posted by EditingEmma 17.45
Lingering on Gracie's Front Path
I am not Willie Thomas. I am not Willie Thomas. I am not Willie Thomas. I am not Willie Thomas.

posted by EditingEmma 19.31
I Might As Well Be Willie Thomas
Well, *that* was uncomfortable.

I got there at five thirty and I'm home at seven thirty. That should tell you something about how awkward that was.

When I finally knocked on the door (after lingering on the path for a good fifteen minutes), Gracie opened it and looked a little bit surprised to see me.

'Hi?' she said, questioningly.

'Hi,' I said.

But she didn't let me in.

'We did say I was coming over, right?' I asked.

'Oh, yeah, right,' she said, and finally moved aside.

I took off my shoes and we both stood for a while.

You could have heard a pin drop.

'So, um, how are you?' I asked.

'Oh, good,' she said. 'You?'

'Yes, good. I'm good.' I gave a forced smile.

Silence.

'So, um, this is the living room...' she said.

I was about to point out that I'd been here A MILLION times before, but I didn't, because then I'd actually have to come up with something else to talk about. So I just nodded.

'Nice,' I said.

And before I knew it, I was being taken on a tour of her house.

A TOUR OF HER HOUSE. A house that I basically GREW UP IN.

Eventually, we stopped in the kitchen.

'So, this is the kitchen,' she said.

Yes, I threw up in that vase, I thought.

'Would you like a biscuit?' she asked, holding out the tin.

'Oh, no thanks, but thank you for offering,' I said.

... No thanks?!

Thank you for offering?!

WHO AM I?!?!

I SO wanted the biscuit...but I was in this weird polite mode. As soon as I'd said no, I regretted it.

'Shall we, um, play a board game?' Gracie asked. I was still staring wistfully at the biscuit tin.

'Er, yes, that sounds delightful,' I said.

Delightful?

Then we went into the living room to play board games (which I let her win, obviously, because I value my life). It was all very...cordial. Almost stiff. Sort of like we were well-behaved Victorian children.

I guess nothing really bad happened, but it just never felt natural. I kept checking the clock and it wasn't moving. Except it was moving, because I could hear it ticking. There were the kind of awkward silences you can actually hear and we had to keep reviving the conversation with small-talk CPR. The whole time I was thinking about the biscuit.

Eventually, her dad caught me raiding the biscuit tin with a crazed look in my eye. I gave some excuse about having to leave and quickly got out of the house.

Now I'm walking home in disgrace, pulling crumbs out of my hair.

Evidence: Friend dates can be just as awkward as romantic dates.

Seriously, I was nervous about this...but I really did think friend-dating would be easier!!! I mean, I know for a fact that Gracie's not going to lunge at my face when I'm least expecting it, or attempt to cuddle me when I'm trying to consume snacks. The threat of teeth bumping has been removed. I don't have to worry about whether my hands are sweaty or whether I've eaten garlic. And *still*, with all of that stuff gone, I can barely have a coherent conversation?! With someone I've known and hung out with nearly every day for five years?!

How is that even possible?!?!

Ugh, one failed attempt to make a new friend and one failed endeavour to hang out with an old one. This whole 'spread the platonic love' thing is NOT going as planned. Now I feel lonelier than ever.

Friday, 7 November

posted by EditingEmma 17.07

Faith got back from holiday yesterday, so we're all going out to see some fireworks.

'Do you know if Claudia's coming?' I asked Steph.

'I asked Faith, she said it's too soon.'

'Eugh, WHAT.'

'They have only been on two dates...'

'But...but...I want to her meet her!'

'I think your eagerness is only making it less likely.'

'What?! I can be cool!'

'Yeah, the twelve hundred pictures I have of you photobombing me and Andy really prove that.'

'Point taken.'

'Andy's coming anyway, and a couple of his mates.'

'Does that mean Meathead Babs?' I asked, with trepidation.

'Unfortunately, yes,' she answered.

posted by EditingEmma 20.18

At the Display

Having so much fun watching the fireworks. At least I would be, if it wasn't for Meathead Babs' loud guffawing.

'*What* is so funny about fireworks?!' I whispered to Steph. 'I have no idea,' she said.

posted by EditingEmma 20.27

Mystery solved. Just heard Babs say on the phone, 'No really, mate, they looked *exactly* like your jizz, that time we ate all that food colouring at Gav's.'

posted by EditingEmma 23.37

A Breakthrough Moment

Back home now, and I think I might have actually had a breakthrough moment with Gracie!!

All evening, I thought I saw her looking a bit uncomfortable at times. My first clue was when Steph and Andy were in front of us, using a filter where Steph's head looked GIGANTIC and Andy had four noses, and Gracie smiled but *didn't* laugh. I mean, if someone isn't laughing at face-contorting Snapchats, there must be something wrong.

Then I noticed she kept staring at her phone, not really getting involved in conversation. I was wondering what was up, and then I remembered it was probably the first time she'd been out with Steph and Andy together. I know she said she was fine with it, but it's probably going to take some getting used to… I mean, if I'm feeling weird about this, it must be ten times weirder for Gracie.

THEN came the breakthrough moment. Faith was smiling goofily at her phone, at what I'm assuming were messages from Claudia. Meathead Babs was busy pretending to lick his hot dog in an erotic manner. Steph and Andy were taking a selfie. Just as I was about to jump into the perfect Emma-sized gap between their heads, I noticed Gracie looking a bit lost and small.

It was like everything went slo-mo. I knew I had a big decision to make. Continue to photobomb Steph, or go and actually be a good friend. Such…tough…life…decisions…

The camera clicked. Without me. (Obviously, I photoshopped myself in as soon as I got home, but I'm halfway on the road to recovery.) If I was really serious about making my friendship with Gracie work, I was going to have to try harder than one awkward game of Scrabble.

'Hey, let's go over here,' I said, putting my hand on her shoulder.

'Why?' She practically jumped out of her skin. 'Where are you taking me?'

'I'm abducting you, obviously.'

'Seriously, where are we going?!'

'For the love of God, I'm not Willie Thomas!!!'

Eventually we got away from the group. She shrugged at me.

'What's going on?' she asked.

I took a deep breath. 'Are you OK? You know, about Andy and Steph?' I gabbled.

She looked a bit taken aback.

'Yeah. Fine. Why?'

'You just seemed a bit…maybe not fine?'

She crossed her arms. 'Did Steph send you? Are you going to go back and talk about how possessive and uptight I'm being?'

It was my turn to look taken aback.

'What?! NO! I just thought you might be feeling weird, which would be completely understandable.'

Her shoulders relaxed a bit, then, and her face softened.

'And it wouldn't mean you were being possessive or uptight, or even that you weren't fine with it,' I went on. 'It would just mean you were adjusting, which would be totally normal.'

She searched my eyes for a moment, as if looking for proof I was tricking her or something. Eventually she must have decided I wasn't, because she said, 'Well… OK. I guess it is a bit weird.'

I nodded like I knew. Which I absolutely don't, because I don't have any siblings. Would it be the same to imagine a friend dating my mum…? GROSS. NO. TOTALLY NOT THE SAME. GETOUTGETOUTGETOUT.

'Do you want to talk about it?' I asked.

'I don't know,' she started cautiously. 'Like, it's nice in a way, I mean it would be nice if Steph came to our family events and things…'

'That would be fun,' I said.

'Yeah. I mean…it will be nice for a while. But they'll probably break up, right? And then what will happen? Will Steph still want to come round mine?'

'Probably jumping ahead a bit.'

'Yeah, but, it's true, right?'

'Well… There might be some potential awkwardness if they break up.'

Gracie sighed.

'But I think that's all it is…just awkwardness,' I continued. 'It wouldn't actually damage your friendship with Steph or your relationship with Andy. Their relationship is *their* thing.'

Gracie nodded, but she didn't seem convinced.

'Is this what's bothering you?' I carried on. 'Their potential break-up?'

'No, I mean, there is that… But it's more like… I don't know.'

'What?'

She chewed her lip.

'I would *never* say this to Steph, so please don't repeat this.'

'I won't.'

'Do you swear?'

'I swear!'

'But you tell Steph everything.'

'I won't tell her, I promise!'

She paused.

'What if I become less important to both of them, than they are to each other? That would be *awful*. I'd feel left out at home, at school… I guess, I don't know, this relationship just invades my life from all angles.'

She put her head down, covering her face in rivulets of red hair. Suddenly I had an urge I'd never had before… To hug her. I mean, we've hugged before, but I mean really hug her. *Squeeze* her.

'GRACIE,' I shouted. 'That is so not even a tiny, weeny possibility! Andy is your brother, your blood. Blood! Blood! BLOOD!'

'Please stop shouting "blood".'

'And Steph is one of your best friends!' I carried on.

She looked up at me, through her hair.

'Don't get me wrong,' I said. 'They're going to have a, um, *different* bond with each other than they do with you. But not more important. No way.'

She looked at me all vulnerable and bushbaby-eyed.

'Do you really think so?'

'YES. *Of course!*'

She nodded.

'Thanks,' she said. 'You know, I actually feel lots better.'

I thought about going for the squeeze-hug, then, but I thought it was still probably a bit premature. So I just linked my arm through hers and we went back over to the group.

'What were you guys doing?' asked Steph.

'Oh, er… ' I looked at Gracie, who stared back at me with pleading eyes.

'Just checking out the cute hot-dog guy,' Gracie finished.

Steph frowned, glancing at the hot-dog guy (who was in his fifties and sporting a handlebar moustache), but didn't ask any more questions. She turned back to Andy.

'Thank you,' mouthed Gracie. And she smiled at me.

And now I'm in bed, still thinking about the talk and the smile and the fact she actually seemed better after our chat. I feel kind of…warm? About Gracie. Warm about me and Gracie. Huh.

Saturday, 8 November

posted by EditingEmma 11.07

I Don't BELIEVE This

I just saw Crazy Holly posting about an email she'd got from the school, and how excited she was to try out her designs for 'banana shoes' in the fashion show.

I DIDN'T GET ANY EMAIL!

Rang Steph.

'I don't believe this,' I said. 'Did you see Holly's post?'

'Yeah,' she said. 'What do you think *banana shoes* means? Like, shaped like a banana? Or made out of actual banana?'

'STEPH. Please focus on the matter in hand. I signed up for that, and I've not heard a peep!'

She laughed. 'Chill out, Emma. They probably just missed you off by accident.'

'Oh yeah sure, an *accident*. I can't believe I finally put myself forward for something at school and I'm getting rejected. Rejected by teachers. Seriously, this really is an all-time low. This is psychologically *scarring*.'

Steph paused.

'Maybe you just didn't make the cut, Emma. I mean, when you're competing against banana shoes...'

She is so unhelpful. Anyway, I've sent Ms Parker a strongly worded email. Let's see what she has to say for herself.

posted by EditingEmma 13.15
Email from Ms Parker:

Oh, I thought you were joking. Have added you to the list!
P.S. Don't even _think_ about missing the first meeting.

It's really no wonder 'the youth of today' are all struggling with their self-confidence, is it, when the people supposed to be inspiring and encouraging them show so little faith.

posted by EditingEmma 14.56
Friendship Progress
I have just officially received a message from Gracie. Not in 'Strengthening our Womanly Bonds,' but in our _private thread_.

Our private thread which has not had a message in it since eight months ago, when I asked her if she'd remembered her ingredients for FT, and she said yes, and I said please can I cut off half your avocados and use them as mine, no one will notice, and she said no.

So do you want to maybe come over later? 14.44

I'm still looking at the message sitting there. It feels like a message from an alien. But I'm going to say yes. I really, *really* hope it goes better than last time.

posted by EditingEmma 22.16
A Friendship Reborn

That was a very, very strange evening. But I think…I *think* it was good. I think it was really good.

When I first got there it was much the same as last time. We played board games and I continued to let her win. We made small talk. I was just starting to despair that we'd ever be properly at ease with each other alone, and wondering if that magical moment of closeness on Bonfire Night was just a one-off that had disappeared into thin air… When suddenly… it was like we sort of…reverted to our twelve-year-old selves.

We started flipping through some magazines and Gracie said, 'Do you think I have weak eyebrows?'

I snorted.

'Why, do some other eyebrows want to take it outside?'

She pointed at a picture of Cara Delevingne.

'I'll never look like her. My eyebrows are so wispy,' she sighed.

'Well…no,' I said, 'but it's not really the eyebrows. It's more like your other features and hair and skin tone and everything else about you.'

'Draw me some eyebrows!' she said, all keen.

So I drew some eyebrows on her. Then she drew some eyebrows on me.

We looked *ridiculous*.

'What do you think?' Gracie asked.

'I think they look like two giant slugs trying to eat the rest of your face.'

Then we started drawing beauty moles on each other and did our hair all big and ending up taking pictures of ourselves in our underwear, pouting and pretending to be *Victoria's Secret* models. As you do. Then we realized we look absolutely nothing like *Victoria's Secret* models and so put the whole ugly incident behind us. But until that point it was really, really fun. I've not had that kind of pure, unadulterated sort of fun where time disappears and you're just doing really pointless, silly things in…well…I can't actually remember.

It was sort of like we both sensed we needed to go back in time to before we discovered alcohol, before body hang-ups, before boys and hormones and confusing feelings and just be Emma and Gracie. Emma and Gracie before all those things started getting in the way. It was kind of like…I don't know, like we were redoing our entire friendship from the beginning.

When I came back in, Mum said, 'Did you have a good time?'

'I did, actually,' I said.

She looked all smug and annoying. So I reminded her of the message from the 'doctor' she got all excited about earlier, who turned out in fact to be not a doctor but a self-professed 'lurve doctor'.

Anyway, I feel sort of…giddy?! It's like I've made a new friend, even though we've technically been friends for years.

Sunday, 9 November

posted by EditingEmma 21.14

Does Being A Good Friend Sometimes Mean Being a Bad
Friend?

So Steph came over this evening… And I lied to her.

I've NEVER lied to Steph. Ever. I mean, there was that time
she wore flares and I told her they looked good, when flares
categorically cannot look anything but disgusting. But I've
never *properly* lied to her.

We were just lazing around discussing what hairstyle Steph
should try next (Steph and her sister are constantly changing
their hair – at the moment she's going natural Afro) when she
suddenly said, 'So, what were you and Gracie being so secretive
about the other day?'

My brain froze. 'Um…'

I couldn't tell her we were only being secretive because
we were talking about Gracie's brother, and Steph is dating
Gracie's brother.

'No we weren't. When do you mean?' I said, unconvincingly.

I *really* wanted to tell her what we'd actually been saying, but
then I remembered my promise to Gracie and her pleading eyes.

'Never mind.' Steph shrugged.

Ughhhhh. What do you do when something that means being a good friend to one person, means potentially being a bad friend to another? Obviously *I* share everything with Steph and I don't want to keep stuff from her, but this isn't my thing to share.

It was hard, but I comforted myself with the fact that earlier on I bought her the best birthday present EVER. I got us tickets to the Women's Premier League. I mean, I'll probably have to stick pins in my arm to try to stay awake, but she'll LOVE it. I can't *wait* to see the look on her face when I give them to her.

posted by EditingEmma 22.04
The New Friend Plan: Step 2
Before Steph left, she said, 'How are your resolutions going, by the way?'

'Ah.' I tapped my nose. 'Funny you should mention. Only a few hours ago, I set the wheels of a brand new beautiful and everlasting friendship in motion. Just in time for the new term.'

All this week, I'd sort of been considering putting the friend mission to one side, seeing how well things are going with Gracie. But then I remembered how exposed I felt without Steph and Faith…just for a few days. *A few days.* What about when Gracie isn't available, too? What about when it's for longer periods of time?! I feel like relying solely on three people probably isn't that different than two.

Plus, given that Steph and Faith are both in new relationships, and Gracie's been making lots of new friends at her

Cambridge prep study group, it seems like everyone else has their own stuff going on. And, well, I don't.

Now that everyone's adding more things and more people to their lives, I think I need to as well. Steph, Faith and Gracie are sewn so deeply through the fabric of my life that I don't even know who I am when I'm not in the context of them. I'm slightly petrified, but I think it's probably time I try to find out.

So, for now, I've decided put the Anika thing down to pure naivety. A youthful indiscretion, if you will. But now I know… if you want to be friends with someone, maybe don't start off too intense.

Which is why it seemed sensible to choose this next person on my list. Hannah Condom. I don't *need* to do tons of research to get chatting to Hannah – her surname is all the conversation starter I will ever need! Step two of the New Friend Plan is a go.

Emma Nash: Hi Hannah, I just wanted to say I've never truly appreciated before that your last name is Condom! What lolz. I wish I had a surname like that. And you'll never forget to use one! X

That should do it. I bet we'll be BFFs by the end of the week.

Monday, 10 November

posted by EditingEmma 08.32
Back To School
Deep joy.

posted by EditingEmma 13.15
I Will Never Be Friends With Hannah Condom
Oh my God. Something horrific has happened. And it's only my first day back at college. And it's not even lunchtime. I kid you not, *actually* horrific.

I was just getting a drink at the fountain when Steph came over to me.

'Emma,' she said. 'Why is it going round school that you're cyber-bullying Hannah Condom?'

I spat water all down my top.

'WHAT?!'

'Apparently you made fun of her surname?'

'Oh my God.' I put my head in my hands. 'I wasn't making fun of it. I said I liked it!!'

Steph smirked. 'You *like* the name Condom?'

'Yes!! It's hilarious!'

'Hilariously awful.'

'It's whimsical!'

Steph's smirk became a grin.

'Oh God. You believe me, don't you?' I said desperately. 'I was being sincere!'

'*I* believe you,' she said. 'Because I know you're a total weirdo. But I don't think anyone else will.'

Just then, I saw a bunch of girls heading my way. Hannah Condom's friends.

Oh God.

They all started whispering in a huddle, then marched over to me.

'Hey, what did you say to Hannah?' one of them said.

'I...' I started.

'She's crying in the loos because of you,' another said.

'Oh God, I'm so sorry, I...'

'At her last school the boys used to fill her locker up with condoms. They used to blow up condoms and write "Condom Head" on them, and leave them sitting in her chair.'

'I'm so sorry to hear that, I...'

'She doesn't need that trauma again, OK?'

'It wasn't meant to be...'

But they'd started walking off.

'Tell her I'm sorry!' I yelled at their backs.

Then I turned to Steph, who was literally suffocating trying to hold her breath in from laughter. Once they'd reached a safe enough distance, she exploded into fits of snorting, raucous guffaws.

'You…total…twat…' she said, gasping for air.

I sat on the floor and buried my head in my hands.

'Oh God,' I repeated. 'Oh God, oh God, oh God, oh God. Steph, what am I going to do?!'

'Do you…have any…classes with…her?' she managed.

'No, thank the Lord!'

'Well then…' Her lungs sounded like they were about to collapse. 'Just avoid eye contact…for the next year and a half… and you're golden.'

Then I stood up, got some water in my hands from the fountain and splashed it on her. The shock seemed to calm her down.

Anyway, I think I can safely say that I will never be friends with Hannah Condom. I will never even be on remotely friendly terms with Hannah Condom.

Please can I go home now? Please???

posted by EditingEmma 19.06

I've Given Up

Just an official post to declare the friend mission is ABORTED. All day I had to stay well out of Hannah Condom etc.'s orbit. I did really well until after last bell, when I saw Hannah walking down the corridor. I started running in the opposite direction, only to bump into bloody Anika Khatri coming the other way. She gave me a look like I was a real freak and by the time I got past her Hannah had caught up, and she gave me a look like I was a mass murderer.

That is two out of three girls on the list I've not only failed to make friends with, but actually actively pissed off. How am I so terrible at this?! How do I have any friends at all? Was it all a fluke? Or was I just better at speaking to people, age eleven? Is that it now? Is all my friend-making done forever??! Oh my God. This is AWFUL.

Seriously though?? What happens when Faith goes backpacking? When Gracie gets a swanky job in New York? When Steph starts procreating with Andy? WHO WILL I TALK TO?!

Maybe I could convince Steph and Andy to let me live in their shed, if I promise to be very quiet and not to scare their children with my unwashed hair and glazed eyes.

Definitely not going in tomorrow. One day back was more than enough.

Tuesday, 11 November

posted by EditingEmma 08.36

Mum wasn't a fan of the whole 'I'm not going back in on my second day' thing, so here I am. Sigh. It's probably for the best. It's the first fashion show meeting tonight and now that I bugged Ms Parker about joining, I'm definitely going to have to turn up.

posted by EditingEmma 16.01

So, I am currently at my first, official *after-school activity*. Waiting for Ms Parker to arrive to commence the *voluntary captivity*. I feel weird and not at all like myself, like Stefan Salvatore when he gets the taste for human blood after 150 years.

WHO AM I?

Anyway, this new, pod-person Emma, who stays at college more than thirty seconds after the bell rings, sat down next to Crazy Holly (who is also helping out with the fashion show). Holly carefully unwrapped a carved lemon from some tin foil and offered me a piece. I respectfully declined. Then she said, 'So why are you here?'

'I like making clothes,' I said.

She nodded profoundly.

'That's what they told me to say, too,' she said and winked.

WHAT AM I DOING?

posted by EditingEmma 18.07

Home

I can't believe I'm saying this but…I think I might have actually…had fun? At school? At school when I *didn't* have to be there?

For a while I watched people leaving out the window, going back to their homes, walking towards their freedom, and I felt quite wistful and helpless… Like I was the guy in *Shawshank Redemption*, wrongfully imprisoned for a crime and left to rot. I sort of had the urge to call out, 'I'M NOT SUPPOSED TO BE HERE. I WANNA GO HOME!' But then Ms Parker arrived and began chatting about the plans for the show, and it actually all sounded really cool.

There were about twenty-five of us and we went around the circle introducing ourselves and dividing out roles. I didn't really recognize anyone except Holly, but the guy who sat next to me was nice. He had very 'high fashion' hair and shoes and managed to look sort of preened in a way that I can never achieve after three hours getting ready, never mind after a day at school.

'Hi,' he said. 'I'm Charlie.'

'Hi,' I replied. 'I'm Emma. What teams are you going for?'

'Design.' He shrugged, as if there were no other answer.

'Oh cool!' I said. 'Me too!'

Then he showed me a pair of paisley trousers he'd been working on and how he'd stitched the seam to be curved like the paisley. A cool trick, which I made a mental note to steal for future designs.

'Did you make this?' he asked, pointing to my top.

'I did.'

'I really like the buttons.'

'Why thank you.'

It was SO NICE to be able to talk to people who were really interested in making clothes, too. As I explained my choice of buttons I waited for him to raise one eyebrow sceptically, or to shout 'Why didn't you use CHOCOLATE buttons' and try to fit a whole pack in his mouth, like Steph did the other day. But no... He listened to me, explaining my choice of buttons, as if it were a legitimate and interesting thing to be speaking about.

This must be what Steph feels like when she's with her football team talking about the offside rule, rather than trying to explain it to my unconscious, sleeping body.

Anyway, I volunteered for design and social media. Holly kept putting her hand up for *every single team* and eventually Ms Parker said, 'Are you sure that's not too many, Holly?'

'I can handle the heat.' She shrugged.

I'm actually really, really excited. If I get design team then I get to make fifteen outfits for the show and people will actually BE LOOKING AT MY DESIGNS. ON A RUNWAY. (Even if it is just some wooden planks cobbled together by Holly, that will probably collapse.)

When I was leaving Ms Parker said, 'It's really nice to see you doing something other than gazing out the window and nodding, Emma.' And she *smiled* at me. It made me feel a tiny bit sickened at first, but then really happy. I like Ms Parker. And for once, she wasn't exasperated with me!... Maybe *she* could be my new BFF?

Emma Nash @Em_Nasher
Would it be weird to make a friendship bracelet for a teacher?

Steph Brent @Brentsy
@Em_Nasher Yes

posted by EditingEmma 19.16
Sigh
So I know I said I wasn't going to mention the unmentionable person, but looking back at that last post feels somewhat disingenuous, because, unfortunately, that very same unmentionable person walked in right in the middle of the meeting.

AGsdhhdjsnv~HSHDHHDHDHDHDH.

GAGH.

Ms Parker had just mentioned that people in lighting and set could 'maybe' use a strobe light, and Holly got so excited she squirted a bit of lemon into Willie Thomas's eye. Willie was clutching his face and swearing and I was just googling 'what to do when you get citric acid in your eye', when he, oh nameless one, stumbled in through the door. Looking all flustered and messy-haired-but-in-an-annoyingly-good-way.

'****,' said Ms Parker. 'Good, you're here.'

'Sorry, I...' He caught my eye and looked away again quickly. I forgot how dark and round his eyes were. 'I had to go see Ms Fray.'

My heart wrenched against my will. Ms Fray teaches him Biology, which he so badly wanted to do well in but was pretty dire at (I know, because I used to help him). He'd probably stayed behind because he was struggling with something. Ughhhh. My heart wrenched again as I remembered that was one of the horrible things I'd accidentally posted about him online.

'That's OK, sit down. Emma?'

'*What?* There's no room!' I panicked. For some reason it crossed my mind that she was suggesting he sit on my lap.

'Er...did you find anything?'

**** went and sat down on the other side of Charlie, who fist-bumped him. Are they friends? How is it possible that **** has a friend I don't know about? Why have I never seen him on his Instagram feed before?! Boys baffle me sometimes. I'm a hundred per cent convinced that girls would never have such non-publicly declared relationships.

In the middle of this inner-rant, I realized everyone was looking at me.

'Oh right, yeah,' I stammered. Willie was still howling. 'If the pain doesn't stop after you've washed it, get some saline solution drops and keep putting them in.'

Willie looked like he was about to cry. Holly reached over and patted him on the shoulder, like he was just being a massive baby. I stifled a laugh and caught Leon's eye as he smirked, and we both looked away again.

This is a bit of a spanner in the works for my not thinking about Leon resolution, to be sure. But I can handle it.

Wednesday, 12 November

posted by EditingEmma 11.15

Stupid Friends

At break, I sat down with Faith and Steph.

'Guess what *I* did last night,' I said.

'What?'

'Went to my first *after-school activity*.'

'Cool,' said Faith. 'The fashion thing? How was it?'

I paused.

'Faith, I'm not sure you heard me properly. I went to an *after-school activity*. I stayed at school *longer than I was legally obliged*.'

She blinked. 'Congratulations?'

'What?! Come on! This is big!'

'I stay behind to finish my art projects all the time,' said Faith.

'I have football practice on Tuesdays and monthly matches on Saturday,' said Steph.

I sighed. 'This is just like becoming a pen-writer all over again,' I said.

'What?'

'So in primary school, you know how you use pencils, and then graduate to pens?'

Faith shrugged. 'Can't remember.'

'Well in our class it was a really big deal. The first pen-writer, *Gail Wandsworth*,' I said her name with venom, 'was treated like bloody royalty. Her pen was bestowed upon her like a knighthood and everyone *clapped*. And she was all, *I'm Gail, everywhere I go I leave a trail of permanent ink that smells like roses and superiority. Gail...* ugh. Then there was Polly Kendrick, and Dan Sharma...'

'Are you going to go through your whole primary school class?' asked Faith.

'Shh,' said Steph. 'I want to see the depths of her bitterness.'

'And by the time it got to me, loser Emma Nash, pen-writer number fifteen, NO ONE CARED ANY MORE. Does my achievement mean any less because I got there a bit later? Do my successes not mean anything on their own? Must they constantly be compared to that of my superior friends and peers?'

'You're right.' Faith patted me on the shoulder. 'Well done.'

'I just don't feel like you mean it.'

'Better show appropriate enthusiasm, Faith,' said Steph, 'You don't want to end up like Gail, buried in a shallow grave with a pen stuck down her throat.'

Why do I bother?

posted by EditingEmma 13.55
Steph came with me to look at the fashion show sign-up sheet, to see what teams I'm on. I got social media and design

like I wanted!! Score!!! Then Steph pointed at a name lower down.

'LEON is doing it?!' she shouted.

'Yup.'

'Agh, WHAT. WHY DIDN'T YOU TELL ME.'

'It's no big deal.'

'It IS a big deal. AGH. That's so ANNOYING. This was something you were just doing for *you*. And he has to ruin it with his stupid…annoying…*presence*!! Ugh, why doesn't he just cheese off, seriously!!!'

'Cheese off?'

'It felt right in the moment.'

'Don't worry,' I said, 'he won't ruin it.'

'AGH!!! It's so UNFAIR.' She shook her fist at a passing Year 7.

'Steph, really!' I took hold of her fist. 'I was a bit shocked and at first I was very…*aware* of him in the room…but after a while I just got on with it and forgot about him.'

'Really?' Steph peered at me.

See. I can't lie to Steph.

'OK, I didn't *totally* forget about him. But I nearly did. I promise. He's not going to ruin it.'

'He'd better not,' said Steph. 'Remember this is something you're doing for you and ONLY YOU.'

'I'll remember.' I nodded. 'Anyway, he's doing set with C-Holz, so I'll barely ever see him.'

'They're letting Crazy Holly do *set*?' Steph exclaimed. 'Isn't that a health and safety hazard?!'

'Probably.'

She got distracted then, thankfully. Because I don't think I was doing a great job of convincing her. But she really needn't be worried. I'm definitely not thinking about him.

posted by EditingEmma 20.19

Why Is My Mother Incapable of Dating Men With Normal Jobs?

Mum came into the kitchen, looking a bit glamorous for a Wednesday night...

'Where are *you* going?' I asked.

'Out,' she said.

Expansive.

'You've got a date?' I prodded.

'...Yes.'

'With who?'

'The nice man we met on Halloween.'

'Oh my God, the pumpkin carver!!!' I practically screamed.

Mum sighed. 'His name is Graham. And he's a *vegetable artist*.'

I stopped. I stared.

'A what?!' I repeated. 'What the hell is a *vegetable artist*?!'

'Must you be so obsessed with my boyfriends' jobs?' Mum sighed. 'Can't you ever just focus on their personalities?'

'I will, once you go out with someone who's an electrician, or a plumber, or in advertising, or sales... What about sales, Mum? What about a nice, normal salesman?'

'I don't want to date a salesman. I want to date Graham.'

'Well then. It's up to you. But I'm afraid I'll have to keep referring to him as the Pumpkin Carver.'

'Vegetable artist,' she replied, through gritted teeth.

She left before telling me what that meant, exactly. I'm sure time will tell.

Thursday, 13 November

posted by EditingEmma 17.01

Friendships Take Actual Work: A Realization

So, in amongst all my terrible friend-making, I've been comforting myself with the fact that at least mine and Gracie's friendship is totally solid now. Well, *I* was in for a rude awakening from the cold mackerel of truth. This afternoon I was sitting with her, giggling at 'worst sex injuries' on the internet (which I've got to say, doesn't inspire me – the most clumsy person in the universe – with much hope for my future) when she said, 'So, when are you going to start dating again?'

'I'm not,' I said.

She laughed.

'What?' I asked.

She realized I was being sincere then, and nodded in a way I imagine she thought was supportive.

'Gracie,' I said. 'People don't have to have a love interest to lead a worthwhile and satisfying life.'

'I know,' she said.

Silence.

'People don't. You do,' she added.

And for some reason, even though it's completely a comment I would usually expect from Gracie, it sort of stung me out of nowhere. I'd foolishly let my guard down, because I think somehow I thought our relationship had just... I don't know... *magically transformed* over the holidays. But no, here we were, just the same people as we were last term.

After she said that she went back to the laptop, as if nothing had happened, and I sat back feeling grumpy and childish. I decided to ignore her until she noticed and then go to lessons. But, clearly too enthralled by genital piercing mishaps, she didn't notice me ignoring her... And during this time, I had time to cool off and assess my options. I thought...

1) I can carry on ignoring her
2) I can snipe back at her
3) I could actually say something

1 and 2 are definitely how I've spent my entire life with Gracie, up until now. I took a deep breath. I so badly wanted to walk off and scribble 'Gracie is a butt' over my work all afternoon (it's very therapeutic). But I thought about my resolutions. If I wanted things to change, I was going to have to change them.

'Gracie.' I broke my silence (that she hadn't yet noticed). 'I feel like we need to chat.'

She looked up from her screen. My heart started thudding. 'About what?'

'Um, important relationship stuff.'

'Oh,' she said. 'All right...'

She leaned back in her chair, looking at me expectantly.

I continued. 'It's just… Er.' Oh God, this was hard. I swallowed. 'I know we're all good now and that's great, but I feel like we can't have a fight, clear the air and then just move on. I feel like maybe we need to talk about how we're going to change our relationship, otherwise we're just going to fight again. And clear the air. And fight again. And it will be an endless cycle of fighting and air-clearing until we have no air left to clear. Our friendship will be trapped in an airless room and die.'

'Uh huh,' she said, looking at me like I'd just put on a hat in the shape of a pineapple.

'Right.' I ploughed on regardless. 'So I'll go first, then. I feel like…sometimes you unnecessarily make me feel like I'm being weird. Like just then. And it's mean.'

'Ooookay,' she said.

'There!' I shouted. 'You're doing it again! Talking about our relationship is *not* a weird thing to be doing!'

She sighed. I waited.

'All right,' she relented. 'I don't think you're weird, but this makes me feel…uncomfortable. I don't really like talking about this. So maybe it's a defence or something, I don't know.'

'GOOD!' I yelled, doing a little dance. 'Progress! Get it all out in the open, Gracie!'

She paused.

'But then sometimes I do think you're weird.'

'Point taken. Your turn.'

'All right, um, hmm. OK. I feel like sometimes I can't say

stuff around you because you make everything into a joke. It makes me feel like everything I say is being mocked. You never take me seriously.'

Just as she said the word '*seriously*' she looked all pouty and I reflexively pouted back at her. She huffed and crossed her arms.

'Oh, I see, this is *one-way* criticism.'

'No, no, I'm sorry!' I yelped. 'It was my facial muscles. They just do silly things on their own. I do take you seriously!!'

She nodded.

'All right, you go.'

I took a breath.

'OK. I feel like…whenever something bad happens to me, you react in a way that makes the whole thing seem worse. Like, OH MY GOD THAT'S *AWFUL*, and then I feel ten times worse…like you're rubbing it in, or something.'

She paused.

'I feel like, that's actually me being genuinely sympathetic. Because if half the things that happened to you last term had happened to me, I'd be *mortified*.' She shuddered.

I know I found my mum's Tinder profile, had a date where literally the only five words spoken were 'Do you want a Minstrel?' and accidentally went out with a thirteen-year-old, but really, does she need to *shudder*?

'See! You just did it, just then!' I shouted.

She sighed. 'It looks like we're set in our ways.'

'No, come on, we can do this. Um… Maybe we could make a signal? So, you know, whenever I don't take you seriously, or you make me feel unnecessarily weird, we could, erm... hoot like an owl?'

She looked at me with a raised eyebrow.

I hooted like an owl.

'Our signal is *not* going to be an owl!' she whined.

I kept hooting.

'Stop it! What about...looking at our phone?'

'Bit confusing. What if I genuinely need to look at my phone?'

'OK. Blink three times?'

'That'll do, I guess,' I conceded.

Silence.

'... I still preferred the owl, though.'

Evidence: Friendships take just as much work as romantic relationships.

Anyway, I feel like this was an important moment for us. For me. Instead of going away feeling like I'd chewed on Crazy Holly's snack bag of lemons all afternoon, we're actually ok. It just takes...effort?

Maybe I should start making an effort with more things... Like, contouring my face. Or eating super foods.

Then again, slow and steady and all that.

posted by EditingEmma 16.39
Damnit!
Aghhh. I'm SO annoyed at myself. I said that I wasn't going to let Leon... I mean, Oh Nameless One...affect me. But here

I am, the first after-school designing session for the fashion show, and what is he doing?

Affecting me.

I came in to start working on a shirt (blue/green silk, buttonless, flowing) and, lo and behold, he was in the room. We made eye contact as I came in and he immediately left.

His friend Charlie came in a minute later.

'Hey, have you seen Leon?' he asked.

'He left.'

Charlie frowned. 'Oh. I'm sure we said to meet here. Hey, amazing material, by the way.'

'Thank you,' I said absently.

And I shouldn't have let it, I know, but it kind of bugged me. Because then all those familiar thoughts started creeping back in. *What's he thinking? Why did he leave the room? Was it because of me?*

How is it fair that as soon as I've managed to kick stalking him online, he starts getting constantly shoved in front of me IRL?

Well, I refuse to dwell on this any longer. Maybe he left the room because it was too awkward. Maybe he left the room because he wanted a sandwich. It makes no difference to me.

Friday, 14 November

posted by EditingEmma 11.15
The 'Race' (That Apparently I'm In Without Even Entering)
Was just sitting around with Gracie when she suddenly said, 'I guess Steph's going to win, then.'

'Win what?' I asked. Had she entered some kind of competition I didn't know about?

'You know,' said Gracie.

'No, I really don't.'

'*You know.*' She raised her eyebrows.

When I didn't respond she sighed, and said, 'She's going to lose her virginity.'

'I...what? How is that *winning*?!'

'Well, she's going to be the first one.'

I paused, stupefied.

'... Do you mean winning against all the rest of us?'

She looked at me like I was really, really dumb.

I blinked three times.

'I'm sorry, I just refuse to believe you haven't thought it.'

'I honestly, swear to God, have *never* thought about it like that.'

Gracie sighed.

'All right fine, you're an oblivious loser, but you're still a loser.'

This is confusing to me on so many levels. Firstly:

- Different people are ready at different times. So does my 'race' begin from the moment *I'm* ready or the moment that my best friend is ready? Surely that would be like starting off Usain Bolt about a year behind everyone else on a track and calling it fair?

- Or is this not about being ready at all? But then does that mean you're just supposed to do it, even if you're not ready? Why would that be winning? Surely doing something you don't want to do just for the sake of it is actually losing?

- Even if someone *is* ready to lose their virginity, they still have to find someone else to lose their virginity *with*, which seems purely circumstantial to me. I can't just order up someone I like enough, who likes me back (and I did learn this the hard way).

- Surely this would all logically entail that people who've had sex are superior to people who haven't. I'm just not sure this makes any sense. At the end of the day it's really just a bodily function, with two people involved instead of one. Or is it the fact that someone else wants to have sex with you that makes you superior? But in that case, all we'd have to do is walk into any old seedy club and I'm sure there'd be hundreds of creepy men there willing to have sex with any one of us.

I showed this list to Gracie. She just shrugged.

posted by EditingEmma 13.19
Can You Tell If Someone's A Virgin Just By Looking At Them?
Gracie seems to think so, because she keeps staring at Steph and saying stupid things about her appearance being virginal or non-virginal.

'Look at that walk,' she said. 'That's definitely a *non-virgin* walk.'

I looked at Steph, walking across the sixth form centre.

'It's not,' I said.

'Well for one thing, she's strutting.'

'Steph always struts.'

'Nooo.'

'Yes.'

'No way!'

'Yes, you just never noticed before because you didn't used to analyse her every move.'

'Look at the way she bites into the cookie!'

I looked again.

'She's hungry.'

Gracie fixed her eyes on Steph and furrowed her eyebrows.

'But then again, that was a very virginal sneeze.'

'Oh for God's sake. She's still a virgin, all right.'

'Was it the sneeze?'

'NO.'

'Well how do you know?'

'I just know.'

'*How*?' Gracie needled. 'I'm going to need solid evidence.'

'Solid evidence like a sneeze?'

She shrugged.

'I just KNOW, OK.'

'All right, all right,' she said.

We sat in silence for a moment.

'But she's got a distinctly *ex-virgin glow*,' she added in quite a disturbing voice.

I didn't say anything else so that she'd leave it alone. Because the truth is… I mean, now that she's said it… I actually don't know whether Steph's had sex or not. I mean, I'm pretty sure she hasn't. But I don't know for *definite*. Ugh, I don't want to admit that!! I don't want to admit there's a possibility she *might* have had sex and *might not* have told me, because we tell each other *everything*.

EVERYTHING.

She definitely would have told me, right?! She would have discussed with me, if she was even *thinking* about it?

RIGHT?

posted by EditingEmma 17.07

Must Leon be EVERYWHERE?! Even When He's Not Technically In The Room?

Just did my second designing session for the fashion show. Thankfully, this time **** was nowhere to be seen…but his friend Charlie was. He started talking to me when I came in.

'Hey, can I ask your opinion, Button Queen?' he said. 'These or *these?*' He held out two kinds of grey buttons.

'Uh…' I said.

It was really nice being asked my opinion about a fashion thing, and I did want to talk to him about it… But also what popped into my head when he spoke to me was, *I wonder if Leon's spoken to you about me? I wonder what you know about Leon right now, that I don't?* etc., etc. And it's unfair of me, I know, but even speaking to Charlie is a little bit of a reminder of the person I would much rather forget.

'Those, I think,' I eventually answered and sat down at my station.

I'm not usually stand-offish, but if I'm really going to stop thinking about Leon, fraternizing with his friends just isn't going to help. I must maintain a safe distance from all things Leon. I mean ****.

Saturday, 15 November

posted by EditingEmma 18.03
Why Did I Sign Up For This, Again?

So, as part of my role on the social media team, it's my job to create the event for the show. And now, sitting and staring at the blank event, I'm wondering why on EARTH I volunteered for this.

'Steph! Help me!' I shouted on the phone.

'Uh huh.'

'What do I say on the event description?'

'Umm…' I could hear her chewing on something. 'Be super chill and casual. Like you're doing this really fun thing people can come to, but ultimately you don't really care whether anyone comes or not.'

'OK. Got it. Chill and casual.'

Hey you crazy cats. Some of us have been making some cool clothes and it would be great if you came to see our show. Or Not. Whatever. No pressure.

Rang Steph back, and read it out to her.

'"Crazy cats"?' she repeated. '*Crazy cats?!* Since when do you live in the Fifties?'

'I was going for off-the-wall,' I said.

'Hmm, works for Crazy Holly, because she legit doesn't care…not so much for you.'

'All right all right, what else needs to go?'

'Um, ALL of it.'

'All right, fine, clearly I can't do casual. I'm going for heartfelt.'

Hello, everyone. We're working really, really hard on this fashion show, and it would mean a lot to us if you came down to see the fruits of our labours. It's for a good cause, so please think of the children.

'Sounds vaguely threatening,' said Steph.

'All right, well…'

'And a bit intense.'

'OK, I'll…'

'And what is *fruits of our labours*? Now you sound like you're in the nineteenth century.'

'Oh my God, I GIVE UP. How does anyone write these things?!'

'Look, you're overthinking it. Go again. You'll get there. I BELIEVE IN YOU.'

Come to our super cool fashion show…

'Hello, Desperate Paul.'

Join us for a night of fun...

'Exactly what Mr Morris would say.'

Be there or be square...

'Oh my God, Emma. I've stopped believing in you.'

posted by EditingEmma 18.10

It took three hours but I finally concocted a casual and fun-sounding event description (no thanks to Steph). Now I just have to 'invite' people.

Oh my God. There are about five hundred people to invite. Hovering over the button...

Done.

... And now there are literally five hundred people invited and one 'attending'.

Me.

OH MY GOD. What have I done?! Why didn't I prepare?! Why didn't I have Steph on standby to click attending *immediately*?! Now she's having dinner, aghhhh!!

posted by EditingEmma 18.19

Called Gracie.

'Gracie, please go online, I just invited you to something.'

'Yeah, I saw.'

'You *saw*?! What?! WHY haven't you said yes yet?!'

'Well, then it would just be me and you attending...'

'Oh my God.'

'Bit keen, you know.'

'Click attending NOW.'

'Um, yeah, I will.'

'You mean you will, when some other people have!!'

'Well…'

'Gracie. That's ridiculous. What if everyone did that? Then no one would ever click attending for anything, EVER.'

'Oh, er, sorry, Emma, my dad's calling me…'

'NO HE ISN'T.'

'What's that, Dad? Oh, all right, yes, I'm coming!'

'Gracie Morton, do not hang up on me!'

'SorryEmmagottagoloveyouuuuu.'

Then she hung up. How dare she!!! *How dare she!!!*

@Em_Nasher
@GracieMorton1 Just listening to 'You've Got A Friend In Me', what a tune

@Em_Nasher
@GracieMorton1 Oh and, 'With A Little Help From My Friends'

@Em_Nasher
@GracieMorton1 'Best Friend'

@Em_Nasher
@GracieMorton1 'My Forever Friend'

@GracieMorton1
@Em_Nasher All right the others maybe, but I just googled & you
are not listening to 'My Forever Friend'

posted by EditingEmma 18.27

Phew, ****'s friend Charlie clicked attending. Feeling marginally less anxious now.

Marginally.

Oh, and **** did too. Not that I noticed.

Sunday, 16 November

posted by EditingEmma 15.22

The Word 'Virgin'

I've been thinking about the word 'virgin', because we've used it a lot recently. I really, *really* don't like it. I think because either way you use it, there's some sort of negative connotation. It's really hard to use it and simply mean 'person who has not had sex'. It usually comes out like...virgin = loser. Which implies if you haven't had sex by age sixteen, you're some kind of weirdo. Or...virgin = pure. Which makes sex seem like this sort of bad, sullying thing.

I've been repeating it to myself under my breath, to try and remove all the connotations and simplify it's meaning.

Virgin virgin.

But it just hasn't worked. I simply cannot use the word 'virgin' in the literal sense.

We should come up with new words like...um... *'non-sexer'*

or '*oui-sexer*'. Always said in French accents. Because nothing said in a French accent can have a negative connotation.

posted by EditingEmma 19.19
Friendship Mission: Reboot
I don't know if it's Gracie going on about Steph's virginity, which is making me feel like Steph's a million miles away from me in adult-land, or whether it's the fact that *a certain person* keeps cropping up IRL, which is maybe…just a tiny, minuscule bit…giving me the urge to click on his profile…but all of a sudden I feel kind of lonely. I reached for my phone to message Steph, about it getting harder to resist clicking on him, and then put it down again. How massively immature would she think I was? I mean, there she is in this new, amazing relationship, and I'm still trying to resist cyber-stalking someone I barely even dated at all. We were so on and off that we never even got to that stage. She's probably *so* bored of it by now.

I was feeling a bit down and lost, when I started to wonder if I gave up too quickly on the hunt for a new buddy.

What happened with Anika and Hannah were setbacks, to be sure, but that doesn't mean the last girl on the list isn't ripe with potential life-affirming friendship…

I mean, where would we be if people didn't see their missions through to the end?! If James Cook and his crew had turned around and said, *Hey, guys, it's kinda cold? Who cares about crossing the Antarctic Circle? Let's go home and buy a snow machine?* (Actually, that's probably exactly what I would have done, but anyway.)

No. I will NOT abort my mission yet, only one week into school. And last up on the list is Kayleigh Spencer, Cat Lover Extraordinaire.

I'm currently in the process of digging up lots of cute cat pictures online and littering everyone's feeds with them. Hello my furry, feline friend-enticers.

posted by EditingEmma 21.34

Right. Obnoxious amount of cat pictures = posted. I'm feeling so much more upbeat than I was earlier. No uptake from Kayleigh yet. But I'm sure it's only a matter of time...

Monday, 17 November

posted by EditingEmma 08.46

When I came in this morning, Steph and Gracie were clucking around like chickens.

'Faith's new girlfriend is coming to Battle of the Bands on Saturday!' Gracie filled me in.

'Oh my God!' Steph squawked. 'The mysterious Claudia.'

'I'm glad she's coming,' said Gracie. 'It will be so nice to meet her.'

'Yeah, come to think of it…Faith hasn't said that much about her,' I pondered.

'I think she's scared of putting too much pressure on it, too early,' said Steph.

Avoiding putting too much pressure on things too early. Huh, there's a novel thought.

posted by EditingEmma 11.39

Walked to Art with Faith.

'So Faith,' I said. 'I hear, Clauuuudia's coming to Battle of the Bands.'

'Yes, Claudia is coming,' she said.

'What's Clauuuuuuudia like?' I asked.

'She's…Well…' I could feel Faith's happiness and discomfort radiating from her in equal measure.

'She's PERFECT,' I finished for her.

'Ugh!' said Faith. 'This is exactly why I *didn't* want to talk about it.'

'Does she have dreamy eyes?'

'Stop.'

'Does she…understand you?'

'You're the worst.'

I am the worst. But I'm also massively, massively trying to distract myself from the fact that, from the event flyer, I can see Leon's band are performing. How can I ignore him whilst he's doing that? Would it be weird to wear an eyeless balaclava?

posted by EditingEmma 13.25

Dear God No

Just sewing some stuff next to Holly, when she said, 'Are you still trying to meet boys on the internet?'

'I was never doing that.'

'Oh, I thought…'

'I was trying to get to know boys that I already sort of knew, using the internet.'

'Uh huh. Well, are you still doing that?'

'No.'

'Why not?'

'Because, actually, I realized I'm quite happy not knowing them.'

'Oh.'

She shuffled in her seat.

'Well that's a shame…'

'Why?'

'My friend Adam, he saw your picture and he said you have a very square jaw.'

'I… What?!'

'He really enjoys a good, square jaw. Do you want to see his picture?'

She was already getting out her phone. She shoved it in my face proudly.

'There,' she declared. 'What do you say to *that,* eh?'

There, staring up at me, was a boy wearing a leather *Matrix* coat.

Forget every other physical description I could give him. In the face of this, they are not worth mentioning. I repeat: A LEATHER. *MATRIX.* COAT.

Holly was clearly waiting for me to respond.

'Um…he has a very square jaw too.'

'I'll tell him you said so,' she said and winked.

Dear Lord.

Evidence: Even when you insist you're fine on your own, there will always be someone in the world who wants to push their strange friend on you.

posted by EditingEmma 19.08

Cat Watch

I regret to say that, despite posting pictures of cats pretty solidly since Sunday night, there has been absolutely nothing from Kayleigh on the feline front. Even when I posted a video of a cat climbing into a sock, which was categorically ADORABLE. What's wrong with her??? Is she made of stone?!?!

I'm wondering if maybe she hasn't seen all my posts… Although I don't know how that's possible, because everyone else in the world definitely has. Earlier Gracie asked me if someone had hacked my account, and Faith threatened to choke me to death on kibble.

Still, I suppose it's not been that long. Onwards I go.

Tuesday, 18 November

posted by EditingEmma 08.44
Don't Lend People Your Things. Ever.

'Oh, Emma,' said Steph, 'I forgot. Here are your gloves.'

She started getting them out of her bag.

'Oh, thanks,' I said, reaching for them.

'But, um…you might want to wash them.'

I paused. '*Why?*' I said, slowly.

'Errrr…'

'*Why, Steph?*'

'Errr…'

'WHAT DID YOU DO TO MY GLOVES?!'

'Just trust me.' She nodded.

'On the contrary,' I said, 'I don't think I'll ever trust you, *ever again.*'

Now my hands are *freezing* because my lovely, warm, knitted blue-and-pink gloves with little roses sewn round the wrist, instead of being on my hands keeping them snug and toasty, are sitting at the bottom of my satchel, wrapped in a freezer bag like part of a crime scene.

Gracie asked why I wasn't wearing my gloves and I foolishly

told her. Now she's more convinced than ever that Steph's no longer a virgin.

'*I told you,*' she said.

'Gracie, you only get to say *I told you* when the thing you told me has actually been proven.'

'And it has been.'

'It's not like she gave me back the gloves with a used condom inside.'

'Ew.'

'Unless you're suggesting the glove itself was the condom, because I don't think that would be particularly comfortable.'

'Ew, no. Look, all I'm saying is they're getting saucy.'

'Well, yes, but...'

'I mean, what is it that *you* think they did with the glove?'

'Given that these gloves were knitted for me by my now-dead grandmother, I'd really, really rather not think about it.'

posted by EditingEmma 15.25

I was passing Charlie in the hallway earlier, and he said, 'Hey, have you seen how many people are coming now? It's gonna be epic.'

I nodded curtly.

When we'd passed him, Steph said, 'Have you lost the ability to speak?'

'Huh?' I asked.

'Why did you just completely ignore that boy?'

'He's friends with You Know Who,' I said.

'Ah.' Steph frowned.

I'm doing SUCH a good job with my pretending-Leon-doesn't-exist resolution.

Wednesday, 19 November

posted by EditingEmma 11.19

I Am Never Coming Into School Again

Something so horrifically embarrassing has happened to me. Oh God. I might *die* of shame. Can a person die of shame?? Because I think if a person could, it would be me.

I'm still so embarrassed I can barely bring myself to write it down, but blogging is therapeutic...so here we go.

Mr Allen handed me back my essay. He looked really red and didn't make eye contact. I was just wondering whether I'd accidentally doodled 'I <3 Mr Allen' on it, or something, when Faith leant over.

'Emma, what's that?'

'What?'

'On the back of your essay.'

I turned it over.

Oh no. Oh. NO. Oh no.

Noooooooooo.

SO MUCH WORSE THAN A DOODLE.

So the other day after Mum said the printer was 'having a meltdown' (which definitely means she was just using it wrong) and she accidentally printed off loads of photos on our computer. She started screaming about 'paper waste' as if she was personally responsible for destroying the entire Amazon rainforest. So I told her to turn round the paper and put it back in the printer… And then, I forgot…

Some of the photos were… Oh God.

The pictures me and Gracie took of ourselves, the other day… When we were pretending to be *Victoria's Secret* models…

Oh God.

You can probably put two and two together.

WHY DIDN'T I DELETE THEM?!?!?!?!? WHY????

I WILL NEVER BE ABLE TO LOOK MR ALLEN IN THE EYE AGAIN.

'What did you get, incidentally?' asked Faith.

'B plus.' I pondered. 'Do you think he was grading my body?! Because if he was, that's *disgusting*.'

'Uh, no.' Faith shook her head. 'I think Mr Allen is a nice person who doesn't think about his students in a sexual way or judge other human beings based on their appearance, and you've terrified the living daylights out of him. Plus, you're definitely an A, baby.'

I paused. 'Thanks. I think.'

Afterwards I showed them to Steph. I thought she'd laugh and make me feel better, but all she said was, 'Oh? When did you take these?' Her voice sounded all crisp.

'Err… a few days ago?'

She nodded and didn't say anything else, so I put my phone away. I shouldn't have shown her… I mean, she's in her first proper relationship, *maybe* losing her virginity and not telling me about it, and I'm messing around with Gracie like a twelve-year-old. She's probably starting to notice what a chronically underdeveloped human being I am.

posted by EditingEmma 14.39
At Least SOMEONE Finds It Funny

I was just hiding in the design room doing an extra session, because I couldn't face bumping into Mr Allen in the dining hall, when Charlie came in.

'Hey, what was up with you in English?' he asked.

I hadn't even noticed he was in my English class. Huh.

Anyway, lying about it seemed futile at this point, so I told him.

He looked stunned for a moment. 'Oh. My. God,' he said.

For a while he didn't say anything else, then he started having a massive coughing fit.

'Are you all right?' I asked.

After a minute or two, I realized the coughing was his way of trying to cover up a HUGE laughing fit.

'I'm sorry, I'm sorry...' he spluttered.

'No, it's fine,' I said, totally relieved. And then I started laughing too.

The laughing was actually what I wanted. To be honest, it's kind of the reaction I was expecting from Steph...

It made me feel better, until his laugh started reminding me of ****'s laugh. Which is when I abruptly stopped laughing, put my head down and carried on working.

posted by EditingEmma 18.08

I Won't Give Up That Easily

I was walking home, wondering whether to send Steph this really funny picture of some monkeys on a moped or whether she'd react the same way she did earlier. I opted to keep it to myself. Then I thought about how it's now officially been three whole days and I've not had so much as a cursory like from Kayleigh. I wonder how mature *she* is? She did post that picture of her cat dressed up as a horse, so it seems like we might be on the same wavelength.

I was still thinking about it, a bit at a loss for what to do next, when I noticed our neighbour's cat, Pudding, sitting on a wall. Suddenly I had a brainwave.

Now, how does one abduct a cat?

Not abduct. Borrow. How does one *borrow* a cat?

posted by EditingEmma 18.35

Cat-Snatching

Right. I've been rooting through the cupboards and found an old can of tuna. Cats like fish, right? So my plan is to wave the tuna in front of its face and lead it into the house. Easy. Then I just need to *borrow* the cat long enough to take some adorable photos with it. How hard can that be? Not very. Tuna, in, snap, snap, out.

I can see Pudding is still on the wall. She must be hungry by now. And I'm quite convinced I see loneliness in her eyes... She'd probably *love* a cuddle. If you think about it, I'm actually being very charitable. Maybe I should forget all this fashion stuff and consider working at a pet spa. It may well be my true calling.

posted by EditingEmma 19.19

Cat-Scratching

Oh my God. I thought cats were supposed to be *nice*. I thought they were supposed to be *family pets*.

Why does anyone go near those things?!?!?!

I went outside and found Pudding sitting in its usual place on the wall. I approached it and it eyed me suspiciously. Then I got out the tuna and waved it under its nose.

'Heeere Pudding Pudding Pudding,' I called. 'You like fish, don't you? Mmmmm.'

Pudding glanced at the tuna, then looked away and yawned. Seriously. It YAWNED.

What are they feeding this cat? Caviar?

I thought, maybe if I just go in for a selfie here? So I did. But the resulting selfie was of me leaning next to a totally disinterested, random cat on a wall. It wasn't even looking in the right direction.

'Can't you look at the camera?' I asked it.

It carried on looking into the mid-distance.

I stood dithering for a little while until I just thought, sod it... Now, what happened next was not my finest moment...

I grabbed the cat.

OK, it was rash, but I was panicking!!! All I wanted was a cute picture! Aren't cats cute and cuddly?!?! Isn't that their WHOLE DEAL?!

No. Apparently, it is not.

Pudding started wriggling and clawing and making HOR-RIBLE noises. I mean, really, truly awful noises. Like I was Cat-

Satan dragging it to the depths of fiery Kitty-Hell. I managed to get it into the living room, where it started leaping around the furniture like a totally berserk thing.

'Stay still! Pudding! Sit!' I was yelling. But it kept bouncing around, knocking stuff on the floor.

After a minute or two, I realized this would be my only photo op, so I started chasing Pudding around trying to get in the shot. Which was obviously impossible. I got a few of me with its rear end as it leapt around, but that was about it.

Eventually I let Pudding out and it rushed down the path. JUST as Pudding's owners were arriving back next door.

I stood in the doorway, facing Mr and Mrs Pudding and Baby Pudding, who were all looking at me totally aghast.

'What's going on?' Mrs Pudding broke the silence.

'Er, Pudding seemed to find its way into our house and er, I was just letting it out,' I said weakly.

They all carried on staring at me. I pulled my shirt up to hide the scratches.

'Her name is Anastasia,' said Baby Pudding forcefully.

Seriously? Where did I get Pudding from?

'Oh, right, yes, of course, sorry. Bye, Anastasia!!' I said in my cutest voice, and shut the door. Good riddance, devil cat.

Now I'm completely *covered* in deep, red marks, I smell like tuna and all I've got to show for it is one picture of me and a cat's bottom.

Still, better than no picture. I guess it will have to do.

posted by EditingEmma 19.31

Picture posted. My caption is: 'Me and Pudding love chasing each other round!!! #lazyevenings #catlovers' with lots of hearts and cat emojis. I've also liked loads of Kayleigh's cat pictures.

Faith already commented, 'All right, come on now. WHO is Pudding?' but I deleted it.

Anyway, still nothing. Nada. Squat. Come on Kayleigh. Take the bait!! The cute, furry, EVIL Satanic monster bait!!!!

Thursday, 20 November

posted by EditingEmma 08.11
GloveGate
Mum just came into the kitchen.

'I'm off, see you this evening!' she said, waving.

And then I spotted them.

THE GLOVES.

Oh God. I'd left them out on the side in the hallway, to remind me to put them in the wash, and she must have picked them up!!

'*Mum*,' I said, panic rising. 'Why are you wearing my gloves?'

'Oh yeah, sorry, I've lost mine and I've got a lot of walking to do today. It's freezing. You don't mind, do you?'

'Errrr. Well, yes. Yes, actually I do. Please can I have them back?'

She frowned. 'Are you serious, Emma?'

'Yes, Mum, it's very important that I…'

'I know you're an only child, Emma, but really, I thought I raised you better than that. At least try and open your mind to the concept of sharing.'

Then she walked quickly out of the house.

OWCH.

'Fine, walk around in Steph's sex-germy gloves all day, see if I care!' I called out to the empty hallway.

I can't believe my mum is out there walking around in those gloves. *Shudder.* Another thing for the avoid-thinking-about-it pile, methinks. Like my aggressive, unrelenting horniness.

posted by EditingEmma 11.25
New Friends Update
Unbelievably, there is STILL nothing from Kayleigh. Should I go cruising for some other cats on my street this evening?? Get a whole litter of them in? Take a picture with so many cats covering me that you can just see my head peeking out?? Dress as a giant cat and start bringing her dead mice??!
WHAT WILL IT TAKE??!

posted by EditingEmma 13.19
Friend Fail: Take Three
I was just in the toilet when I heard a familiar voice from outside.

Maths Champion Kayleigh aka Cat Queen aka My New Best Friend.

I thought, *This is my opportunity.*

I rushed out of the loo and washed my hands. She was standing by the dryers, talking to another girl. I moved over to them.

'Sorry,' I said. 'Just got to dry my hands.'

She smiled quickly at me and then carried on talking. I listened to their conversation for a moment, praying there was some way I could shoehorn cats into it.

'So then my dad grounded me, it was so unfair...'

At least you got to stay in with your cat?

'I know, you didn't even get to wear your new dress...'

Could I say I design cat dresses?

'What's for lunch today?'

'I think it's turkey.'

TURKEY! YES!

'My cat loves turkey,' I said, turning to Kayleigh.

She looked briefly puzzled. 'Oh right, yeah, mine too,' she said. For a minute I thought she looked kind of...sad? But I ploughed on anyway.

'Wanna see her?' I asked. 'She's so adorable.'

Then I got out my phone. Kayleigh and her friend leaned in.

'She looks kind of...afraid?' said her friend. 'Is she all right?'

'Oh, she's fine.' I fake laughed. 'It's just a game we play...'

Then, suddenly, Kayleigh started squeaking. At first I thought she was cooing over the cat. I was all pleased with myself and started playing my inner triumph trumpet, when I realized she was actually crying.

I stood rooted to the spot in utter terror.

'I'm sorry,' she blubbered. 'It's...it's...'

Kayleigh's friend put her arms round her shoulders, and then nuzzled into her neck.

'I'm sorry, Kay,' she said.

Then Kayleigh started wailing. I mean really WAILING.

Kayleigh's friend turned to me. 'Her cat died,' she half-whispered. 'Two weeks ago. Tragic bus accident.'

Oh. My. God.

You. Are. Friggin'. Kidding. Me.

It all clicked into place. Of COURSE she hadn't liked any of my cat pictures... She hadn't been posting anything about cats recently either. Oh my God.

Kayleigh's wails got louder.

'Oh my,' I started. 'Oh dear. I'm so sorry. I...um...I don't know what to say. Maybe I'll just leave you to...'

Then Kayleigh flung her arms around me. She drew me into the hug and started sobbing on my chest. I was so close I could smell her shampoo. My face was sort of pressed against her friend's face on the other side, and we both tried not to make direct eye contact.

'Thank you,' she said. 'Thank you for getting it. Not...' She choked a little. 'Not that many people get what it's like to lose a pet you really love. I mean really get it.'

'I...um. Yeah. I get it,' I said.

Not technically a lie. I had a fish once. I think it's name was Jimmy. Or was it Timmy?

'I just can't imagine it getting better,' cried Kayleigh.

'I know, I know,' soothed her friend, and looked at me, as if urging me to say something comforting as well.

'I, uh, can't imagine how much it hurts,' I added. I was INCREDIBLY uncomfortable at this point, and all my words were coming out very wooden and stilted.

Then Steph walked into the toilets. At first she barely took any notice of the huddle and went to wash her hands. Then, when she glanced in the mirror and noticed I was part of it, she did an actual double take. She turned round and gaped at me.

'HELP,' I mouthed silently over the top of their heads. But she just shrugged at me and carried on gawping. Good to know I can always count on her in a time of crisis. We all stood there for another thirty horrendously awkward seconds.

'Oh, look at me.' Kayleigh eventually let go. 'Pulling myself together now. Pulling myself together.' She slapped her own cheek a couple of times. 'I'm really sorry.'

'It's OK,' I said.

'Sorry to put a downer on things. She's really cute.'

She pointed at the fraudulent cat picture on my phone. I started to feel very, *very* guilty.

'Er, thanks,' I said, looking at Steph. 'Is that the time? Oh God, Steph and I said we'd meet a friend, didn't we, so...'

And then, THEN is when Steph decided to find her voice.

'Whose cat is that?' she asked and leaned in.

My heart plummeted. I felt it slipping down, down, down into my shoes.

'Mine, Steph,' I said in desperation.

'Cat?!' she snorted. 'You don't have a *cat*.'

And that was that. It was done. No going back. Kayleigh and her friend both looked at me, and I knew they could see the truth in my eyes.

Kayleigh gasped. Actually *gasped*. They both stared at me for a couple more seconds. Then her friend threw her arm back around her.

'Come on, Kay,' she said.

And they hurried out. Kayleigh was still looking at me like I'd killed her cat myself.

AGGGHHhhhhghhhhhhhhhhhhhhhhhhhhhhhhhhhhhhhhh-
hhhhhhhhhhhhhhhhhhhhhhhhhhhhhhhhhhhhhh.

'Um, what just happened?' asked Steph.

I sighed. It's official. Game over.

I WILL NEVER HAVE NEW FRIENDS.

On the bright side, at least I got closer with her than the others. I was right about her. She *is* a very warm person.

On the downside, she now thinks I am a very cold, strange, sick and twisted person.

I don't believe that in attempting to find friendship, I have made two girls *cry*.

ACTUAL CRY.

posted by EditingEmma 16.29
Friend Fail: Take Four

Now I think it's *my* turn to cry. On top of failing to make new friends, I'm now failing to maintain my old ones. At lunch, Steph went running after some girl on her football team to tell her practice was cancelled. Gracie said, 'See. A *non-virgin* run.'

I don't know if it was the Kayleigh Spencer thing that had got me all worked up and upset, but I reacted badly. 'OH MY GOD,' I yelled, lunging for Steph's phone, sticking out of her blazer pocket. 'That's it! YOU ARE DRIVING ME UP THE WALL.' I put in her passcode and opened up her message thread with Andy.

'I'll show you,' I said.

'Ew, no!' said Gracie, biting her lip. 'I don't want to see their saucy messages!'

'Emma,' interjected Faith. 'What are you doing? Put it back.'

But I was a woman possessed. I scrolled further and further (unfortunately discovering that they call each other 'chicken' – does everyone's head instantly turn to mush when they fall in love?) and then found what I was looking for.

'AHA!' I declared. 'Look, they're talking about how far they've been with other people, and neither of them have had sex. This is only from three days ago.'

'Emma?' I heard Steph's voice from above me. 'What are you doing?'

I looked up. She was standing over me.

'Oh, I just had to prove something to Gracie.'

She took her phone out of my hands. 'Were you reading my messages?'

She sounded *really* annoyed. I could feel my neck turning red.

'Um, only to prove a point.'

'What point?'

She stared me down. I felt like a rabbit caught in head-lights.

'We steal each other's phones all the time,' I said, genuinely confused. 'Remember last term when you made me a fake dating profile?'

She shook her head. 'I said sorry for that. And that was different, it was a joke. I mean, these are my private messages.'

'OK…It's not like I don't already know EVERYTHING about you,' I countered. 'One time I saw you coming out of the bathroom naked doing a fart. You don't get to know someone much better than that.'

She didn't even smile. Really? Not even for the naked fart story?

'Yeah, but what I say in private to my boyfriend is…personal.'

'So-*rry*,' I said.

And I was! I was actually sorry. But I also felt kind of hurt, even though technically I was the one in the wrong, and everything I was saying was coming out all sarcastic.

'Look, I know stalking people is your thing—' (OWCH) '—but I feel like maybe you're normalizing it a bit too much. Everyone's got to have some boundaries.'

I opened my mouth, genuinely taken aback. 'I said I'm sorry!' I yelped.

'OK, well, I'll just change my passcode and we can forget it.'

CHANGE HER PASSCODE?! Is she serious?! What the hell is she talking about? I felt a stab of betrayal. Even though it is her phone.

I sat quietly for the rest of the day with tears prickling my eyes. That was horrible. I've never had a disagreement with Steph before. I didn't mean to get so defensive… I was just upset that she minded me going through her messages. Which is obviously stupid because they're her messages. But…she's never had 'boundaries' with me before!! What are these 'boundaries'?!?! And how do I make them go away?!

posted by EditingEmma 20.58
Assessing the Day

I've had a chance to calm down now, and reflect on what has been a pretty catastrophic day. I am, and imagine always will be, completely MORTIFIED by what happened with Kayleigh. That's it now. I'm out of options. I don't have the energy to make a new list... The friend mission really is drawn to a close this time.

I still feel upset about the thing with Steph earlier, but I know it was my fault. I keep thinking about what Mum said, about how sometimes being a good friend doesn't mean clinging on too tightly. Clearly, I'm not doing a good enough job of giving Steph space. I must give her *even more* space than I already am.

As it seems I'm genuinely incapable of making other friends I'm going to really, *really* try to be a good friend to the ones I've got, and if space is what she wants then, even though it makes me sad, space she will have.

Friday, 21 November

posted by EditingEmma 17.08
Friday's Events

1) Did A Lot of Hiding
Faith sat down at lunch.

'Emma, I just heard Kayleigh Spencer and her friends talking about you and something about calling the RSPCA. Please stop making enemies all over school. It's making it hard for me to walk the halls.'

Then Kayleigh Spencer walked past to get a tray and we both ducked.

2) Became Crazy Holly's New Purpose In Life
Every time I saw her, she would waggle a picture of *Matrix* Coat Boy at me across the room and raise her eyebrows up and down faster than I thought humanly possible. Damn, those coats are really shiny. Even on a teeny, tiny phone screen, I could see it glinting at me from thirty metres away.

3) Wished Everyone Would Shut Up About Battle of the Bands

Well, not *everyone*. Namely, Gracie. She's acting like it's a proper party, not just some lame school thing.

'And I thought I'd curl my hair, even though it takes AGES. Do you think I should use the straighteners or—'

'Gracie,' I interrupted, 'You know there aren't going to be hordes of new, fit, talented musician boys attending, don't you? You know that it's probably just going to be Willie Thomas playing a trumpet?'

Gracie sniffed. 'You never know.'

'But I do know. I do. You know where your hopes are, right now? Yeah, well, lower them, keep lowering them until they hit the floor and then sink them way, way below ground, and then you're probably about the right level.'

'Bands outside of our school can enter, you know. And lots of people might bring their friends!'

I decided it was best to just smile and nod.

4) Discovered My Mother Has Hidden Powers

I got home to the smell of burning.

'Mum?' I called out.

No reply.

'Mum?' I called again.

I walked into the living room, getting a bit worried by this point that Mum was lying in the kitchen passed out from fumes, when I saw it. A charred, blackened picture of Mum's stripper ex-boyfriend Olly, in a Speedo and a sailor hat. It was lying in a smoking bucket in the middle of the room.

I stood staring at it for a bit, when Mum finally appeared carrying a white rose and a tangerine. Covered in glitter.

'Mum?' I asked.

'Yes?'

'…What are you DOING?'

She ignored me and carried on towards the bucket, putting the tangerine down beside it.

'Mum? Hello? Earth to Mum?'

She sighed.

'It's a spell to get over Olly. Heather told me about it.'

I blinked.

'Don't look at me like that, Emma. It's not like I actually *believe in magic*.'

'Oh, right, sorry. The spell-casting threw me off a bit.'

'I thought it might help.'

'HOW?'

'Well, I thought it might be cathartic.'

'And was it?'

'Well… I was distracted. I used a satsuma instead of an orange and I kept wondering if that would make a difference. Then the smoke alarm went off.'

'Mm-hmm,' I said.

'Oh just go upstairs,' she snapped.

'What about the pumpkin carver?' I asked. 'I thought you were dating him now?'

She went a bit red.

'I am. Which is why it is especially imperative I banish any last thoughts of Olly from my mind.'

I nodded. I knew how she felt.

'Can I ask one more thing?'

'What?'

'Did you have to use *that* photo? I mean, let me rephrase, did you have to SCAR ME FOR LIFE by using *that particular photo*?'

'We didn't take any pictures together, OK. We're not like you lot with your constant click click click selfies. His advert is all I have.' She stroked his photo-nipple as I retreated.

As I left the room I heard her chanting under her breath, 'A hex on my ex! A hex on my ex!'

Dear God.

posted by EditingEmma 21.37

The Thing I Did Today That Was Really Bad

There may have been something I left out of the day's events because I was embarrassed. And then I realized that's stupid... because what's the point of having a blog if you're not going to be totally, uncomfortably honest? (And also, if the only person allowed to read it is yourself.)

It was after school in the design room. Most people don't stay late on Fridays, but I'd stayed to finish off a couple of last-minute bits on a sleeve (leather band across the upper arm). When I went to get my coat I noticed another coat hanging next to mine. But not just any coat.

He-Who-Must-Not-Be-Named's coat.

He must have been in here at lunch, doing set stuff, and left it. (He's always forgetting his coat. It's completely endearing.) It looked so familiar and yet so weirdly like something from another lifetime. Just sitting there. Being Leon's coat, the same as ever. Existing and carrying on in the same, coat-like way through all of our human drama. And that's when I did the bad thing.

I leaned in to smell it.

And I stayed there. Smelling it.

And it smelt of his shampoo and custard creams and Chewits all wrapped up in bubbles somehow. I don't know why his smell reminds me of bubbles, I'm not even sure if bubbles smell of anything. But that's what he smells like to me. It doesn't sound like a particularly good smell, but it's *amazing*. And as I was breathing it in, everything I'd ever felt for him and all our memories seemed contained in that one moment. (Smell is weirdly powerful.)

And then I heard the door opening and jumped away in terror and the coat's owner was there, standing in the doorway. I didn't look at his face in case he could see what I'd just been doing in my eyes. I don't think he saw. Please please please please please please please please say he didn't see. I scuttled past him and when I got outside I started running.

Please please please PLEASE say he didn't see!!!!

I feel so dirty and ashamed. I can't believe it. I really, *really* thought I was better than that, now. One *second* of weakness and I feel like I've stepped about six months backwards.

How is that possible?!?!

I wanted to message Steph about it, but managed to content myself by having an imaginary conversation with her instead, so at least that's something.

Saturday, 22 November

posted by EditingEmma 12.39
The 'Big Night' has Arrived
Usually Steph would come get ready with me for BOB but, continuing in the name of giving her more space, I've left her to it. She's probably getting ready with Andy, so I'll go with Gracie.

I'm staying at Steph's after in preparation for her traditional birthday sleepover/family lunch tomorrow, so I'll see her then. In all honesty, I'm looking forward to that more than the event. It's funny…everyone's been going on about this for weeks, and now it's here I'm just sort of not in the mood for it. I think (AGH) it must be old feelings suddenly crashing back in for Leon. I just can't wrap my head around it… I genuinely thought I was getting on my way to being over it. Now I feel like what I imagine it must be like to build a house, and then suddenly realize it was actually a tent after a strong gust of wind. Is it really true that being reminded of his *smell* can send me hurtling way back from the finish line? Or have I been lying to myself this whole time? Was I never really getting over it at all?

Steph will know the answers. I can't *wait* for it just to be the two of us. I have so much I want to talk to her about.

And I feel a little jump in my stomach every time I look at the football tickets I bought her. She's going to *love them*. I'm so excited to see her face when she opens them.

In the meantime, I'll just focus on making my new dress to wear tonight. I was seriously considering staying home for BOB and heading straight to hers, but then I remembered Faith's bringing Claudia with her and is really excited/nervous about us meeting her, and I'm really trying to be a good friend.

Everything will be fine if I just keep cutting, sewing, hemming. Cutting, sewing, hemming... Ahhyeahhh. I'ma look so gooooood.

posted by EditingEmma 16.02

Hmmm. Posted a picture of the new dress (which I LOVE) but it hasn't really got as much attention as I thought it would... I mean...some people have liked it. But not like with some other stuff I've made. I usually get way more than that.

Are people just not on social media? Getting ready for Battle of the Bands, maybe?

Hmm. Maybe I'll wear my jeans tonight, instead...

posted by EditingEmma 16.59

My Mother Has Instagram

Was just about to leave when I got stopped in my tracks.

I refreshed my phone for notifications and saw a terrible, some might say shocking, sight.

Mum had liked the picture of my dress.

'Mum!' I called out. 'MUM!'

'What is it?' she called out, emerging from a cloud of smoke in the kitchen. (Cooking gone wrong or another spell? I didn't dare ask.)

'Since when do you have INSTAGRAM?'

'Since today. Graham showed me how to do it.'

I gaped at her. Unbelievable.

'He uses it to sell his art. The other day someone followed him and then bought twelve of his aubergine penguins.'

'That's...'

'And two of the broccoli giraffes, I think.'

'Mum,' I said. 'If you insist on this, could you and your... *aubergine penguins*...please stay away from me. I mean it. No comments. No likes. No interaction.'

'Oh come on, they're good! Look!' She shoved the picture of the aforementioned penguins in my face. They were actually weirdly impressive, but that's so not the point.

'I mean it,' I warned.

'All right, all right, she said. 'But I don't know what you're getting so sensitive about. You could use the boost.'

I looked at the amount of likes on my dress. She's right, damnit. Oh God, how pathetic is it that the only person liking my picture is my parent?!

posted by EditingEmma 18.01
At Battle of the Bands
Ugh. I can't believe I'm EARLY for an event that I didn't even want to attend that much in the first place. Gracie knocked on my door an HOUR before she was supposed to, and judging

by her walking speed you'd think the school was handing out a million pounds to the first person through the door.

'Gracie, can we *slow down*,' I said, already out of breath.

'I want to get the best scoping spot,' she said.

'Scoping spot?!'

'Well, I don't want to miss any new potentials.'

Seriously?

'Seriously?'

'All right, Ms Judgey Face, just because you've decided to go it alone... Some of us are still on the lookout,' she said.

'Apparently, quite literally on the lookout,' I said.

And now, we are sitting in the two chairs positioned opposite the door, and to the side a bit. We actually moved the chairs several times before Gracie deemed them to be adequately placed. Apparently directly opposite the door is '*too* obvious', whereas opposite but a metre across is 'just the right amount of obvious'.

In all honesty her logic has completely gone over my head, but I'm not going to argue because we're right by the snacks table.

posted by EditingEmma 18.26

Staring at the Door

Not a single person has walked through it yet. We are literally the only two people in the hall. Even the people who set up the band area left to go out and come back again.

On the plus side, we did get first dibs on all the mini-dough-nuts.

posted by EditingEmma 18.50

YES! A PERSON CAME THROUGH THE DOOR! And it was...

Willie Thomas.

Carrying a trumpet.

'OH MY GOD!!!' I screamed, practically falling out of my chair. 'I can't believe I was right!!!'

Gracie went all pink.

'I should get a job as a *fortune teller!!!* Oh my God, what if I really can see the future?!'

'You can't,' she snapped. 'You made an educated guess and anyway, he's only the first person to walk in. There could be tons of attractive boys coming. All the cool people turn up late.'

'Like us, you mean?'

She ignored that one.

'Admit it, Gracie, I was right.'

'I...'

'I WAS RIGHT.'

'You weren't, actually.' She gestured towards Willie's instrument. 'That is a trombone, not a trumpet.'

I was so right.

posted by EditingEmma 19.41

Is Anyone Good At Meeting New People?

Me and Gracie were just fighting over the last mini doughnut when Faith emerged in the distance, hand in hand with a dark-haired, olive-skinned figure.

'Oh my God,' said Gracie, 'Faith's here, with CLAUDIA.' She started squealing.

'All right, calm down,' I said. 'It's not like she's here with Adele.'

'It is a bit like she's famous, though,' Gracie replied. 'I've seen so many photos.'

'I wouldn't open with that.'

'Oh, because you're too cool for internet stalking,' Gracie said sarcastically.

'*Obviously* not. The other night I hit her first Instagram post. I literally could not have been any deeper into stalking. But I'm not going to let *her* know that.'

They got closer.

'I'm sort of…nervous,' admitted Gracie.

'Me too.'

'Are we really weird?' Gracie chewed her lip.

'Um, no, we're just um…unrefined in the art of meeting new people.'

They got closer and closer.

'She's very well dressed,' said Gracie.

'She's HOT,' I said.

'Shh, she'll hear you!'

'Nah, they're still too far away. She's hot she's hot she's hot she's HOT.'

'Shhhhhh!!!'

They approached.

'Hi, guys,' said Faith. 'This is Emma and Gracie.'

'Hi,' said Claudia, 'I'm the hot one.'

Bollocks.

Gracie smirked at me. 'See, she *could* hear you.'

'Yes, I got that, thanks.'

'How are you guys?' asked Faith.

'Um, OK,' I said.

Silence. Gracie looked at me urgently. We really must get better at talking to strangers, without being totally off our faces.

'Except, uh, there are no party rings,' I went on. 'I mean, if you're going to infantilize us by serving biscuits and squash, at least do it properly and give us some party rings.'

Gracie shot me a look as if to say, *Don't talk to Faith's new girlfriend about party rings,* which I found a bit hypocritical. It's hardly like she was offering up heaps of sparkling repartee.

'I like your outfit, Emma,' said Claudia. 'Faith said you're into fashion?'

'Thanks. Yep, I am.'

'Have you applied for any internships in the summer?'

The question froze me to the spot like a bitter, winter chill. My eyes widened.

'I, um...no.'

She nodded and smiled, but I could *feel* that she was slightly disappointed in me. Like Ms Parker when I answer every question in English with 'It's a metaphor for desire.'

'I, uh, I'm helping out with the school fashion show this term,' I babbled.

'That's cool.'

'It's for *charity*,' I added.

She smiled again, kindly but also as if she were looking down on me from a great height.

'*I've* applied for the Cambridge Immerse Engineering course in the summer,' interjected Gracie.

I opened my mouth, speechless.

'Oh amazing!' said Claudia. 'How long is it?'

'You never told me!' I said, indignantly.

Gracie ignored me. 'It's two weeks, and you stay on campus. It's split into three sections – energy, life sciences and materials – which is great as you get a flavour of lots of different areas.'

'Oh wow, that sounds incredible. Well, good luck, I really hope you get it.'

Claudia beamed at Gracie and Gracie went all red and googly-eyed. I felt like a jealous sibling. The one who missed out on the lollipop at the dentist's.

'Oh, Claudia, come say hi to some people in my sketch club,' said Faith. 'Are you guys coming?'

I looked across the room. Kayleigh Spencer was standing on the edge of the group. I caught eye contact with her and her lip quivered.

'Uh, I think I'll stay here,' I replied.

I really have made the rest of my school life very difficult. As if it needed to be more difficult than it already was.

posted by EditingEmma 20.01

Steph popped up behind me and Gracie.

'Hey, guys,' she said.

'Hey,' said Gracie. 'You're late.'

'She's not late,' I said. 'It only feels like she's late, because we've been here since sunrise.'

Gracie huffed.

'Oh, did you guys come together?' asked Steph.

Gracie nodded.

'Look who's here!!' she whispered, pointing at Claudia.

We watched them for a second. Faith gave Claudia a little kiss on the cheek and then Claudia gave Faith a little kiss on the nose, and Faith pretended she hated it but you could tell she was loving it, and they were giggling and...well...a bit nauseating, if I'm honest.

'What's she like?' asked Steph. 'Have you met her yet?'

'She's really nice,' said Gracie.

'She's...' I searched for the right word.

'Yes...?' prodded Steph.

'She's got a *powerful presence*,' I decided. 'I don't know why, but after only two seconds of knowing her I felt really desperate to impress her.'

Gracie laughed patronizingly, like, *Oh that's so cute.*

'Whatever, Ms Cambridge Submerge,' I said.

'It's *Immerse.*'

'You were showing off, too.'

'I really have applied for the Cambridge Immerse Engineering course.'

'Yes, all right, but you never even mentioned it to me. *Me*, who you've known for five years, and after five minutes with Claudia you're bragging about being the next bloody Einstein.'

'I was not *bragging*!'

'Uh, yes you *were*!'

We both started blinking furiously at each other, until it looked like our faces were twitching.

'All right, all right, guys, jeez.' Steph raised her hand. 'I get it, you're both in love with Claudia.'

Then Steph went over to go say hi. I wanted longer with her, but I must let her fly…then I'll have her aaaallllllll to myself tonight and tomorrow.

posted by EditingEmma 20.55
Hiding in the Loos
Was just getting into a heated debate with Gracie about whether it's pronounced 'scons' or 'scones', when I noticed I'd lost her.

'Why would you miss out the "e"? It makes no… Gracie. Gracie. Hello?'

Then I turned around to see what she was looking at.

'Oh my God, who *is* that?!' she squealed.

And standing there, in the flesh, was Holly's friend Adam. In his leather *Matrix* coat. Again, forget every other physical description I could give him.

A LEATHER. *MATRIX*. COAT.

Gracie squinted from the brightness. 'What is he wearing?!'

Then Adam turned around. His eyes zeroed in on me. I tried to hide behind Gracie, but it was too late.

'Oh my God. Emma, why is he waving at you?!' she said.

'Er, long story,' I said, reluctantly peering out from behind her hair.

'*Oh my God.* Please tell me that's not the latest instalment in your absurd dating saga.'

'No,' I hissed. 'He's just Holly's friend.'

'Then why is he coming over to you?' She raised her eyebrows.

I looked. Oh God. It was true. He *was* coming over to me. Where to hide?!

'You know what, Gracie,' I said. 'You're right.'

She was about to look triumphant, when I said, 'There *are* new and interesting guys here tonight, just like you said. And, well, here they are.' I gestured to Adam, still striding over to us with a determined look in his eye, coat flaring out behind him like a cape. 'Enjoy!'

Then I ran off to cower in the loos. I suppose I can't hide in here for ever, but I'd really like to try. Aghhhh!! I can't believe Holly brought *Matrix* Coat Boy!

I suppose I'd better go out there, now. Hopefully, Gracie won't take off Adam's coat and strangle me with it.

posted by EditingEmma 21.19
Watching The Bands
Gracie didn't strangle me, but she *is* pretending I don't exist. Probably preferable.

Crazy Holly is currently up on stage doing a...well... CRAZY drum solo. You can barely hear any of the other instruments in the band over her crashing. Every now and again the harmonica player (yes, I did say harmonica) looks back at her and glares, but she's just having way too much fun to notice. The bell ringer looks inordinately grateful just to be on stage and is swaying about smiling. The person on the didgeridoo looks like he doesn't even know where he is.

Where did she meet these people?! What a motley crew.

In fact, I think that's their band name.

Oh wait, no, excuse me, it's Hotley Crew.

posted by EditingEmma 21.31

COMEDY GENIUS

Hahahah. I literally cannot stop laughing. This is TOO brilliant. Holly got way too into her drumming and threw her sticks into the air. They landed on the harmonica player's head and she stormed off the stage in a huff. Then, stick-less, and harmonica-less, Holly decided to just get up on her stool and start dancing.

The mental image of Holly dancing, floating her arms about her like a tranquillized octopus, to the sound of a subdued didgeridoo, will never, *ever* leave me.

Claudia leant over and murmured, in awe, 'Do you know that girl?'

'Ohhh yes,' I said.

posted by EditingEmma 21.37

Of Course

Just as I was starting to enjoy myself and forget about…ugh, OK, so not saying his name hasn't been working out for me so far, LEON, his band started setting up. Fantastic. Because everyone knows it's really easy to forget about someone when they're in front of you on a stage, looking really attractive and holding a guitar.

Even watching him attempting to coax Crazy Holly down

off her stool with a biscuit didn't stop the plummeting feeling in my stomach.

Neither did him saying 'this song is for Anna' into the microphone and smiling at her across the room. She smiled back, looking perfect and pretty as ever. That didn't help either. Nope. That was probably the thing that pushed me towards tears.

Suddenly I was finding it very hard to breathe. It felt very stuffy and the walls felt closer in than they did ten minutes ago.

As I ran out of the room, I accidentally knocked into Charlie. 'Hey, are you all right?!' he asked, but I just kept running.

Now I'm sitting in the hallway.

posted by EditingEmma 21.55
Still sitting in the hallway
Brilliant. Just...brilliant. I was just settling into the shadows, when I noticed an incredibly tall, familiar-looking figure walking towards the entrance.

The figure stopped and squinted at me, lurking in the darkness. '...Emma?' the figure said.

Great. Just...great.

'Greg?' I replied weakly.

He folded his arms and smiled. 'Well, this is a surprise,' he said.

'It's my school,' I said.

He laughed. 'Yes, I know, I thought you'd probably be here. I meant it was a surprise to see you sitting by yourself in the hallway.'

'Oh...right. Yes,' I said dumbly.

We stared at each other for a little bit. My heart was

thumping in my chest. Seeing my ex-boyfriend was definitely what I needed tonight of all nights.

Not.

He really does have nice hair. And such a kind face. He was smiling at me so openly.

'So um, what are you doing here?' I asked.

'My friend Shannon's playing,' he said.

'Oh, right…cool,' I replied, flying into mild, instinctual hysteria at the mention of 'Shannon'. Who-is-Shannon-is-she-really-just-a-friend-and-if-they're-dating-HOW-DARE-HE-MOVE-ON-SO-QUICKLY.

'Are you OK?' he asked. 'Why are you sitting out here?'

I came back to the moment and looked at him. His eyes were full of genuine concern.

My heart broke a little then. I could see in his face that he still cared about me, after I treated him so appallingly. I didn't mean to, but I did, because I always really wanted Leon. And here I was, selfishly panicking at the thought that he might have moved on to someone who actually wanted to be with him.

'I was just calling my mum,' I answered lamely.

'Right.'

We were both silent.

'Are you sure?' he asked, reaching for my hand.

And then my heart broke even more. Because in that moment, I wanted to jump into his arms and have him hug me and tell me everything was all right. I wanted to be comforted. I wanted to be wanted. But I still didn't really want him.

I looked down at his hand, holding mine. It would've been

so easy to give into it. But you can't just decide to be on your own when it suits you, and then give in again when you're feeling low and pathetic.

I pulled my hand away. Greg looked mortified.

'Look, Greg…' I said.

'No, you don't have to say anything. Sorry.' He looked so sad and flustered.

And the last little bit of my heart that was still together fell totally apart.

Arghghghghhh.

He opened the door and I walked in front of him, pretending to go back inside, and then came straight back out to lurk in the shadows again.

Now I'm just sitting here. Mulling. Twiddling my thumbs. Oh my God. That was…*awful*. I would just go home, now that I've fulfilled my duty and met Claudia, but I'm supposed to be staying at Steph's. God, we've got AGES until her parents come to pick us up.

posted by EditingEmma 22.10

Still sitting in the hallway by myself when, of course, Holly's friend Adam spots me. Oh God. *No no no*. He's coming over to me.

'Emma?' he breathed.

'Hi, yes,' I said.

He took a long gulp of air.

'Wouldyoulikeadrink?' he rushed, brandishing a bottle of scary, intense Russian vodka from inside his long coat. (What else could he have hidden in there?! The possibilities are endless. His coat is sort of like a weird, creepy version of Mary Poppins's bag.)

He stared. I stared. My head was bleeping *say something, say something* like an alarm. Eventually, I said,

'Um, I really need the toilet. A number two.' I nodded.

If that doesn't get him to go away, I don't know what will.

posted by EditingEmma 22.37
Still In The Toilets

Yes, I am still in the toilets half an hour later and no, I am not actually doing a poo. I was just sitting down on the loo, feeling a bit weird and hollow, when I heard someone sniffling in the cubicle next to me.

I knocked gently on the door.

'Um, are you OK?'

No answer.

'I mean, clearly you're not OK. But if you'd like to talk about why you're not OK, then, um, you can. But obviously, you don't know me, so if you don't come out I'll assume you just want me to go away. I'll stay here for ten seconds...'

For some unknown reason I started stroking the door frame, as if the person inside might sense it.

'Three...two...'

Then the door opened.

And Anna came out.

Her make-up was smudged and her eyes were all teary, but somehow she still looked...*together*. Like her crying had only given her some windswept, soaked-in-the-rain vibe. *How?* Anyway, my heart skipped a beat and she glanced at my hand, which is when I realized was still stroking the door frame.

I stopped.

'Emma,' she barked. 'No offence but you're really the last person I want to speak to.'

'OK, no, sure, I'll just…' I said, backing away, and stumbling over the bin.

Then I went outside. The last person she'd want to speak to? As in, the very last? That seems a bit harsh. I mean, I know we're not friends and we both liked the same person which is always a bit awkward, but there are still plenty of people I'd rather speak to *less* than Anna. Piers Morgan, for instance. Or a member of ISIS. I stood dithering for a minute. Then I did something that was probably very unwise. It probably went past 'unwise' and into the territory of 'the really, really stupid'. I went back inside.

And knocked on the door. Again.

'Anna?'

I heard the sniffling pause.

'I'm really sorry to bother you again, um, can I just ask, I mean, or it's going to really bother me all night and probably for the rest of my life, but *why* am I the last person you'd want to speak to? Did I do something?'

There was a tense moment before she spoke again. 'Are you serious?'

'Um, yes.'

The door opened again. She sat back down on the loo and

I took this as my invitation to go inside. I closed the door behind me. And then there we were. Enclosed in our tiny prison of female intimacy.

'Well, he's all yours now,' she said.

My heart started hammering in my chest.

'Err...what?'

'You don't have to pretend.'

'I... No. I really don't know what you're talking about.'

'I'm breaking up with him.'

I paused, before asking the obvious question. It seemed a bit intrusive but I'd already followed her into the toilet, so that ship had probably sailed.

'Why?' I asked hesitantly.

'Because I know what you've been doing behind my back.'

I frowned. She frowned.

'What?' I said.

'Seriously. You two are free to go out now. I'm not going to stand in the way any more.'

'Anna. I haven't been doing anything behind your back.'

'I saw the messages,' she said, then added quickly, 'I was using his timer to bake some muffins. They were already on the screen. I wasn't going through his phone or anything.'

(Ha. As if she has to explain herself to *me*, even if she was.)

'Anna, I haven't spoken to Leon in weeks!'

'Please don't lie, I saw them.'

'No, really,' I said, and got out my phone. I rifled way, way far back in my messages, to our conversation that I still haven't been able to delete. 'Look, all these are from *before summer*.

Then there are a couple from, um, when that blog went up before half-term. But apart from that zero contact.'

She took my phone from my hands and stared at it. Then she started crying again. I stared in horror for a second.

'Do you not believe me?!' I asked.

'No, I do,' she said.

Oh God, I thought. Why is she still crying?! What should I do? I sort of wanted to put my arm on her shoulder, but my instincts were telling me it was best not to touch her. In the end I just stood there awkwardly for a bit longer until she stopped. She wiped her eye with her hand and I broke some loo roll off, put some moisturizer from my bag on it and handed it to her.

'Thanks,' she said, wiping her barely disturbed make-up.

Then she took one look in her compact mirror, stood up and smiled at me.

'That's better. You coming?' she asked.

'No. I think I need to sit down for a while.'

'OK. Bye, Emma,' she said.

It was all very dignified until she had to squeeze past me and I felt her boobs against mine.

Now I'm sitting here in the stall alone, making sense of the past fifteen minutes. I don't know what to think. Possibly, I've lost the ability to think. In one night, I've managed to upset one ex-boyfriend-who-is-lovely-but-I-just-don't-love, and patch up my other ex-boyfriend-who-I-still-have-feelings-for's relationship.

Great.

posted by EditingEmma 23.06

Sitting With Adam

I came out of the loos, with *every intention* of going back inside. But I looked through the door and Claudia and Faith were dancing together, wrapped in their own little love bubble. Andy had arrived and Steph was hugging him. Gracie was chatting to her Cambridge study group. Leon was on stage scanning for someone, presumably Anna. Crazy Holly was teaching her band to octopus dance. Greg was doing lame-dancing with maybe-just-a-friend Shannon. Even Mum was out tonight with the pumpkin carver.

All my friends were off doing their thing, I'd failed catastrophically at making any new ones, and I was still as lonely and pathetically hung up on the same person as ever. In that moment, I'd never felt more like Emma the Unloved.

I really, *really* wanted to talk to Steph, but I knew I should leave her alone. Just because I'm having a crap night, doesn't mean I should ruin hers as well.

I looked down the corridor, at Adam, sitting alone swigging his vodka in the gloomy, flickering hallway lights and it just seemed more like where I belonged.

When I sat down next to him, he looked all pleased and moved his *Matrix* coat out of the way to make room. He's a little strange (obviously, because he's friends with Holly) but honestly, I just feel so relieved to not have to be around crowds of people right now. So, I choose vodka with a stranger.

Vodka with a stranger... It could *almost* sound quite cool

and grown up… If we weren't sitting in my school hallway, and the stranger wasn't dressed up as Keanu Reeves circa 1999.

I'm typing quite a lot as he talks at me, but either he hasn't noticed or he just doesn't care. He's waffling on about the correct feed for garden squirrels.

posted by EditingEmma 23.38

We moved outside because teachers kept circling the hallway.

And then behind some trees because teachers kept circling outside.

Must they make drinking on school premises *quite* so difficult?

posted by EditingEmma 00.38

It suddenly got very late when did it get so kate

Adam is not so bad really, he is the vodka bearer.

My horn is telling me to kiss him but I know that wouldb be bad

Very bad

I will not kiss higm, I will not play intyo my sad horn's trap

My sad sa d horn

posted by EditingEmma 0.45

OH MY GHJOD. WHEN DID I GET TEN MISSED CALLLS.

Oh no no onononoononooooo I must find Steph. STEPPPPP-PHHHHHHHG

posted by EditingEmma 01.42

Andy seems very angry like when Graci e is angry they have the same pinkness and botht their lips disappear

Septet is here. STEPH not Septet. Hahah. In a car. When did that happen?

Sunday, 23 November

posted by EditingEmma 12.31

Woke up in Steph's bed, staring up at Kurt Cobain. What HAPPENED last night? I honestly didn't think I'd drunk that much vodka. Russian vodka is clearly just as stereotypically lethal as they say it is.

I instinctively turned around for a spoon, but when I put my hand out the other side was empty.

My heart dropped.

It all came flooding back.

I sat up in bed, my heart pounding. *Steph's birthday lunch.*

'Steph?' I croaked. 'Steph?!'

I got out of bed. Her special blue mascara was lying out half open on her chest of drawers. I rushed over to her wardrobe... Her favourite leather ankle boots were gone. The house felt deathly still and I could tell they'd left. I knew it, but I really didn't want to believe it. I picked up the phone.

'Hello?' she said.

'Steph? Where are you? Are you there already?'

'Yep.'

'Why didn't you wake me?' I whimpered.

'Um, I kind of assumed, given that you were still vomiting at 4 a.m., that you probably weren't up to it.'

'I can come now?' I said desperately. 'I can be there in forty-five minutes.'

I started rushing to put clothes on. *Crap.* I only had last night's gross, stained clothes. I'd got patches of mud all down my jeans, and on my top as well?! How on earth did I do that? They'd have to do…unless I could I pull off one of Steph's crop tops?

'Don't worry.' Steph broke my train of thought.

'Look, I'm so sorry, Steph,' I garbled. 'I'm an idiot. I got really upset about…*Ugh.* Lots of things. I wanted to talk to you about it, but…'

'It's all right. You don't need to make excuses.'

'No really, I…'

'Gracie told me about Adam.'

'Oh my God, NO, it wasn't like that. It was…'

'Look, I can't really talk right now, but Gracie's probably free.'

'What?' I faltered. 'I want to talk to you! It's your birthday! I want to be there. I can still make it.'

More silence. She cleared her throat.

'It's fine, Emma. Andy came with. After he helped you out of the car last night, he slept on the sofa. Anyway, the table's only for five, so don't worry about it.'

Silence.

'Oh…' I said. 'I see.'

'Look, I've got to go. They're bringing the cake. Bye, Emma.'

'Oh. Bye, Steph,' I said. '… Happy birthday.'

I put down the phone. The huge, sinking stone in my stomach got heavier.

'What are you looking at?' I said to Kurt, watching me with judging eyes.

I dived into Steph's open wardrobe and buried myself in her football kit. It smelled like Steph (like her perfume mixed with the outdoors). I'm not sure how long I lay there for, but eventually I decided it was time to go home and put the muddy trainer I was clutching back in her bag.

What is it with me and smelling people's things, these days?

I can't believe I overslept. I can't believe she didn't wake me.

I can't believe this has happened.

posted by EditingEmma 14.05
Oh No
Walked in the door and Mum said, 'Hi, you're back early... What's this?'

She pulled a twig out of my hair.

And then I remembered.

Running through bushes.

OH MY GOD.

WHYYYYYYY.

So it was after I saw the ten missed calls from Steph. Her parents were supposed to be picking us up at half twelve, and it was already quarter to. I looked out from behind the trees and saw their car in the parking lot. My heart plummeted.

Steph was standing by it, phoning me, and her mum was standing next to her looking a bit concerned.

I remember thinking, even in my *very* heavily intoxicated state: Steph's parents categorically CANNOT see me emerging from the bushes, in the middle of the night, with a boy I don't know. It may as well be my mum watching me emerge from some bushes, in the middle of the night, with a boy I don't know. But the thing was, the car park was in the middle of where I was *supposed* to be, in the school, and where I *actually* was, hiding in some trees.

Things were looking very, *very* bad for me.

'What's wrong?' Adam asked.

'I have to go.'

'All right,' he said, taking a step out of the trees.

'NO!' I cried. 'I can't go that way!'

'Err…'

He looked around him, clearly as stumped as me for another escape route.

I remember thinking, then, that I knew what I had to do. In the moment, I can honestly say it well and truly felt like the only possible option available to me.

I ran.

I ran as fast as I could. I ran like Seabiscuit. I ran *all the way* around the back of the school field, so that I could re-enter through the back of the school and come out the front like I'd been in there all along.

By the time I got to the car I'd basically nearly collapsed from exhaustion. I was red, puffy and half an hour late. I remember silence on the way back because EVERYONE in that car was well and truly beyond annoyed at me.

Steph said, 'We saw you running across the back of the field, Emma.'

And then I passed out.

Aggghhhhhh!!! What a TERRIBLE evening!!! So I did get drunk...but Steph still shouldn't have taken Andy instead of me, right?! I should have just told Steph I was upset about stuff...but I was trying so hard to give her space!

Well, now she REALLY has space!!! Oh God!!

Plus, I keep getting flashbacks of Greg's pained face as I took my hand away. And a crying Anna. And Leon searching for a crying Anna. And then, to top it all off, I spent the rest of the evening hanging out with a guy in a leather *Matrix* coat. Aghhhhhhhhhhhh. I can't believe I got so upset I missed the *only* thing I was looking forward to the whole evening!!! And now I'm even more upset!! I *really* wanted to go today. I really wanted it to just be the two of us, and her family. Like every year. And now Steph's there with ANDY.

posted by EditingEmma 16.04
I Can't Do Anything

This is awful. I can't even make clothes to distract myself. I accidentally sewed a sleeve onto the boob part of a t-shirt. Kind of like a really pathetic, floppy attempt at a Madonna cone bra. And then when I saw it, I didn't even laugh.

Andy is in my place right now. *My* place.

MY. PLACE.

I can just see him there now...telling jokes and making Steph's parents and sister laugh merrily...talking with them about *the news* like a real adult…sitting in MY chair and holding hands with MY Steph and…and…eating MY olives. I feel so invisible and sad and betrayed. I'm like…Dickie Greenleaf. And Andy is The Talented Mr Ripley. And NO ONE HAS NOTICED THAT I'VE DIED.

WHY didn't Steph wake me?!

Ugh. I have so much pent-up frustration. I started doing jumping jacks. Mum came in.

'What on Earth are you doing?'

'Jumping jacks.'

She watched me.

'Why are you watching me?'

'I just don't think I've ever seen you do physical exercise before. It's very strange.'

I lay down on the floor, seeing spots.

'And now it's over,' I said.

'I knew it wouldn't last,' she replied and lay down next to me.

We both lay there for a little while, staring up at the ceiling.

'What's wrong?' she asked. 'Why aren't you out with Steph and her parents?'

I opened my mouth to speak…then closed it again. I burst into tears. Mum hugged me, but didn't ask any more questions.

I can't believe I'm *not* at Steph's birthday. I haven't not been at Steph's birthday since… Well. Since her tenth birthday. But that wasn't my fault, because I hadn't met her yet. Steph's voice on the phone keeps ringing in my ears. She sounded so distant… She went without me. She didn't seem to mind that I wasn't there.

posted by EditingEmma 22.08

Going to sleep in Mum's bed. She didn't say anything when I came in, just glanced up from her book and put a pillow out for me.

I want Steph.

But I don't think she wants me any more.

Monday, 24 November

posted by EditingEmma 07.37

Was RUDELY awoken by my mother, poking me in the back.

'I told you to get up *half an hour ago*,' she barked.

'I told you I'm *not going to school*,' I said, from under the covers.

'Oh yes, you are.'

'Oh no, I'm not.'

She tried to rip the covers from on top of me but I clung on like a limpet. Then she BUNDLED ME IN THEM and ROLLED ME ONTO THE FLOOR.

'How dare you PHYSICALLY ASSAULT ME!' I yelled, from within my bundle.

'You're going to school, even if I have to roll you there myself,' she said.

She thinks she's got the upper hand, but I will prevail.

posted by EditingEmma 08.14

Lurking In The Next Street

Waved goodbye to Mum as I left the house. I even thanked her for 'helping me to see the light'. She looked briefly confused but didn't seem to smell a rat, which only proves how foolish she is and is therefore basically asking to be tricked.

Now I'm waiting. Waiting and watching in the shadows of Mornington Road. Soon she will go off to work and the house will be mine, all mine. Hmm, now, what will I do with my lovely free day?

I mean, watch *Gilmore Girls*, obviously. But it doesn't hurt to pretend to consider other options.

Come on. LEAVE ALREADY.

posted by EditingEmma 08.55

FINALLY. She departs. Excellent timing, because I've walked up and down Mornington Road so many times I'm pretty sure the people at number twenty-one think I'm trying to steal their car.

Now… Goodbye, world and sunshine. Hello, darkness and unrealistically fast-paced yet compelling, smart and witty dialogue.

posted by EditingEmma 11.09

CRAP

I'd just settled into a relaxing bath, when Mum phoned me.

'Hello, love,' she said. 'How's it going?'

'Er, fine? What's up?' I asked.

Panic. Fear. Is this a trick?

DOES SHE KNOW?

'Just thought I'd give you a bell on your break. Are you OK?'

'I'm OK,' I replied.

'Well, I got you some profiteroles.'

'Oh, thanks, Mum.'

Ughhhh. No, don't be nice to me!! Oh God. Starting to feel TERRIBLE about lying. Why did she have to buy me profiteroles!!!

'All right, I'll see you at home.'

'What?! I'm not at home!'

'I mean later.'

'Right, yes. Duh. See you later.'

'I'm not back until seven, but they'll be waiting in the fridge for you!'

My heart stopped.

'Err, I thought you were in Hertfordshire today?'

'I am. I'm just popping them back now.'

NOOOOOOOOOOOOOO.

'Oh, you don't have to do that!!! You have more than enough to worry about!!!'

'Well, I don't want them to go off.'

'They're profiteroles, not raw chicken.'

'Consuming bad dairy can lead to abdominal cramping and vomiting or diarrhoea. Do you want diarrhoea?'

Unbelievable.

'No, I don't want diarrhoea.'

There's absolutely no point arguing with her about refrigeration or expiry dates.

WHAT CAN I DO?!

posted by EditingEmma 11.15
Great. Just Great.
For the second time today, I'm lurking on Mornington Road waiting for Mum to leave. But this time I have wet hair in a towel and I'm wearing a pink, fluffy dressing gown.

Oh come on.

The same old woman who thought I was trying to steal her car earlier is peering at me out of the window. I waved at her and she held up her phone and pointed at it, as if to warn me that she might call the police.

What crime is it, exactly, that she thinks I'm going to commit in my sloth slippers?!

posted by EditingEmma 11.41
Back inside now. Staring at the profiteroles, feeling empty and hollow.

I was sort of managing to bury myself in *Gilmore Girls*, but now I feel really, really low.

And I've started stalking Steph online. When did that happen?

How did I suddenly get back to Year 11 without even noticing?

posted by EditingEmma 15.05
I've looked at so many pictures of Steph it's like I can't really see her face any more. Only all her individual features. You know, like when you say a word over and over, like, um...platypus... and it stops being a word and just becomes a jumble of letters?

Platypus. Platypus. Platypus. Plat-y-pus. P-l-a-t-y-p-u-s.

Steph's nose. Steph's big brown eyes. Steph's hair. Steph's mocha-coloured skin. All the parts that make up Steph.

Steph. Steph. Steph. S-t e p-h.

Nothing makes sense any more.

When did she start liking Andy more than me? Did I change? When did I become so unlovable?

Why did I ever buy that hideous green jumpsuit in Year 9? I loathe myself.

posted by EditingEmma 20.07

You know what doesn't help self-loathing? Eating twenty profiteroles.

posted by EditingEmma 22.07

A Pearl of Motherly Wisdom

My mother, i.e. the woman who felt musically satisfied by listening solely to Nilsson's 'Without You' for over a decade, just told me I must stop watching *Gilmore Girls*.

Clearly, something in my life needs to change. Thank you, and goodnight.

Tuesday, 25 November

posted by EditingEmma 08.01

Lurking around at home again. Today was easier, because Mum left before I would have left for school. I just watched her drive off.

I wonder if I can watch *Gilmore Girls* at the same time as staring at photos of Steph?

posted by EditingEmma 08.34

Easy. Laptop in one hand, phone in the other. I'm surprised by what an amateur question that was, really.

posted by EditingEmma 12.01

Got a message from Gracie, asking me when I was coming back. Never, is the answer. Thinking about it, I could *actually* stay in here for ever. Seriously. I could call up the school and tell them we're moving. The school would think I'd left, Mum would think I was still at school and, hey presto!, all along I was just in my room. Then when it was time to go to uni, I could tell Mum I'd got a place etc., etc., she'd probably give me some funds to set me up for a term or something and then I could just move upstairs into the attic. It would be a bit of an adjustment but I'd be fine... Probably... That guy in *Black Christmas* was fine, right? It was everyone else who got murdered.

posted by EditingEmma 18.14

Another message from Gracie. Ughhh. I've been ignoring them so far but I might have to answer soon:

Are you coming in tomorrow Emma? 16.31

I guess not. Call me later? 16.47

Are you OK? 17.12

Did something happen with Steph? 17.40

Do you want to talk about it? 17.41

OK obviously you don't want to talk 18.10

But please tell me you're not sitting in darkness staring at her picture? 18.11

And then I burst into tears. Because I am. I am sitting in darkness staring at her picture. And it's awful. All these feelings and memories from my horrible summer spent sitting pining over Leon are flooding back. But this is *worse*.

Evidence: Clearly it is just as easy to get obsessed with friends over social media as it is a ghosting ex-boyfriend. Who knew?

Aghhhhh. HOW did I end up back here?! Making myself miserable, stalking someone over the internet?! This is completely going against my resolutions... I had meant 'no stalking' in relation to boys, but this is just as unhealthy…as well as completely, utterly absurd. This is Steph we're talking about. STEPH.

I've been convincing myself she doesn't care any more. That I'm too immature for her now. That she's moving away from me and moving on with her life. But I don't know that. Maybe she's been upset, too. Maybe I'll go in tomorrow and we'll sort this out.

Sent Gracie a message back:

I'll be in tomorrow x 18.12

Wednesday, 26 November

posted by EditingEmma 08.29

Just got into school. I'm even *a little bit early*. Feeling so nervous about seeing Steph that I turned around and started walking home several times. But I'm here now.

Right.

I've got her tickets in my pocket. The plan when she gets here is… I'll say I'm sorry I got so drunk and explain about being upset, I'll give them to her, and then she'll say sorry for not waking me up and taking Andy, and everything will be wonderful and rosy and yes. Everything will be fine.

It's going to be painful to talk about it but ultimately friendship strengthening, I bet. I'm almost excited for all the emotions we're going to share. We'll probably both cry.

posted by EditingEmma 08.44

Steph came in and my heart started POUNDING. She glanced at me as she was walking over, and you know when it becomes like there's only you and one other person in the room? Well, I had that. Whatever Gracie was babbling about next to me got completely tuned out. I took a deep breath and prepared myself for our dramatic make up.

Then, in the middle of my preparations, she sat down...and *started talking to Gracie*!!! (Who, as it turned out, was talking about the proper way to care for koi carp.)

Is that IT?!

... Do I mean *nothing* to her?! Was I right? Was she was totally fine this whole time, whilst I sat in darkness pining over pictures of us from when we still thought wearing matching hats was a really cool thing to do?

OK, then... I guess she doesn't need my apology. She can just take Andy to everything from now on. Which is clearly what she wants to do anyway.

I don't believe I've spent all this time trying to give her space and be a good friend, and being so upset about our argument... and it seems like she hasn't been thinking about me at all.

posted by EditingEmma 14.01
Salt In My Wound
I don't believe it. When I came into Maths, Steph wasn't sitting in her usual place, i.e. next to me. She was sitting next to... wait for it...

Boring Susan.

BORING SUSAN.

I kid you not. I've legitimately been abandoned by my best friend, for Boring bloody Susan. I think if someone had stolen from me or...*poisoned* me...I'd still rather sit next to them than Susan.

I walked over to them.

'Hey?' I said, questioningly.

'Oh hey.' She looked up from her book. 'Mr Crispin asked me to sit here today, because Susan missed the first few days. She needs to copy my notes.'

'I was in Wales,' said Susan. It really is amazing how anyone could get their voice so monotone. Quite a skill.

'OK,' I said.

Steph went back to her book and I walked away. If sitting next to Boring Susan instead of me isn't a sign she doesn't care any more, then I don't know what is.

Now I'm sitting next to Gracie. I just caught Steph's eye (was bound to happen at some point, given how all I'm doing is staring at her). Damnit!! I won't give her the satisfaction of thinking I'm pining for her!

Who cares about Steph anyway? Because I have Gracie. My new Maths buddy. And we're going to have tons of fun. TONS. OF. FUN.

Every time Gracie says something I laugh really, *really* loudly.

'What's so funny?' Gracie asked.

'Er, what you just said...' I said, craning my neck to see Steph and Boring Susan.

'Move the decimal point?'

'Yes,' I said, 'Hilarious. You should do stand-up.'

Then she sighed. What's wrong with her? Does she not realize we're supposed to be having tons of fun?

posted by EditingEmma 14.29

This Is Going To Be Harder Than I Thought

After about ten minutes, Gracie slammed down her pen and said, 'Emma. *Please* stop talking.'

'I...what?' I stuttered.

'I'm sorry,' she said, biting her lip. 'I know you and Steph mess around during lessons... And I'm sorry she's sitting with Susan.'

'Oh, really?' I said. 'I hadn't noticed.'

She rolled her eyes.

'But, I'm not Steph. I don't want to mess around. I...well... if I'm going to get into Cambridge to do engineering, I *have* to do well in Maths.'

'Oh,' I said. 'I understand.'

Gracie looked quite relieved and went back to her books.

Right. I'm clearly going to have to readjust here. Somehow I'm going to have to have to make it appear to Steph as if we are having *tons of fun*, without actually interacting with Gracie at all.

posted by EditingEmma 15.04

BRILLIANT. I've definitely cracked it. What can I say? Some can solve Maths problems, some can solve *life* problems. So every time Gracie works out a new fraction or something, I peer at her book all wide-eyed and scandalized, like she's written me a really hilarious, secret note. Then I do a fake, silent laugh, which Steph won't know is silent because she's on the other side of the room and couldn't hear me anyway. And, because the laugh is silent, it won't disturb Gracie either.

Ingenious!!

posted by EditingEmma 15.15

Or not. After five minutes of fake-scandalized-laughing, Gracie turned round to me and said, 'Emma. *Please* stop peering over my shoulder and fake laughing. It's really off-putting.'

'What?! I'm just, um, intrigued by your mathematical methods.'

'No, you're not. You're trying to make Steph jealous. A) It's not working and B) I've only been sitting next to you for one lesson, and I'm already lagging behind.'

'All right, all right, I'll stop. Sorry.'

Translation: I clearly have to be more subtle. Now, what else to do…

posted by EditingEmma 15.20

I was halfway through making us matching graph paper hats when Gracie said, 'That's IT. I'm sorry, Emma, I'm moving seats!!'

'What?!?!' I yelped. 'I wasn't peering at you!'

'No, you were *trying to put a hat on my head*.'

'Very, very slowly, so you wouldn't notice.'

She bit her lip. 'I'm sorry. I can't do this. I'm sorry.'

Then she GOT UP AND LEFT.

SHE LEFT ME!!!!

I can't believe I have been abandoned by not one, but TWO best friends.

Evidence: In trying to focus on my friends, I've somehow driven away all my friends. How did that happen?

posted by EditingEmma 18.09

Back home now. And I am mad. I am really, really mad. I just spent the last two days of my life pining over someone who'd rather sit next to Boring Susan in Maths than me. Screw stalking Steph! Why should I sit here moping over her, when she doesn't even care about me any more?

You know who will always care about me? Me. Through the good times and the bad, me and *me* are always mighty good friends. Back to my ME resolution, i.e. staring mindlessly at my *own* various social media profiles.

Yes. This is brilliant. Who needs other people when you can entertain yourself by looking back through your old posts and making yourself laugh? They were so long ago that you've forgotten what you wrote, and it's like having a friend with the EXACT same sense of humour as you.

Evidence: The friendship mission is solved. I AM MY OWN NEW FRIEND.

Thursday, 27 November

posted by EditingEmma 11.06

Faith sat down next to me at break.

'Emma, it's Hope's engagement party tomorrow, will you be my plus one?'

'Of course!' I said. I'd been stewing over Steph all morning, but I felt my mood lift a little bit.

We ate in silence for a moment.

'Look,' said Faith, 'I know what you're thinking. Why aren't I taking Claudia? Well, it's not for the reasons you think. Well, obviously I would need to come out to my parents first. But even if I had told them, it's actually just too soon in the relationship to introduce her to my ENTIRE family, all right?'

'Yes, I...'

'And just because people are in relationships, doesn't mean they have to start automatically taking them to everything instead of their mates.'

'No, I know...'

'So you can stop with all your questions.'

'I *didn't say anything!*'

Faith sniffed. 'You were saying it in your mind.'

I actually wasn't thinking anything other than, *Thank God someone wants to spend time with me*, but I just nodded.

posted by EditingEmma 13.10
Sacré-Bleu!
Something big has happened. I was just about to bite into my lunchtime KitKat, when Gracie sat down next to me with a very grave look on her face.

'Emma, did you see that Anna and Leon broke up again?'

The KitKat hung in the air. Had Anna broken up with Leon because of me? Did she not listen to what I said?! I looked at Gracie's phone.

Leon Naylor is single
1 hr

The sight that last term had me floating on air just made my heart sink. I never thought I'd say this, but I've honestly had *enough* of all this drama. If it's absolutely nothing to do with me, then fine, obviously they can carry on and do what they like, but if this is *anything* to do with what Anna said to me in the girls' toilets then it's completely ridiculous.

UGH. I have to find her.

posted by EditingEmma 13.15
Operation Get Anna Alone
I keep lurking round corners, waiting for my opportunity. I feel like a serial killer. And also, a little bit more empathetic for

anyone trying to get a girl on their own to ask them on a date. I mean seriously, it had never really bothered me until this very moment, but why *do* girls travel in packs?! Her stupid friend Patricia follows her *everywhere*. She can barely bend down to tie her shoelace without Patricia, my new arch-nemesis, getting in there first.

I peer round the corner at Anna, opening up her Tupperware of delicious muffins and sharing them round. Ugh, they're never going to go away now there's free food involved!!

posted by EditingEmma 13.17

I really want a muffin. Why aren't I friends with Anna, again?

posted by EditingEmma 13.20

FINALLY thought I might get her when she went to the loo, but then, lo and behold, *Patricia* got in my way yet again!!!

Anna got up and it was like a little alarm bell went off in Patricia's head. I saw her looking around her, all distressed. *Panic. Panic. I cannot possibly coexist for five seconds without attaching myself to Anna's side. Who am I when I am not standing next to Anna? Identity crisis. Identity crisis.* Then she seized her bag and went scurrying after her.

Are you *kidding* me?!

GO AWAY PATRICIA.

Seriously, if Anna ever went missing, Patricia's is the first door I'd be knocking on. She probably sleeps with a little Anna doll made out of Anna's real hair and fingernail cuttings.

posted by EditingEmma 13.36

FINALLY

Eventually, I decided I was clearly just going to have to approach Anna *and* her Siamese twin. I saw them going off on a little walk and ran down the end of the corridor so that I could pretend to just 'bump into them' coming the opposite direction. It kind of went like this:

Anna and Patricia are approaching.

They don't seem to have noticed me.

STOP GIGGLING AND NOTICE ME.

Oh God, what do I do?!

Don't come off like you're ambushing her.

DON'T come off like you're ambushing her.

'HI, ANNA,' I yelled, stepping across her.

Yep, definitely came across like I was ambushing her.

'Er, hi, Emma?' she said.

Patricia was looking at me all frowny. I was still standing over Anna a bit, and I'm quite a lot taller than her so it probably all seemed vaguely threatening. I stepped back, trying not to tower.

'Hey, can we, er, chat?' I asked.

'Sure,' she said.

I looked at Patricia, but she didn't get the hint. Just carried on standing there.

'Are you all right?' asked Anna.

'Um, yes, fine,' I said, leaning 'casually' on the wall. Oh God, NOW it looked like I was coming on to her!! Seriously, why can I never just convey normal body language?!

I ploughed on. 'I just wanted to check. I mean, I just wanted to check you, uh...remembered what I said at Battle of the Bands?'

She nodded. 'I remember.'

'OK,' I said. 'It's just I...um, I saw that...' I stopped.

'You saw me and Leon broke up?' Anna asked.

'Well, yeah.'

'Don't worry,' said Anna. 'I don't still think he's cheating on me.'

'Oh, OK,' I said, exhaling. 'All right, well, cool, sorry I just didn't want you to have the wrong idea. All right, see you later.' I smiled awkwardly and tried running off. I was thinking, thank GOD this conversation is over.

'He still likes you, though,' she said, to my retreating back.

I stopped.

I turned.

'Eh?' I said.

Patricia was staring at us both, wide-eyed in horror.

'He wasn't cheating on me, technically, but it didn't matter.' She shrugged. 'He was still going through his old conversations with you. It's hardly the dream relationship,' she said.

'Um...' I said, like the sharp-witted intellectual I am.

'Anyway, I decided I'm not going to be picked up and benched when it suits him,' she continued.

'Uh, what?' I asked.

'I mean, I'm not going to be second best,' she said.

Patricia was flipping her head backwards and forwards between us. She waited, anticipating my response. Suddenly,

I had the overwhelming urge to start singing 'Independent Women', but stopped myself.

'No, I can't imagine that somehow,' I said, finally.

Then Anna sort of smiled. And I sort of smiled. Patricia still looked aghast. Then her and Patricia wandered off.

Obviously, there's a lot to discuss here, but first things first. WHAT is benching?!

posted by EditingEmma 14.16
Benching Is Real

Now I get what on Earth she was talking about. The urban dictionary definition of 'benching':

> *Benching is when you start dating someone you think is nice and who has potential, but you're not crazy about them. You don't know whether to keep dating them, or dump them and move on to the next one. This is where benching happens; instead of going for either of the above polarized options, you put your date in your mental 'maybe' folder and 'bench them' so you date around to see what else is out there.*

Who knew there were so many horrible ways to treat people?!

Well. Leon, clearly.

I really do think Anna's got it wrong, though. I think *I'm* the one being 'benched', here. Or are we both being benched?! Just swopping in and out of an endless benching cycle?!?!

Yeah, well, not any more. I refuse to think about this ridiculous situation for even another SECOND. Whether I still have feelings for him or not, I'm sick of being picked up and dropped by him, too.

I really want to talk to Steph about this.

posted by EditingEmma 19.18

I stayed after school for an extra designing session, finishing off a blue shirt, then came home and posted it. Four likes in thirty seconds.

I should probably put my phone away now...

Or. You know. I could just sit here and watch the likes as they come in. Yup. I've probably achieved enough for today anyhow.

As it turns out, not being distracted by constant Snapchats from Steph means I'm actually getting lots of stuff done. I bet having a fight with her best mate is how Coco Chanel got started.

Friday, 28 November

posted by EditingEmma 13.25

Was doing a lunchtime designing session when I heard someone come in and pull up a chair beside me. For a brief, magical moment I thought it might be Steph.

It wasn't. It was Charlie.

'Hey,' he said.

'Oh, hey,' I replied.

'Wow, my face doesn't usually elicit such disappointment,' he joked, putting his hands under his chin and putting on a big smile. 'What's wrong?'

'Oh, nothing.' I smiled back weakly.

'Same thing that was bothering you at Battle of the Bands?' he asked, pulling up a chair.

I was quite taken aback. I don't even remember seeing him there.

'Oh, um, no. I'm fine,' I said.

'Sure you are.' He raised an eyebrow, but at least he dropped it then.

posted by EditingEmma 20.05

The Weirdness Of Surname Changing

At Faith's sister's engagement party. It's actually quite fun. Faith and I are just sitting at the end of the table, talking crap and sneaking gulps of champagne when her parents aren't looking.

We were just about to start on mains, when Faith's mum said we should raise a glass to 'the future Mrs Simon Wind'.

'Oh, are you taking Simon's name then?' I asked Hope.

And her and Lilian laughed like I'd said something *hysterically* funny.

'Of course I am,' said Hope.

'Why? Wouldn't you?' asked Lilian.

'Er, I suppose it depends on the name,' I said.

Then they both burst out laughing again. I felt like Mr Bean; apparently hilarious to others but always a bit confused as to why. Faith glanced sideways at me, smiling and shaking her head.

'I enjoy watching you interact with my family,' she whispered.

'Seriously though, *Wind*?' I whispered back. 'Why would she trade Connelly for a name that sounds like a fart?'

Faith snorted. 'I agree,' she said.

'Hope *Wind*,' I said, shaking my head.

'So it depends on the name for you, huh?'

I nodded. '*If* I ever got married. IF.'

'But IF you did?'

'Yeah, it's not that I'd *never* take anyone's name. I just don't think it should be *assumed* that I would.'

'What do you mean?'

'Like, the way it is now sort of implies the husband owns the wife, doesn't it? But it wouldn't if all couples considered all options and just decided what they prefer. Like…double-barrelled, or either changing to whatever sounds best, or like… not changing at all and keeping their own names.'

'What if you'd been marrying Leon?' Faith asked.

I wrinkled my nose.

'Emma Naylor. Sounds so dull. Leon Nash is much better. But if I was marrying Leonardo DiCaprio…'

'Emma DiCaprio does have a certain ring.' Faith nodded.

'It's quite nice that, if you ever get married, your names won't be caught up in all this. There's no default "ownership" setting for you guys,' I said.

'That's true,' said Faith.

'What's Claudia's surname again?'

'Diaz.'

'UH! INCREDIBLE! Faith Diaz. Amazing. If that does ever happen, you should take hers.'

Faith smiled.

Emma Nash @Em_Nasher
Question: would you change your surname? Thoughts?

Gracie Morton @GracieMorton1
Yeah I think I would

Holly Barnet @HoHoHo
@Em_Nasher Only if the FBI finally caught up with me

posted by EditingEmma 21.38

Dancing Has Begun

In the loos hiding because I'd really rather not be involved in a middle-aged conga line. What is it about ABBA that has this universal effect of making all adults above the age of fifty go completely bonkers? I mean, I like ABBA as much as the next person. I too am a dancing queen, when I get the chance. But seriously, they all get *so excited*. Maybe it's something in the sound that only middle-aged people can hear which gives them this biological urge to jiggle themselves around? Sort of like how only dogs can hear really high-pitched noises?

I was just watching Faith's Uncle Phil bumping his hip maniacally against Faith's Aunt Carol, when Faith raised her voice over the music.

'So, now that we're drunk enough, I have two uncomfortable questions to ask you,' she said.

'All right...' I sneaked a sip of champagne in preparation.

'One, how are you feeling about Leon and Anna breaking up? Again?'

I shrugged. 'Not all that much.'

'Really?' She raised her eyebrows.

'Really,' I said. 'It's so boring. I'm bored of it.'

'Good.' Faith nodded.

'And Anna said something about not being...'

'Woah, WOAH!' Faith sloshed her champagne glass about. 'Hold the phone. You spoke to Anna?'

'Er, yes.'

'About her break-up with Leon?'

'Yes.'

'OK… Interesting. Continue.'

'Well, she said this thing about not being benched by him and I really agreed.'

'What on earth is *benching*?!'

'Um, like when you like someone, but you're not totally sure, so you keep them hanging around and don't really make a decision about it.'

'OH!' Faith yelled. 'I get it. Like Greg?'

I winced. 'I did really like Greg. But…yes. Accidentally, I suppose.'

Faith shrugged. 'Don't beat yourself up. You made a mistake. You're sorry. You won't do it again. Next question…WHAT is going on with you and Steph?'

I downed the rest of my champagne in one.

'Um…nothing.'

'Really?' Faith raised her eyebrows again. 'I accepted the *I'm-totally-fine-about-Leon-and-Anna*, Emma…but really…'

'I AM totally fine about Leon and Anna!!!'

Faith sighed. 'Look. Me and Gracie didn't want to ask, because we don't want to get involved, but it's getting ridiculous now. Don't you think you should talk to her?'

'I tried.'

Faith's eyebrows practically lifted off her forehead.

'Oh yeah? *You* tried to talk about a problem instead of ignoring it and hoping it would go away?'

'Hey!' I yelled. 'I did! I came in ready to talk and she clearly didn't want to.'

'Yeah, sounds like you tried really hard...' said Faith.

'I'm not sure I like this, Faith,' I asserted. 'I'm usually the one asking *you* awkward questions about your feelings.'

'Yeah, well, we're in a room full of my family, so we can't talk about me.' Faith smiled smugly.

'OK, well, I feel like it's kind of the same thing as it is with Leon. I'm not going to be benched by Steph, either, while she puts her boyfriend first.'

Just at that moment, Uncle Phil grasped at Faith's shoulders, kicking his legs out either side behind her. As she was being whisked off, Faith yelled,

'FYI, Emma, I don't think you're on the bench. For Leon OR Steph!'

And she conga-ed away into the night. With Uncle Phil flapping his legs behind her like a strange, middle-aged-man-cape.

And now I'm sitting on the toilet, contemplating, listening to the sounds of 'Waterloo' coming from the next room. I believe that's how all great thinking is done.

posted by EditingEmma 22.09
My Comedy Act Continues

Caused another riot when I said if I got married, IF, that my mum would walk me down the aisle. Once she had finished wiping a tear of laughter from her eye, Faith's Mum asked, 'But what about your dad?'

'I don't really know my dad,' I said.

'But he's alive?' she asked.

But he's alive?! Is that the only criteria he has to meet, in order to walk me down the aisle whilst my poor mother, who has cared for and looked after me for the past however many years, watches from the sidelines?!

When I get home, I'm going to give my mum a giant hug.

posted by EditingEmma 22.49
Faith Is a Oui-Sexer!!!

I don't believe this. Faith waited until THE END OF THE EVENING to drop this massive bombshell.

'So can we not talk about you *at all*?' I asked. 'Even though our conversation is definitely getting drowned out by the sound of Phil Collins?'

Faith glanced from side to side.

'Well, actually…I do have news,' she said.

'You had sex?!' I said, on autopilot.

She smirked.

'Oh my God, you *did*!!!'

'Shhhhhhhh!!!' Faith put her hand over my mouth. 'My Aunt Carol hears like a bat!'

'But you did?!' I continued.

'Yes, and now you can stop saying it every time I say I have news.'

'Oh my God. OH MY GOD. FAITH.'

'I know.'

'You've gone to the other side!'

'I didn't *die*.'

'You're a *oui-sexer*.'

'A what?'

'I decided I didn't like the term "virgin" so I came up with non-sexer and oui-sexer instead.'

'I'm not sure it'll catch on.'

'How do you feel?! Do you feel different?'

She laughed. 'I feel the same.'

'Tell me everything! Were you scared?'

'Emma, you keep making it sound like a murder went down.'

'Sorry. Were you nervous?'

'Yeah, I was a bit. I mean, Claudia's not a virgin. Sorry, non-sexer. So I thought I'd feel like the bumbling buffoon. But it wasn't like that at all. None of that mattered. She made it so easy.'

Faith smiled.

'You do seem different,' I said. 'Peaceful. Glowing. Confident. I mean, you're always confident. But now you're all… SEXY confident.'

Faith did a little joke pout. 'Thanks, Emma.'

I can't *believe* one of my friends has had sex. Actual sex. S-E-X. THE SEX.

Surely this makes me more of an adult by association?

posted by EditingEmma 23.41
My Jealousy Horn Is Tooting
Back home now. A little bit drunk. Thoughts turning… Aghhhhhh.

So it seems that, inadvertently, through no fault of her own, Faith has accidentally enraged the dormant beast that is my horn. Despite my head and my heart being VERY happy for her, there's always that pesky vagina, lurking like the shark in

Jaws and causing me all sorts of trouble. It's like, as soon as it heard that one of my friends was getting some action, it got all jealous and started pestering me. *What about me, Emma? Don't forget I'm here, Emma. I have needs too, Emma.*

SHUT UP, VAGINA.

posted by EditingEmma 00.58
Blame My Vagina For Everything
Oh God. OhGodohGodohGod. I think I may have done something I shouldn't have done. I mean…something I really, *really* wish I hadn't done. And now I really, really want to talk to someone about it but Faith won't understand and Gracie, i.e. Ms I-Don't-Masturbate, would definitely judge me for my base behaviour. Steph is the only one who would really get it, but we're not speaking.

Oh God.

I spoke to Dev.

DEV.

So I'd been masturbating for nearly an hour and was sort of feeling a bit better, but not really. My jealousy horn was being slightly less obnoxious, but still whispering insistently in my ear. I was wondering what more I could really do about it, when I spotted that Dev was online.

Dev
Dev is a boy who lives in Leeds. He's friends with Steph's cousin Bart, and used to visit Steph a lot when we were thirteen. I don't remember much about him, apart from that he wore a

backwards cap that said 'YOLO' on it. Then he followed me and started talking to me. It seemed innocent at first, but then one day he asked me 'if I was horny'. And I was, obviously. So I said yes. And then, um, things sort of escalated from there. I used to send him NAUGHTY messages (naughty for thirteen-year-olds) and giggle over them.

It was a totally safe, if a little strange, way to explore all my early horniness... I mean, come on, who doesn't have a Dev at some point in their life?! But I was sort of ashamed of it. It felt like a much bigger deal to me than it was, at age thirteen. Then one day I admitted my sordid secret to Steph and she burst out laughing. I was really afraid for a moment that she was going to judge me, but then she said, 'OH MY GOD. ME TOO.' It turned out she'd also been naughty-messaging Dev. We compared all our hilarious cringe messages from him and didn't stop laughing for about a year.

I'd totally forgotten about him until today.

Our conversation:

Emma: Hi.
Dev: Oh hey, long time no speak ;)
Emma: Indeed.
Dev: What can I do for you...?

You know what, I can't even go on. Just think, there's one of my friends having intimate, caring sex with her girlfriend and *I'm* still having my needs met by seedy online conversation with some weird boy who introduces himself by saying, 'Hi,

I'm Dev, do you know my name means "Godlike"?' No wonder Steph's outgrown me.

AGHHHHHHH I feel so *dirty*. I can't BELIEVE I spoke to DEV!!!

posted by EditingEmma 01.05
Typed out a message to Steph to tell her about the Dev thing, then deleted it.

I miss her so bad.

Saturday, 29 November

posted by EditingEmma 12.44

Something Strange Is Happening

When I went to take the bin out this morning I was greeted with an incredibly bizarre sight. Possibly, one of the strangest things I've ever encountered. There, sitting on the step in front of our door, was...wait for it...a tiny, tiny chair. Like, fairy people tiny. I almost didn't see it and nearly crushed it with my foot it was so small. I blinked a few times and it was still there. I called to Mum, inside the house.

'Mum? Why have you ordered a tiny chair?'

'What are you talking about?'

'There is an inexplicably tiny chair sitting on our doorstep.'

'You're seeing things,' she said.

'Come outside!'

She came out and we both stared at the chair. Then I reached out to pick it up.

'NO!' she yelled.

'What?!'

'It might be a trap.'

'A trap for WHAT?!'

'…Your hand.'

'Are you SURE you didn't order this?'

'I'm not going senile, Emma. Maybe it's one of your little friends, playing a joke on you.'

'I mean, if this is a joke I'm really not seeing it.'

'That Steph always did have a peculiar sense of humour.'

'Ugh, come on, let's just go inside.'

'WAIT.'

She disappeared off into the house, then reappeared with a spatula.

'Just in case,' she said, and leant down towards it.

Then she carried the tiny chair into the house. On the spatula.

posted by EditingEmma 18.29

I messaged Faith and Gracie and neither of them know anything about the mysterious chair. I even messaged Steph, because I was so stumped, and all she said was:

No idea. Sx 18.01

I can't believe she's not even curious about a teeny, tiny chair randomly arriving at my house. I guess she really doesn't care any more.

Mum put it in my room and I'm looking at it now. It's wooden and green and painted up the side with little flowers.

Totally, totally bizarre.

posted by EditingEmma 21.19
Sum Total Of My Day
Cringed about things I said to Dev. Tried not to think about
Steph. Or Leon. Posed outfits against my tiny bit of wall and
tried to get the look/lighting *just* perfect. I'm definitely getting
better and better at it.

Oh, and stared at the tiny chair.

Sunday, 30 November

posted by EditingEmma 15.08

Mum came into my room.

'I suppose you're just going to keep staring at yourself online today?'

I shrugged. 'I'm not *just* staring at myself. I'm staring at other people too and comparing myself to them. Look at Faith's girlfriend. She's a writer, feminist campaigner and illustrator. She actually *makes money* from her designs. Look!'

Mum raised her eyebrow. 'I'm more interested in what you're doing. What about all your resolutions, hmm? Stop moping online? Spending time with your friends?'

'Ha, yeah. It's a little hard when your friends don't want to spend time with *you*. And when you're incapable of making new ones.'

Mum frowned. 'I thought you *had* made a friend. What's his name? That boy doing the show with you?'

Then I frowned. 'Huh? Who?' I said, dimly.

'Oh, now what's his name... Charles?'

'Do you mean *Charlie?*' I scoffed.

'That's the one,' she said. 'Isn't he on the design team with you? You mentioned him a few times. I just assumed.'

'Oh,' I said. 'Well, yeah, he is. But...'

Suddenly, I felt another light-bulb moment coming on. Only this one didn't make me feel like I was on the brink of a great discovery. It made me feel like I'd been a huge, gigantic idiot.

... Had I really been ignoring an *actual* potential friend?!

I started thinking about it. Who did I meet this term who I actually had something in common with, rather than trying to force a conversation with? Charlie. Who had been supportive of everything I'd been doing? Charlie. Who found my mishaps entertaining, instead of cringeworthy? Charlie. Who noticed when I was upset and asked me if I was OK?

Charlie.

AGGHHHHHHHHHHHHHHHH.

How can I have been so UTTERLY STUPID?!

All this time... All this time I've been trying to make friends with bloody Anika Khatri because she was loud and...and... Hannah Condom, because her last name was Condom! All this time I've been abducting cats and...and...drinking with strange boys who wear *Matrix* coats because I was lonely... through all that, I had an actual friend just waiting there?! All this time, I've been ignoring that actual friend purely on the basis that he knows Leon?!?! Leon who I said WASN'T GOING TO AFFECT ME?!

I can't believe it. I can't believe in trying not to let Leon impact my life, I've actually let him impact it more.

I *have* to fix this.

The friend mission is BACK ON!!!

posted by EditingEmma 19.30
New Day, New Friends

I've been feeling *so* down and defeated, but I'm starting to see a ray of hope. It's time to 'get back on the horse', as it were. I *am* capable of making friends...I made one without even realising!!! Welcome to OPERATION: BEFRIEND CHARLIE.

Step 1: My New Maths Buddy.

The plan: Charlie's in my Maths class where, conveniently, I currently have no one to sit with. So, my devious scheme is to start talking to him about something urgent when I come into the classroom. We'll get so distracted and caught up in our wonderful, engaging conversation that when Mr Crispin comes in, I'll just *have* to sit down next to him.

Ingenious.

I'll say that I was in the design room, admiring the beginnings of his new jacket, when a button came off in my hand (which, obviously, I ripped off). I'll apologize profusely and say I have no idea how it came off, and then offer to sew it back on for him so he thinks I'm *super nice*.

The jacket will be fixed, and we'll be on track on our journey to Friend Land. It's win-win.

Monday, 1 December

posted by Editing Emma 13.58
It All Went Wrong, But Sort Of RIGHT!!!

No one will be surprised when I report that, incredibly predict-ably, Operation: Befriend Charlie did not go down as I planned. However…I think it might have actually gone *better*?

I hung around in the design room for ages after lunch, just waiting for the chance to cut a button off his jacket. Everyone had left the room so I finally seized my opportunity…and the scissors.

I headed towards the jacket with a deranged look in my eye, the instrument raised above my head, poised to cut…my shadow looked like Edward Scissorhands.

I descended on the jacket, pulling it towards me. But, as I pulled, about to snip off one tiny button…the rail came with it.

I cut.

Right through the jacket.

And then…THEN…is when I hear a little cough.

I turned around.

Charlie was standing behind me. Looking totally, totally confused. And a little bit upset. And a *little* bit like how you might look if you were standing in front of an escaped tiger at a zoo.

We stared at each other for a moment. I still had his jacket in one hand and the scissors in the other.

'What…are you doing?' he asked.

And then I burst into tears. I just BURST into tears. In front of him. It all came pouring out. I just stood there crying and crying and *crying*. Charlie looked even more afraid.

'Oh God,' he said. 'Oh God, I…um.' He came towards me. 'There, there,' he said, patting me on the shoulder.

I cried harder.

'No, no!' I yelled. 'Don't comfort me! I just wrecked your jacket.'

'Right, yeah,' he said, but he kept patting my shoulder anyway. 'And why were you doing that, again?'

'I…I wanted to make *friends* with you,' I sobbed.

'By…cutting up my jacket?'

'Aghhhhhh!' I wailed. 'It was an accident! I thought it would give us something to talk about! I'm terrible at making friends!'

'Er, well, if this is anything to go by…yes.' He laughed.

'And I'm terrible at *keeping* friends,' I carried on.

'Hey, no, I'm sure that's not true.'

'It is! It is!' I wailed.

'What about your mates? The fit girl who looks like Rihanna and is always changing her hair?'

'Steph,' I replied. 'I… We… I don't think we're friends any more.'

'What happened?'

'Well, it started…when…' I took a breath between sobs.

'Go on.' He sat down, gesturing for me to sit next to him.

'My other friend…Gracie…' I started, sitting down. 'Said Steph might not be…a virgin any more…and I was upset she didn't tell me.'

Then Charlie burst out laughing.

'What?!' I stopped crying. 'What's funny?!'

'It's just, if you were a group of guys, there wouldn't be any question of *not* telling your friends. Everyone's bragging about losing their virginity before it's even true.'

'Really?!' I asked.

'Really,' he laughed. 'Anyway, go on.'

And I told him. And I actually calmed down. Afterwards I felt *so* much lighter. I told him about how I've been feeling like I should give her space… whilst sort of feeling hurt that she would want space. And then accidentally giving her too much space, partly because she's dating Gracie's brother and I've had to keep some things from her for the first time ever, and partly because I didn't want to bother her with being upset when she was off having a great time…and then accidentally missing her birthday because of this…but then it seeming like she didn't care anyway and that she was fine just taking Andy, and feeling generally like she was outgrowing me.

'Wow,' said Charlie.

'I know,' I said.

'And…what's happening now?'

'Now, she's not even sitting next to me in Maths any more,' I said. 'She's sitting next to Boring Susan.'

'Oh my. That *is* a slap in the face.'

'Right!!!' I said.

'I mean…God…I think if someone stole from me or… attempted to murder me…I'd probably still rather sit next to them than Susan.'

I smiled. I knew, then, that we were going to get on.

'Anyway, look, it will be fine. I've seen you two together. You're like, in love or something.'

'Really?' I asked.

'Yeah, I saw you once doing cross country. You'd collapsed by a tree and everyone was stepping over you. And then, from way ahead, Steph ran back and started poking you with a giant stick, until you started crying. I remember thinking… *that's real love.*'

'She gave me a piggyback in the end.' I smiled. 'Steph could've won but we crossed the finish line together. Last.'

'See. You'll be fine.' He patted me on the shoulder again, more confidently this time.

I smiled.

'And I think you're ignoring lots of good stuff. I mean, you have other friends right? Gracie? And the blonde one?'

'Faith.' I nodded.

He was right. I do have Faith and Gracie, and this time last year I didn't really have Gracie at all. I'm not a *total* friend fail.

'And I'll sit next to you in Maths,' he went on.

I almost started crying again, but managed not to. 'That would be nice,' I said. 'I'm sorry I ruined your jacket.'

'It's fine,' he sighed, looking wistfully at it. 'Maybe I can sew it up. Just promise never to come up with any devious plans to make friends with me again. You don't need an excuse to talk to me.'

'Thanks,' I said.

'Now…wipe your make-up. You look quite scary,' he said. 'Especially holding those scissors.'

I think… I think I officially have a new friend. Sort of. A fledgling friend. I can hardly believe it.

Now I just need to not destroy any more of his possessions, and we should be OK.

posted by EditingEmma 19.07
Muting People Who Are Better Than You

So initially, I followed Claudia because I thought it might inspire me. But I regret to report she is actually having the OPPOSITE effect.

Is there anything she isn't good at?! Does she ever sleep??? I mean, seriously? Last weekend she and her mum went to a political rally together. Last weekend, me and *my* mum watched *Howard the Duck* (an underrated classic, I don't care how many Worst Movies lists it features on) and ate a multi-pack of Twiglets for dinner.

I'd only just started to feel pleased about my own productivity levels. But with Claudia spamming me with all her stupid brilliance, I see how pathetically low they truly are.

Rang Gracie.

'*Poetry reading*?!' I exclaimed. 'POETRY READING?!'

'It's OK,' soothed Gracie. 'We've got our "things" and that's much better.'

'HOW?!' I shouted.

'Well, I mean, if you think about it, Claudia's got so many talents... How's she going to know what to do with them?! How's she going to know who she is? What's her *brand*?'

I don't care what Gracie says, I've muted her. She is INVIS-IBLE to me. Now I won't have it thrown in my face what an unworthy human being I am every five minutes... I can bury that fact way, way down in my psyche, and then start to believe again that I am a good person.

posted by EditingEmma 23.38
Going to bed. Despite having spent the evening being taunted by my own inadequacy's I am actually feeling in an alright mood. I'm so happy that I finally noticed Charlie. I think of how he made me feel so much better about stuff today, despite barely knowing me, proves I'm onto something potentially great here.

Tuesday, 2 December

posted by EditingEmma 10.41

When Charlie came into Maths today, I'd prepared him a special graph paper hat.

'You can do better than that,' he scoffed. 'It's a graph paper fedora or nothing.'

We made SO MANY graph paper hats. Graph paper boater hats...graph paper berets...even a graph paper capotain!! Now that's my kind of maths lesson.

I hope Steph's having fun *doing her work* next to Susan.

posted by EditingEmma 13.45

Having High Standards Is Good – But How High Is Too High?

Was sitting in the sixth form centre with Gracie when I remembered, in being totally wrapped up in all this Steph stuff, I'd forgotten to ask about her 'scoping'.

'So was there anyone who caught your eye at Battle of the Bands, in the end?' I said.

'No one who met all my criteria.' She shrugged.

'*Criteria?*'

'Yeah, you know, dark hair, good sense of style, funny...'

'Haha, oh right, *that* criteria. Let me just get out my check-list and we can compare,' I joked.

Then she legitimately *pulled out a check-list from her blazer pocket.*

I kid you not. Here it is:

Gracie's Boyfriend Criteria
- Between six foot and six foot three, because I need a tall guy, but over six foot three is a bit *too* tall.
- Dark hair. Preferably wavy and short.
- Dresses well (smart, never scruffy). Chest size 39 in.
- A bit hairy, but not too hairy.
- Funny. But not immature humour *à la* Emma. Understated, witty jokes.
- Smart but not so smart he's impossible to understand.
- Puts people at ease – lovely, kind. But <u>popular</u> too.
- Good at fishing, sporty and at least Grade 8 violin.
- Ability to speak another language.
- Good time management skills.
- Meat eater.

I gaped at the list.

'OK, first of all, my sense of humour is not *immature*.'

She raised her eyebrows. 'The other day when someone farted in assembly, you literally didn't stop laughing about it until the next morning. Then we went back into assembly and just being in the room set you off again.'

I bit my cheeks. Just the memory of it was making me… *No*. I would prove I could rise above fart humour.

'That aside. I have many other questions about this list.'

'Mmhmm.'

'Well, you've underlined *popular*.'

'And?'

'To go out with a popular person, doesn't it follow that you would be popular?'

She looked blank.

'Moving on. Meat eater?'

'Mmm, I'm just not sure I could be attracted to a vegetarian. What if you were having a steak, and they ordered an… *omelette?*' She shuddered.

'Would that legitimately stop you from going out with a person?'

'Yes.' She nodded.

'Right. And what is too hairy?'

'When you can't see the skin underneath.'

'How will you know if they're hairy or not? Isn't that something you find out later? Would you go out with them for a bit then dump them as soon as they took their shirt off?'

She snatched her stupid list back and blinked at me furiously.

'No no, um, I wasn't…' I said, cautious of slipping back into our old dynamic, 'I just…it's quite specific.'

'You're being mean about my list.'

'*I'm* being mean? I think the *list* is mean.'

'Yes, well, you would say that.'

'What's that supposed to mean?!'

'Nothing.' She bit her lip.

'What?'

'Nothing.'

'No please. Do go on.'

'Well, I just think it's fine to have standards...'

I paused.

'Are you saying I *don't*?'

Silence. Her lips were so thin now you couldn't even see them.

'Are you saying I don't have standards?!'

'No, but...well, yours are just...lower.'

EXCUSE ME?!?!

'Yes, well, I suppose you don't have to pass an exam, solve a riddle and navigate your way out of a maze whilst juggling flaming knives to go on a date with me, if that's what you mean.'

Then we both sat in silence and stewed in our bitter juices. Just because I want a boyfriend, not a personal assistant, doesn't mean I have 'low standards'. I mean 'time management skills'? What is that? It would really serve her right if she met a candidate (yes, candidate, not fellow human being) who finally ticked all her stupid little boxes, and then he broke up with her because she eats her peas one at a time, or something. (Which she does do and it is very, very annoying.)

Evidence: Dating is clearly a struggle for everyone. Not just me.

posted by EditingEmma 16.50

Another Mysterious Package!!

Was just putting my key in the door and heard Mum bounding down the corridor towards me.

'What is it?' I said, stepping inside.

'Come into the back room,' she said.

'Why?'

'Just come!'

'Is this about carpets again? Because I've told you before, I can't see all the different shades of beige like you can. It's all just beige to me.'

'JUST COME.'

So I followed her into the back room. And there, sitting in the middle of the floor, taking up half the space, was a GIANT teddy bear. I mean, *really* giant. Almost like a real bear. It had a love heart necklace around its collar, that read 'BE MINE' on it. The love heart was about the size of my head.

'Ugh!' I screamed. 'What is *that*?!'

I take it you didn't order this, then?'

I just looked at her.

'Did I order this? Did *I* order this? What on earth would prompt me to buy this monstrosity?'

'I don't know, you might have been punishing me for that time I didn't get you the giant lion at London Zoo.'

'I... *What*?!'

'You were very upset. You wanted to ride its back and pretend to be a warrior, or something. But it was a ridiculous amount of money...'

'No, Mum. I have not been biding my time for ten years, waiting for the right time to exact my revenge, because one time you wouldn't buy me a giant lion.'

'Well *I* don't know! Where did it come from?!'

We paused, looking at the humongous bear. It looked back at us. Its black, beady eyes were sort of haunting.

'Wrong address?'

'It had "Nash" on it.'

'Was there a card?'

'Duh, I didn't think to check for that.' Her voice dripped with unnecessary sarcasm.

'I'm just thinking aloud!'

'Is there anyone else? What about that Greg boy? Could he be trying to woo you back?'

I refrained from commenting on the word 'woo' with great difficulty.

'Really, really not. Greg, quite rightfully, will probably be happy to never see my face again, let alone spend money on buying me presents.' My stomach clenched, thinking of our hands breaking apart.

'Leon?'

'Pah!' I snorted. 'Aside from all the other reasons it's definitely not him, Leon would *never* be this tacky. What about your new man? The pumpkin carver?'

'*Vegetable artist.*'

'All right all right, *vegetable artist.*'

'Definitely not. He's against corporate capitalism. He did make me this, though.'

She reached for a little heart-shaped piece of carrot dangling around her neck and blushed. Again, I refrained from commenting.

'What about *your* ex, hmm?' I went on. 'Could it be the stripper? I mean, Olly?'

Mum paused.

'I suppose. I mean...it *could* be...'

I nodded. 'I think he's our only viable option.'

'Oh Lord. Maybe you're right. What should I do?!'

'Contact him?'

She took a breath.

'I'd really rather not speak to him. I mean, I'm dating Graham now.'

I sighed.

'I guess we've got a new housemate, then,' I said, looking back at the sad, pathetic bear. Its head rolled to one side, almost as if it heard me...

posted by EditingEmma 23.03

My Mother Is EVIL

I'd nearly finished brushing my teeth, and I went into my room and turned the lights on. My heart stopped dead. There appeared to be someone already in my bed.

'UGHHHHHHH!' I screamed, throwing my toothbrush up in the air. It hit me in the head, just as I realized 'someone' was the giant teddy bear, propped up, lying on its side, on one elbow. Waiting for me.

'Mum! MUM!' I called out. 'That's terrifying and PER-VERSE. Please get this...*thing*...out of my room!!!'

She emerged from her room, pissing herself laughing.

'I wish I could have caught that on camera,' she said.

'Get it *out*. You almost gave me a heart attack!'

'Just put it on the floor.'

'No way. I can't go to sleep with that *thing* staring at me.'

She rolled her eyes. 'Don't be ridiculous.'

'All right, put it in *your* room, then.'

'No,' she said.

After a somewhat slapstick half an hour of shoving the teddy back and forth at each other, we ended up leaving it blocking the corridor. No one can really walk up and down the house now, but at least I can sleep peacefully.

Wednesday, 3 December

posted by EditingEmma 08.31

Left Mum dithering around about messaging Olly this morning.

'What do I *say*?' she pleaded.

'Hmm. How about, if you ever send me something this creepy again, I'm going to have you arrested?'

'You're not helping,' she said.

I genuinely thought that was very helpful.

posted by EditingEmma 15.45

Boys And Girls CAN Be Friends (I Can't Believe I'm Even Having To Write This Post)

Gracie said an absolutely ridiculous thing to me at lunchtime. I was speaking about Charlie and how nice it's been getting to know him. I referred to him as my 'friend', and she said, 'You're not friends.' She shook her head all solemnly.

'What? Why?!' I squealed.

Had he been bitching about me behind my back?!

'Boys and girls can't *really* be friends.'

'Of course they can.'

'Nope,' said Gracie. 'One or the other of them always ends up fancying the other, and then it's ruined.'

'That's crap!' I screeched.

'*Is it*? Look at you and Leon. Friends for years, and then what happened...'

'All right,' I said. 'But me and Leon were different. We were friends but there was always...something else.'

Gracie shrugged, as if she'd made her point.

'No, I'm sorry. You can't base this on one example.'

'It happens all the time.'

''Cause you know so much about this, Gracie,' I continued. 'Being friends with so many boys.'

'*Exactly*,' she said.

'Exactly *what*?'

'Exactly my point.'

'So you're telling me the reason you've got no male friends is because you did, once upon a time, and they all ended up fancying you?'

'Well...'

'Having known you for six years now, and never having met these boys, I can only assume this is evidence based on a secret double life?'

'That's not...'

'Or before the age of eleven? Because if that's the case, I think we probably need some post pre-teen evidence before we go around making such huge claims.'

'*All right, all right*,' she said, but clearly still believing that I'm wrong and she's right.

I tried a new tack.

'So what about Faith?'

'What about her?'

'Well, she likes girls. Do you ultimately believe that you'll never have an entirely platonic relationship with her? Do you think one day she's suddenly going to realize she's been lusting after you all this time and pounce on you when you're getting changed for PE?'

Gracie sighed. 'Faith's *different*.'

'HOW?!'

'Because...Faith's a girl.'

'Wait, wait, wait. This is opening up a *whole* other can of worms.'

'Shall we talk about something else?'

'Why? Because you know I've speared you?'

'*Speared* me?'

'So straight boys and girls can never be friends, but gay girls can be friends with straight girls. Got you. What about gay boys and straight boys? I take it that's a no?'

'I don't...'

'Or straight boys and gay girls?'

'I...'

'What about transpeople? Or non-binary? Where do they stand in this?'

'Emma...'

'Ooh, ooh, what about bisexuals?! Can they be friends with ANYONE?'

'I...'

'I think Theo Wilson in the year above is bisexual. Maybe you should go and let him know he's destined to lead a lonely, friendless life.'

'All I was saying,' said Gracie, incredibly pink by now, 'is that either you or Charlie will, at some point in your lives, end up fancying each other.'

'I'll prove you wrong, Gracie Morton. Don't think I'll forget this.' I shook my sausage at her, on the end of my fork. 'I'll be ringing you on my deathbed just to tell you how wrong you were.'

Gracie nodded. 'I do believe you'd actually be that sad, yes.'

posted by EditingEmma 16.50
I Don't Believe It
I was just hanging around with Holly, working on the clothes (or in Holly's case, throwing random objects in the air and not catching them as practice for her next gig), when she dropped a bombshell.

'So, you and Adam, huh?' she asked.

'Erm, no, we haven't spoken since the Battle of the Bands.'

'Did you get his gifts? Have any squirrels sat in the squirrel chair yet?'

So *that's* what that was!!!

But also *oh*.

OH.

Ohhhhhhhhhhh.

'What's this?!' Charlie overheard us and interrupted.

'Emma's new beau,' said Holly.

'He is NOT my new beau,' I said to Charlie.

Beau?

'Please, tell me more,' said Charlie, cracking up. 'Squirrel chairs, you say?'

'I don't have time for this!' I shouted, diving past him for my phone.

I quickly rang Mum.

'Mum? Mum?! Did you speak to Olly yet?'

'No.'

'GOOD. OK, phew. I know who's been sending us the gifts. It wasn't him, it was some guy I met last week. Anyway, I'll sort it, so don't worry.'

There was a silence.

'I haven't *spoken* to Olly yet,' she said slowly. 'But I *have* sent him a message telling him to stay away from me, that it's over and that I'm sorry that he's still pining for me but he needs to accept it and move on.'

Woops.

'Um, eek, sorry.'

'Sorry?! You're SORRY?!?!'

'Well, in my defence I didn't tell you to accuse him of pining for you. That was all you.'

There was a silence, and then, 'You will be sorry, Emma Nash, you *will* be sorry.'

By the time I hung up, Holly had told Charlie everything and he was practically pissing himself laughing.

'You are NOT helping,' I huffed.

Ugh. I wonder if I can camp out here for the night?

posted by EditingEmma 19.07

Came home and everything was strangely fine. The house was quiet. Mum was sitting on the sofa reading a book. She barely looked up as I came in.

'Hi, Mum,' I ventured tentatively.

'Hi, Daughter,' she answered.

The clock ticked. A floorboard creaked. Huh, I guess she isn't going to yell at me, then… Maybe she's forgotten about it?

I retreated slowly as she turned another page.

posted by EditingEmma 19.29

AGHGHMM

My heart won't stop pounding. I'm utterly, utterly terrified. I WILL NOT SLEEP IN THIS HOUSE.

I'd just put my school stuff away and sat down on my bed to take off my shoes, when I noticed I was sitting on something kind of lumpy… It was under the covers. I thought, Has a sock come off in the night? Has a pillow somehow made it down the other end of the bed? I threw back the covers and there, lying in between my sheets, was the sight that will haunt me for ever.

The decapitated teddy bear head. Its creepy eyes looked lost and pleading.

'MUM. MUM!' I screamed. 'WHAT THE HELL?!?!'

I stormed downstairs.

'You're sick, do you know that! *Sick!!*'

'I can't imagine what you mean,' she said. Her tone was calm and even.

'Ugh, stop leaving things in my bedroom! STOP MUTILAT-ING STUFFED ANIMALS.'

@Em_Nasher
If I'm dead tomorrow, it was my mother & here is the evidence

@Faith_18
@Em_Nasher Your mum's really got to find a better way to deal with her anger

@Em_Nasher
@Faith_18 Watch out, Faith, or you might end up on her list

Thursday, 4 December

posted by EditingEmma 08.34

Mum had already gone to work when I left this morning, but she left her book out on the table.

Revenge by Martina Cole.

Subtle.

If she really wanted revenge, she could just stop preparing food and giving me lunch money. I'd probably starve within a week. But I don't want to give her any ideas.

posted by EditingEmma 13.54

Making New Friends Is Liberating

So, I've been trying to forget about it, but I'm still massively cringing about the whole Dev thing. Every time I close my eyes there he is in my imagination, licking his lips in a really weird way or putting a rose between his teeth or something. I still haven't mentioned it to any of my friends.

Then earlier I was in the design room, still thinking about Dev and wondering about what his life is like. (I concluded, remembering the 'YOLO' hat, that probably the less I know the better.) Charlie walked in to put one of his finished shirts away. He must've noticed me wincing because he said, 'Why do you look so horrified? Is it my shirt?'

'Oh no, sorry, the shirt looks great! I was just, um, thinking about something.'

He sat down on the edge of my desk.

'What on earth were you thinking about?'

I paused, wondering how much information to give.

'A YOLO hat.'

He gut-laughed. 'Worn ironically?'

'No.'

'That *is* a distressing thought.' He nodded. 'Anything else?'

I wasn't sure we were good enough friends for this, yet… But I *really* wanted to talk about it with someone. So I told him. Afterwards, he paused for a moment, and said, 'And?'

'That's it,' I said.

'That's *it*? Oh Emma, so what?'

'I just feel like my friends are moving on with their lives, and I'm reverting back to being a thirteen-year-old. Plus it's so icky… Why can't I control my horniness? I can't believe I stooped so low.'

'OK, first things first. Trust me, you're not going to be turning to…*Godlike Dev*…for ever. Secondly, you seem like you're doing all right with your life to me. Look at all this you're doing!'

He gestured towards my outfits.

'And thirdly, I've done *so* much worse than that in the name of my horn. Really, truly. Have you SEEN some of the messed-up shit that's on the internet?'

I laughed.

'Practically every time I have a wank I'm overcome with

guilt. I want to unsee everything I just saw in the past five minutes and surround myself with fluffy white kittens and drink hot milk.'

'Why hot milk?'

'You try looking sexy drinking hot milk. It's impossible. Natalie Portman herself couldn't pull it off.'

I laughed. And everything felt a bit lighter.

'Do you really only wank for five minutes at a time?' I asked.

'Yeah. Why? How long do you do it?'

I shook my head.

'Oh, Charlie.'

Anyway, it hadn't really crossed my mind to tell Charlie before...but I'm glad I did. I actually feel loads better. I think our fledgling friendship is becoming a...um...large bird?

posted by EditingEmma 18.17
I Am A Social Media Star
So, apart from having made a new friend, another silver lining to the big, dark, ugly cloud of fighting with Steph is that at least my Insta profile has gone WAY up in quality. I'm practically a professional now. It's probably because normally, you go through the filters and they mostly look really similar and eventually you get bored and just pick one, but now I have aaaaaallll the time in the world to really think about it, and get it to fashion Instagram stardom level.

Evidence: Friendlessness is clearly the path to success.

Friday, 5 December

posted by EditingEmma 09.40

I was just getting my bag off the rack and the handle got caught and I ended up spilling the entire contents all over the floor. Boring Susan went skidding on a sanitary towel, and Anna bent down to pick it up and hand it back to me.

'Oh, so sweet!' cooed Gracie, as she walked away.

'What?'

'You and Anna are like...*friends* now.'

I wrinkled my nose. 'No, we're not.'

'But she smiled at you! You totally are.'

'No, Gracie. This is not a Hollywood movie. Just because we both decided Leon's not worth our time, I'm pretty sure we still have zero else in common.'

'But wouldn't it be so nice, to both get something out of your horrible break-ups? A new pal?'

'Lots of things would be *nice*, Gracie, that will never, ever happen. Like Britney and Justin getting back together.'

She thought for a moment.

'You're probably right. Anna is way cooler than you.'

posted by EditingEmma 11.17
How Much Checking Social Media is 'Normal'?
Was hanging out with Gracie when she started talking about how worried she was about becoming obsessed with her phone. She said, 'Yeah, I think it's becoming a real problem…like, I literally check my Instagram about…ten times a day.'

Ten times?!

TEN TIMES?!?!

She thinks *that's* obsessive?!?! I literally checked mine ten times when I just went to the toilet!

Oh my God. If that's obsessive, then what am I? Do I need to think about this? Or is Gracie the abnormal one here?

Yes, that's probably it. Gracie's definitely the weird one.

posted by EditingEmma 17.01
Reasons Why Leon Naylor Needs To Move
A lot this term, it's felt like I can't get away from Leon. But today…today was utterly ridiculous. It was like I was Road Runner and he was Coyote. Or maybe I was Coyote. Anyway, he was bloody EVERYWHERE.

1) He Was In The Design Room
Which is fine. I'm used to him hanging around there by now. But he was standing *right* by the pink thread I needed and I couldn't go get it. And then I ended up using green and trying to convince myself the combo would look 'zany'. I was doing a good job of believing it, until Charlie asked me why I was designing clothes for the Muppets.

2) He Was In The Hallways

Does he ever go to lessons? Why is he in the hallway so much?

3) He Got The Last Slice of Pizza

I wanted that pizza! As if it isn't enough to ghost me, bench me and look completely adorable and achingly sexy whilst doing it (shut up shut up shut up brain) HE TOOK THE LAST PIECE OF HAM AND PINEAPPLE PIZZA. He knows how much I like ham and pineapple pizza!! And he was just ahead of me in the queue...How dare he eat it so brazenly, right in front of me!

4) He Was In My Head

That was the worst part. I tried to blame it on the pizza-thieving, but even I couldn't kid myself I was thinking that hard about pizza.

No, I was thinking about the pizza-eater. (And a little bit about the pizza.)

It's been getting steadily worse since the coat-sniffing relapse, but...agh...I hate how pathetic this is. But it's got *even worse* since him and Anna broke up. I'm trying not to let him move back into my head...I really am...But somehow he just creeps in there.

This is one thing I definitely *can't* talk to Charlie about.

I really want to talk to Steph.

posted by EditingEmma 21.31

Mum came creeping into my room.

'Why are you in bed at nine thirty?' she asked.

'I'm tired,' I lied.

'Look,' she said. 'I know you've been upset, so...'

She paused and sighed.

'What?' I prodded.

'You know that hotel commission I won.'

'Yes?'

'Well, as a thank you, they invited me for a free stay this weekend.'

My ears pricked up.

'I was going to ask Graham, but...do you want to come?' she asked, through gritted teeth.

'Do I want to come?!' I yelled. 'Do I want to come and be pampered in an amazing hotel?!'

'Well, do you?'

'Uh. YES, Mum. I want to come.'

'All right,' she barked, pointing her toothbrush at me. 'But I better be *bloody* relaxed when I get home, Emma. There will be no ruining of my relaxation, do you understand?'

'Yes,' I squeaked.

'You will be quiet as a mouse, all weekend,' she went on.

'As a mute mouse,' I said, nodding very fast.

'As a *dead mouse*,' she said, and retreated.

Emma Nash @Em_Nasher
I'm officially going to a HOTEL! A fancy pants hotel, with
massages and table linen and probably mattress toppers.

Emma Nash @Em_Nasher
Mmmm. Mattress toppers.

Saturday, 6 December

posted by EditingEmma 12.21

Mum being nice didn't last long. This morning she woke me up by throwing something at my head.

It turned out to be a box of chocolates.

'Another *delivery*,' she spat.

'Mmm, thanks,' I said, popping a chocolate in my mouth.

'I thought you told this boy to STOP?'

'I did!!!' I cried, through a mouthful of orange creme.

'It's getting a bit weird now, Emma.'

'I know it is! I don't want this any more than you do!'

'She says, smeared in chocolate.'

'Look,' I started, 'I can't help having a reflex reaction to chocolate, Mum. I'll call Holly again this afternoon.'

'You'd better,' she said, and left the room.

She came back in two seconds later, grabbed a chocolate, and left again.

My call with Holly went like this:

'Holly?'

'Emma Nash, Beans and Mash, what can I do for you?'

'Um…'

'Or do you prefer Greens and Splash? Queens and Rash?'

'I have no idea what you're talking about.'

'Neither do I.'

'I was just wondering if you'd spoken to your friend Adam yet?'

'Ah, Adam Day, Spoons and Hay.'

'Holly?! Did you?'

'Yeah, I did. It made him like you even more.'

'I…what?!'

'He likes when girls play hard to get.'

'But that's the thing, I'm *not* playing hard to get.'

'All right, I'll pass on the message.'

'Yeah, but, can you pass it on *seriously*? Because I really mean it.'

'I'm always serious.'

NOT reassuring.

Right. We're on the way to Mum's relaxing spa weekend now, away from memories of Godlike Dev and where Adam and his *Matrix* coat and bizarre gifts can't find me. I can just unwind and stop thinking about EVERYTHING.

posted by EditingEmma 15.01

Massages Are Weird

I was really looking forward to my very first massage, but, in all honesty, I'm not sure I'll be doing it again. When the lady came in she was talking in very *breathy* tones. At first I thought maybe she'd just run up the stairs or something, and needed a moment to recover, but then she kept talking like that and I figured it was supposed to be *relaxing*.

'Soh, Hemma,' she breathed, 'howh would youhhh like to feeehhhl after todayhhh?'

'Uh…relaxed?' I asked.

She nodded, as if I had said something very interesting.

Has anyone ever given her a different answer?

'Soh, Hemma, sniff these forhh me, what scent arehh you drawhhn to?'

She put two different oils on the back of each hand and waved them under my nose.

'Uh, the lemony one?'

She nodded again, as if it all made perfect sense.

'Of course, the relaxahhhtion oil.'

What do all the other oils do?

I was already quite baffled by this point, but then she put some quite aggressive animal-noise soundtrack on and left the room. She said to lie on the table, but she gave me NO INSTRUCTIONS.

How undressed are you supposed to get for a massage?!?!

I stood there flapping about, getting incredibly stressed. (Clearly the oils weren't doing their job.) The monkeys screeching weren't really helping, either. Is finding yourself in the middle of a rainforest supposed to be relaxing? Because I think, if I did find myself there, I'd probably be dead within about ten minutes.

I didn't have my phone so I couldn't google it. In the end, I just went for it and took everything off, and lay down under the towel. With the rainforest sounds I felt like a vulnerable piece of meat, waiting for a tiger to come and maul me.

When she re-entered it didn't get much better. She just sort of...*stroked* me a lot, which was kind of weird because I have no idea about this woman, apart from that her name is 'Dorothy'. I started wondering a lot about 'Dorothy' and her life; what were her hopes and dreams? Had she always wanted to be a masseuse? Did she have that special someone in her life? What was her relationship like with her mother? Then I tried imagining it *was* someone I knew, like, uh, Gracie. But that was even weirder.

Next she laid some hot stones on me and they REALLY BLOODY HURT. I had to bite my lip from calling out in pain. I was thinking, Is she doing it wrong?! Is she actually going to murder me? Am I going to be on the news tomorrow morning? 'Girl hot-stoned to death by murderous masseuse.'

THEN, joy of joys, she started pressing the stones a bit harder into my back and I really, really needed to fart. I have to say, lying naked in a dark room with a stranger pressing some hot objects into your back, and trying really, really hard to keep a fart in, is not particularly my idea of a 'relaxing experience'.

posted by EditingEmma 16.31
I Think I Have A Problem
So, I came out of the massage after having an hour away from my phone, and was getting a bit...twitchy.

Then I got even more twitchy. Because when I did get my phone back, I realized that the Wi-Fi in this place is not working...and neither is my data.

I tried the on-off trick, i.e. the only thing I know how to do, and still *nothing*. I asked at reception and the lady said, 'Have you tried the on-off trick?'

Figures.

Then I started sort of…convulsing. Going all red. Wanting to shake things.

Mum said, 'What's the matter? Why are you fidgeting?'

'I'm not sure,' I whimpered.

I think I might have a problem…with controlling myself on the internet. Well, what's new? I hear you ask. Yes, absolutely, controlling myself on the internet has always been one of my number one problems. But the thing is, I think, *maybe*, I foolishly thought that because I wasn't stalking *Leon* any more… my relationship with the internet was actually fine now. When, in actual fact…

It's not.

Don't get me wrong, I've been spotting the signs… I mean, like when Gracie said she only looks at her Instagram ten times a day, like that was a lot, or something. I didn't know *exactly* how much I check my various profiles, but I suspected it was a lot more than ten. But now, sitting here jerking and trembling because I can't connect, I'm wondering just how many it actually is. It's only been an hour or so and I'm already like this… What's wrong with me?!

posted by EditingEmma 17.03
Painful Confirmation

Just out of interest… And, you know, because I have nothing else to do… I went onto my own internet history.

Dear.

God.

I don't even want to write it down.

This morning, between the hours of 9 a.m. and 1 p.m., I checked *my own* Instagram...

TWENTY-SIX TIMES.

Twenty-six times in four hours!!! Oh my God, if you added up all the rest of the day... OK, so let's say thirty times in four hours. That's *once every eight minutes.*

Every. Eight. Minutes.

And how many hours in a day are there, when I'm not sleeping? Sixteen?

16 X 60 = 960 minutes. (Thank you, calculator.)

960 divided by 8 is...

120.

A HUNDRED AND TWENTY.

A HUNDRED AND TWENTY?!

I check my own Instagram, on average, a hundred and twenty times a day?!

Oh my God. I've never actually recorded how often I do it before. When you click and take a quick look you can just sort of forget it ever happened, but here staring me in the face is raw evidence of my sadness. I don't even go to the toilet this many times a day!!!

This surely, surely can't be right, can it? *Can it?!*

posted by EditingEmma 20.16
At Dinner. Hour Five Of Phonelessness
'How was your massage?' I asked, clenching my fingers.

'Lovely, thanks,' said Mum.

Silence.

'How was yours?' she asked.

'Oh, yes…great.'

'Good.'

Silence.

'Are you OK?' she asked.

I looked up, desperately.

'Mmmhmmm,' I snivelled.

Dear God. Fifteen more hours left.

Still… at least this will bring down my daily phone-checking average. Looking at the statistics from today, I might almost be considered normal.

posted by EditingEmma 20.29

I Am Never Having A Massage EVER AGAIN

So apparently… APPARENTLY… I wasn't meant to take all my clothes off for the massage.

Oh my God.

I was just saying to Mum, 'I don't know if it's for me. I'm just not sure I feel comfortable being totally naked.'

And Mum practically choked on a bit of her chicken. She literally *cannot* stop laughing. I'm in the toilet right now, because her laughing is just too annoying.

'You…you…*you took your pants off*,' she wheezed.

'Was I not supposed to?!?!'

'NO!!!!' she yelled, rocking back and forth.

'Oh my God!!!!' I yelled. 'WHY DIDN'T YOU WARN ME?!'

'I didn't think you'd take your PANTS off!' she practically screamed. 'You strange, strange child!'

'Oh my God.' I digested this news. 'But I was under the towel. Do you think she noticed?!'

'YES!' cried Mum.

'Oh *Dorothy*. I'm so sorry.' I buried my head in my hands. 'Why didn't she say something?!'

'She's probably...' Mum choked. 'She's probably just going to file the sexual harassment complaint as we speak.'

'Oh my God.'

I don't believe this.

I made Mum SWEAR never to tell anyone. EVER.

posted by EditingEmma 23.30
Parents Always Spot When Something Is Wrong
When she'd finished her chicken, and laughing about the incident which we will never mention ever again, Mum cleared her throat.

'Emma,' she said suddenly. 'I want to talk to you.'

I put my fork down. 'About what?'

'About you.'

'What about me?!' I squeaked. Did she know about my habit?

'I feel like I need to say something,' she went on. 'I try to stay out of things as much as possible, except when I feel you're really spiralling out of control and, well...'

'Oh my God!' I yelled. 'Was this why you brought me here?! To make me go cold turkey?!'

'What?' Mum frowned. 'I mean Leon and Steph.'

My stomach clenched.

'Oh,' I said.

'I think cutting both of them out isn't really working for you.'

'I've not *cut them out*,' I said. 'Anyway, Leon's the one who stopped speaking to me. Again.'

'I think you've stopped speaking to each other, and it's not healthy.'

'But I'm trying to get over it. That's how you get over something.'

She nodded. 'I know. And I think it's much better than you going out with different boys, left, right and centre. But I think getting over someone and cutting them out only really works if you resolve stuff first. But everything's just been left all up in the air with you two.'

I opened my mouth. I closed my mouth.

'I'm speaking from experience,' she said. 'Well, put it this way. The spell-casting didn't work. But after I sent Olly that message about the bear—' she glowered at me '—we actually ended up talking. It gave me some closure and…I'm feeling much better.'

'I'm really glad things are going well for you and the pumpkin carver, Mum.' I smiled. 'You deserve it.'

'Thank you.' She smiled dreamily. Probably thinking about his aubergine penguins.

'And then Steph. I know sometimes actually telling someone how you feel can seem worse in the moment than just burying it. But if you don't do it, then it gets worse over time.'

I picked up my fork again, and started shovelling food in my mouth. She can't make me talk with a mouth full of mashed potato.

Now I'm in bed, still thinking about it. And there's absolutely nothing to distract me. No Netflix. No updates. No pictures. Not even any of Claudia's accolades to make me feel bad about myself. Nope... Sitting here all alone, next to Mum snoring in the dark.

I guess...ugh. I hate to admit it, but maybe she's right. Gracie and I let our relationship go sour, and then when we had that big, horrible fight it was *awful*...but it did make things so much better in the end. Should I be trying to talk to Leon and Steph? In my defence, I did *try*! With both of them! I mean... I tried a bit. The responsibility isn't just down to me, is it? And it seems like both of them are fine without me. I mean, that's the assumption I've been going on.

Aren't they?

Oh God, the thought of actually talking to either of them about stuff, now, feels so intimidating I can barely contemplate it. Sleep now.

Sunday, 7 December

posted by EditingEmma 13.04

Just got in the car to go home. As we were leaving, Dorothy came out to speak to the receptionist and our eyes locked for just a moment. I'm pretty sure I saw fear in them.

I can never, *ever* return to this hotel.

posted by EditingEmma 15.06

HOME

HOME. INTERNET. I'm pretty sure I just made up for my one hundred and twenty checks per day in the past half an hour.

Maybe I shouldn't be thinking of this as a bad thing... Maybe...maybe all this tapping is actually building on important abilities? I mean, it must be training my hands, right? My manual dexterity is probably at the level of a brain surgeon's.

Anyway, Mum's been nagging me about putting our photos up so I'd better do it. I don't know why she cares so much. She's only got about three followers. And one of them is Uncle Ralph. I'd pay good money for Uncle Ralph to unfollow me.

posted by EditingEmma 17.27

Photos posted. In all seriousness, what I would usually do now is just sit and stare at the likes coming in. Is this where I'm going wrong?! Should I put my phone down and forget about it?

Yes, that's what I'll do. I'll just to log off for a bit…relax… No big deal.

posted by EditingEmma 17.47

Number of Times I Checked My Own Various Profiles Since Deciding Not To

H̶H̶ H̶H̶ IIII

Ughhhhh. OH MY GOD. Fifteen times in twenty minutes?! If you include all the various platforms…THAT'S MORE THAN EVERY EIGHT MINUTES. That's…EVERY FOUR!!!

I must stop this. I don't know how, but…surely I'm getting old faster this way? Pouring all this time down an invisible time sink? Surely my wrinkles are going to grow all over my face without me even noticing?

Right. Phone going away. AWAY.

posted by EditingEmma 18.52

This is unbelievable. Bloody unbelievable. I just logged back on (after impressively waiting ONE WHOLE HOUR) and I had looaads of notifications!! I was thinking, I bet my funny moose impression next to the stuffed moose head went down a real treat. I clicked on them and thought, hmm, that's strange, loads of people I don't know have commented. Have people *shared* my moose impression?! (It was pretty funny.) Then I saw Heather had commented on something: 'Oh Allie you look beautiful!'

And the penny dropped.

All the notifications were for Mum.

ALL the notifications. Were for MUM.

I mean...not *all* of them. Crazy Holly was a real fan of my moose photo. But seriously?! Why is everyone loving this photo of Mum just *standing* by a windowsill?! WHAT IS SO GREAT ABOUT STANDING. I can stand!!! I have been known to stand *all over the place*! But how many people can channel the soul of another species in a way that 'makes one feel as if they were really a large ungulate, standing upon a Canadian mountain range, contemplating the ability to close one's own nostrils'. (Holly Barnet). Aghhh. When did she get so many more followers?!

How does she know this many people????!

Thirty-one likes for the (stupid) windowsill picture and six for the moose. Not that I'm keeping score.

posted by Editing Emma 20.58

FORTY likes for the windowsill and still six for the moose. Oh this really leaves a sour taste.

posted by Editing Emma 21.01

Yes! Seven for the moose!

Oh, what? No. It's the same notification I've already seen, but it came up on my phone as well as my laptop.

That's so cruel.

posted by EditingEmma 22.38

Fifty-five likes for the windowsill, still six for the moose, and my humiliation is complete.

Thank you, and goodnight.

Monday, 8 December

posted by EditingEmma 07.51

Had an actual dream about getting another notification.

Who am I?

posted by EditingEmma 16.05

No. Nonononono

I was just walking towards the gate with Gracie and Faith, when I looked up ahead and spotted something potentially terrifying. Now I'm lurking behind the gym, which is a bit awkward because I can see everyone inside doing their exercise. I'm pretty sure Willie Thomas thinks I'm checking out his physique.

posted by EditingEmma 16.38

Gracie and Faith finally clocked that they'd lost me (which took them a whole *three minutes*, by the way). They came back to where I was standing.

'Emma, what are you doing?'

'Oh well, thanks for noticing, guys, I could have been abducted, blindfolded, pushed into a van and heading towards the M25 by now.'

'*Come on*,' whined Gracie, 'let's go home.'

'Look!' I said, gesturing to the gate.

Gracie and Faith turned in the direction I was pointing.

'What?'

'See that person, leaning by the gate in black? Is that...is that Holly's friend?'

Gracie's eyes widened in fear.

'Maybe.' Faith squinted. 'Hang on, let me go and investigate.'

Good old Faith. She walked up to the gate, stood around checking her phone as if she was waiting for someone who wasn't there yet, sighed and turned around. She's so collected. If that were me, I'd have been looking side to side all shifty, got my phone out and dropped it, then fallen over attempting to pick it up.

She circled back to us.

'Yup, it's him,' she said.

'WHAT IS HE DOING HERE?!' I shouted.

Faith shrugged. 'Waiting for Holly?'

'Holly went to the post office to pick up her new abstract drumsticks.'

'Oh God,' said Gracie, 'he's waiting for *you*.'

'What are abstract drumsticks?' asked Faith.

'I have no idea.'

'GUYS,' said Gracie, 'hello?! Emma, what are you going to *do*?!'

'I don't know. Stay here until he leaves?'

'How long will *that* take?!'

'Um, let me just check my crystal ball.'

Gracie blinked at me three times.

'I'm sorry,' I said. 'This is just a bit stressful. What would you suggest?'

Gracie sighed. 'I guess there's nothing else to do, is there?'

'Right. We might as well set up camp, then.'

I put my blazer on the floor.

'Uh, *we*?' asked Faith.

'You're not *leaving* me?!' I screeched.

'It may come as a shock, Emma, but there's actually quite a lot I'd rather be doing than hiding from some weird dude who has a crush on you. *You're* the prisoner here. I'm free.'

'I don't *believe* this!'

'Bye, see you tomorrow.'

She started walking off. I looked at Gracie.

'And what about you?' I asked.

Gracie looked wistfully after Faith, then sat down on my blazer.

'All right,' she said. 'But please can you sit there and block out Willie Thomas doing squats.'

'Deal,' I said.

posted by EditingEmma 17.30
FREEDOM

I've escaped!! Finally!!! After ten minutes of sitting there, I could feel Gracie's resolve was waning. She was getting all restless and whingey.

'Ugh, he's *still* there!!!' she said, shifting on her bottom.

We both peered over at him, standing stock-still and staring into the distance. Everyone had gone home by now.

'How about a game of Boggle?' I said, in a last-ditch attempt to get her to stay with me.

'I do love Boggle…' She bit her lip.

'Excellent,' I said, opening it on my phone.

Then she shook her head.

'No, I'm sorry, Emma,' she said firmly, standing up. 'I've got to get home. My dad's making lasagne.'

I knew I'd lost her then. There's no way I can reasonably compete with lasagne.

'FINE. GO. I hope you're happy and full!!' I shouted

'Ughhhhh,' she said. 'I feel bad leaving you here.'

'Don't,' I said. 'Go on without me.'

Then Gracie came up with an ingeniously ingenious plan.

'Unless…' she said.

'Unless?!' I repeated, clutching at a feeble straw of hope.

'You could maybe hide under my coat.'

I rolled my eyes. 'Is that it?! Is that your big idea?! Hiding under your coat?'

Then she started walking off.

'No, no! Wait, wait! Come back! Gracie!'

She carried on walking.

'I just meant, he'll probably notice you have four legs! Gracie! Come back!'

She paused reluctantly and sighed. 'They're just about to close the gym, so all these guys will come out. I thought we could slip by him in the crowd.'

At that point, I was willing to try anything. Five minutes later, I was shrouded in darkness, hidden under Gracie's coat.

We must have looked like one of those ludicrous fake horses in a play. Except even more ludicrous.

'*Emma*,' Gracie hissed, 'stop hugging me from behind. You're so *weird*.'

'But it's so cosy in here.'

'Willie Thomas is on the move. There are a few other people trailing behind. Do you think five people is enough to mask us?'

'It'll have to do,' I said.

'What?'

'It'll have to do.'

'You want a Frube?'

I stuck my head out of the coat. 'I said, *it will have to do*. Why, do you have a Frube?'

'Get back under!'

'OK, OK. Let's go.'

We began shuffling. It really was incredibly difficult and I kept accidentally kicking the back of Gracie's feet. It also became increasingly hard to breathe down there.

'Oh, um, hi, Willie,' I heard Gracie say.

Making conversation with Willie Thomas on my behalf. Now that's true friendship.

Eventually, we made it past and waited until we were a safe distance away, before breaking apart and doing a celebratory dance.

'WE DID IT!' I yelled.

'Woop woop!' Gracie laughed.

'Shall we go back to yours for a game of Boggle?'

'I'd like that,' she said. And then, 'Are you only asking because of the lasagne?'

'I do like lasagne.'

posted by EditingEmma 19.51
Ideas v. Reality

I was at Gracie's, letting her beat me at Boggle and eating tons
of food, when suddenly she started babbling about this movie
where this hot guy meets a woman in a coffee shop, decides he's in
love with her and waits at the same place at the same time every
day to buy her mocha latte, until she agrees to go out with him.

'It's so romantic,' she sighed. 'That sort of stuff never happens in real life.'

I stared at her, stunned. Truly stunned.

'You mean, like, someone meeting someone once, and then
sending lots of over-the-top gifts to their house?'

'Exactly,' she sighed wistfully.

'And when that person asks them to stop, waiting for them
outside school?'

She registered my meaning.

'*Oh*,' she said. 'I don't think it's really the same with Adam.'

'Why is it not the same?'

She thought for a second.

'Because…he's *weird*.'

'I agree. Completely. But…why is he any weirder than that
man in the film?'

'He just…*is*.'

'No no,' I said. 'You're going to have to give me a solid
reason.'

She shrugged.

'Is it because he's less attractive?' I asked.

'Um, yeah maybe.'

'But aren't most people less attractive than film stars? I mean, is it one set of rules for super attractive people and another set for others? How is that fair?'

She kept thinking.

'It's not the attractive thing,' she said. 'Adam looks fine. I don't know... He's just...creepy.'

'Based on what?'

'The gifts.'

'And if the guy in the film did it?'

'... Different.'

'IT SO ISN'T!' I yelled.

'It is.' She nodded.

'*I* think,' I ventured, 'that if some hot guy you met once *actually* started turning up every day trying to get you to go out with him, you'd be really put off.'

'Not if he was the man of my dreams...'

'But how would you know? How would you know whether he was the man of your dreams or not, until you actually went out with him? Before that, he's just *some guy*.'

Then she got out her little list and waved it at me.

'So let me get this straight. You'll double-check the list with the stalker guy, and if he meets all the criteria his stalking is romantic, and if not, his stalking is just...stalking.'

'Um...yes.'

Evidence: Our ideas of romance are SO backwards.

Tuesday, 9 December

posted by EditingEmma 11.21
The Dreaded 'Queef'

When Faith came into the sixth form centre for break, I thought she looked a bit…peaky.

'Are you all right, Faith?' I asked.

'What? Oh, yes.'

Silence.

'You look a bit ill.'

Gracie shuffled away from her.

'No, I'm OK.'

More silence.

'Apart from my sick vagina.' She buried her head in her hands.

Gracie and I looked at each other.

'What's wrong with your vagina?!'

She took a deep breath. 'I can't even…'

'What? What is it?'

'Can I ask you something?' She looked up, with desperation in her eyes.

'Yes.'

'Has your vagina ever…made a noise?'

I suppressed a laugh. 'What kind of noise?! You mean like, burst into song?!'

'Obviously not,' she snapped.

Man, she was moody today.

'*Oh*,' Gracie said suddenly. 'OH.'

Faith reached over for her hands.

'Has it happened to you, too?'

Gracie grimaced. 'In yoga,' she said.

'Ohhhhh,' I said, finally getting what they were talking about. 'You mean a queef?'

'SHHHHH,' whispered Gracie. 'Emma!'

'*Queef*,' I repeated. 'What a silly word.'

'*Why*?!' Faith continued. 'What kind of cruel universe is this?!'

'Did it happen with Claudia?' I asked.

Faith nodded slowly.

'Oh *God*,' Gracie said, like she was about to throw up.

I blinked at her three times.

'I know,' Faith said, putting her head back in her hands.

'Oh my God, that's…what did you *do*?!' Gracie went on.

I blinked and blinked and blinked.

'Was it…was it *awful*?'

By this point I was leaning towards her and blinking so much I practically fell out of my chair. Gracie finally got the hint and pressed her lips together.

'Faith,' I said, 'it's fine. You love Claudia. Claudia loves you. You're in an actual loving, stable, caring relationship. It's not going to be ruined by a *queef*.'

'No, I know,' she said, sitting up. 'But it was SO EMBAR-RASSING.'

'How did Claudia react?'

'She just carried on.'

'There you go! See, she doesn't care!'

'*I* care,' said Faith. 'I couldn't relax afterwards. I kept waiting for it to happen again. I'd get into it a bit, but then remember it and tense up. I was like that woman trapped in her car by Cujo, and every time she thought it was safe the dog would rear its ugly head again.'

'I'm pretty sure that was Stephen King's intention,' I said. 'That Cujo would become a metaphor for a queef.'

'I didn't even know it was a *thing*,' Faith moaned.

'Have you never done yoga?' Gracie asked.

'And you know what the worst part is. I looked it up, and there's nothing you can do! It's *irrepressible*. Do we not have enough to worry about with our vaginas?! Is there nothing they don't expel uncontrollably? Blood? Gas? What next? Ribena?'

'They are troublesome fiends,' I agreed.

'You can't keep it in?' Gracie paled.

'No. Because it's not like a regular fart. It's just...trapped air with nowhere to go.'

There was a moment's silence as Gracie digested this news.

'You're a real expert on queefing now,' I said.

'Knowledge is power. The more I understand it, the less I will fear it,' Faith said.

I patted her on the back.

posted by EditingEmma 13.08

Lunchtime Awkwardness

Over the past couple of weeks, Steph and I have somehow managed to miss each other at lunchtimes. Either I've been in the design room, or she's been with her football team, and sometimes I've asked Gracie to go with me early.

But today we ran right into each other.

I came out holding my tray with Gracie. Steph came out holding her tray with Faith.

We all stood awkwardly for a moment, until Faith rolled her eyes. 'Guys, let's sit here?'

So we did.

Faith and Gracie started chatting whilst I remained deathly quiet. So did Steph. I couldn't help wondering why *she* wasn't saying anything. I mean, I knew why I wasn't…because I was upset. But even if Steph didn't want to be friends with *me* any more, surely she'd still be chatting to Faith and Gracie?

Eventually Faith said, 'So how's your stalker, Emma?'

Steph looked up from her mashed potato.

'By the way,' Faith went on, 'have I yet pointed out the irony of you, Ms Internet Stalker, getting a real life one?'

'No, but very helpful, thanks.'

'What happened yesterday, anyway? Did he go away?'

'Um, me and Gracie shuffled past him under a coat,' I said.

Steph frowned, clearly confused as to what the hell we were talking about.

Faith gave a short, sharp laugh. 'You're kidding.'

'No, she's not kidding,' said Gracie, wrinkling her nose. 'It took *for ever*.'

Suddenly, Steph got up. 'Sorry, forgot something,' she mumbled and left. Faith and Gracie were still talking about Weird Adam, and I watched Steph as she retreated from the hall.

Huh. If I didn't know better, I'd say it seemed like she was… upset?

Was I imagining it?!

I probably was. I bet she really did have to go.

posted by EditingEmma 22.09
What Is The Saddest Thing Someone Could Ever Do?
I think I may possible have just done it.

Aghhhhh. I don't even want to admit it!!!

OK. I was looking at my Instagram profile, assessing my general aesthetic and pondering which posts were getting more attention etc., etc., etc. And there was the picture of the moose with barely any likes or comments.

And…Mum's phone was sitting next to me. Out on the coffee table.

… I think you can probably put two and two together.

I can't believe this. I can't believe I've stooped so low. So incredibly low.

I liked my own post.

I LIKED. My OWN. POST.

PRETENDING TO BE SOMEONE ELSE.

Not even someone else... PRETENDING TO BE MY MOTHER.

Oh my God. It's sad enough when the only person who gives a post any attention is your parent. Let alone when it's actually you, disguised as your parent.

This is an awful, awful day. Who *am* I?! Why don't I just make some fake profiles and give myself likes all the time, like the strange people on *Catfish*? Hell, why don't I just make an entire neighbourhood of fake acquaintances? What's the difference between real people and made-up people anyway? God, I'm sickened by myself. Sickened and appalled.

...Especially because...well, I was joking but...now that I think about it...That's actually sounding like quite an appealing prospect.

I need help.

Wednesday, 10 December

posted by EditingEmma 13.38
Faith and Gracie Take Action

Today, the same thing happened at lunch again. I went early with Gracie, and Faith and Steph just happened to already be there.

I stopped in the aisle, suddenly smelling a rat. 'You two are doing this on purpose, aren't you?' I barked at Gracie.

She bit her lip. Then Faith started waving us over. I blinked three times at Gracie.

'Hey!' she said. 'I haven't done anything to merit a blink! That was an inadmissible blink!'

'Yeah, well. That's what you get for INTERFERING,' I said, still blinking.

We reached the table. For a while it was much the same as yesterday, i.e. Faith and Gracie chatting away whilst me and Steph stared at our food.

Then Faith asked Steph how it was going with Andy.

'We're not speaking,' she replied, without looking up.

I'm not proud of it, but my heart almost leapt out of my chest in excitement. I sneaked a glance at her, dabbing around at her fishcake with her fork.

'What happened?' continued Faith.

'I...I got some period blood on his bed.' She grimaced.

There was a silence. Words rose up in my throat. Anger bubbled in my stomach. I tried not to speak...I really did... But I just...couldn't...hold...it...in...

'So what?!' The words burst out.

Everyone stared at me. The seal of our silence had been broken. There was anticipation in the air as we waited for Steph's response.

'Well, exactly,' Steph looked up from her fishcake, into my eyes. The direct eye contact made my already leaping heart start doing the tango. '*So what*, right? But when he saw it he got all weird, and then all overly polite and patronizing, like, *Oh it's OK, Steph. Don't worry about it, Steph*, whilst looking like he was going to throw up.'

'Oh no.' Faith shook her head.

'I think he *genuinely* thought he was being nice.'

'He's my brother and I love him,' said Gracie, 'but, oh dear.'

'I mean, it's RIDICULOUS,' Steph went on. 'The boy spends half his time on video games fake-shooting or watching zombies eat people, and he goes all faint about a spot of blood?'

'Yes but this blood is *different*, Steph,' I said. 'Because it came from your *vagina*.'

Steph laughed. It felt really, really good to be laughing together.

It felt really good to be bitching about Andy together.

No no no. Bad thought. Go away.

'WHY does that make it gross?' Steph yelped. 'I mean, he doesn't find my VAGINA gross. I can tell you that much.'

'Ew, TMI,' said Gracie. 'Brother, remember. Brother.'

'Sorry,' said Steph.

'Maybe it's some innate thing about menstruation and pregnancy. Like, they see it and something inside them says, *I'm not ready to be a daddy*,' suggested Faith.

'Then surely no blood would be scarier?' I said.

Faith laughed. 'Eh, they're not that smart.'

'So what happened after?' I asked, gaining confidence now.

'I got really pissed off and left.'

'Left him to clear up your unholy mess,' I laughed.

Steph rolled her eyes. '*Ugh*. I can just imagine him dabbing at it with a cloth and wincing.'

'Well, I think you did the right thing. Screw that,' I said.

'I think you're completely right to be annoyed,' Faith ventured cautiously, giving me side-eye, 'but maybe it's something to talk over? And not a reason to just throw the whole relationship away?'

Steph bit the inside of her cheeks and nodded.

'Thanks you, guys,' she said. She looked all sad. I *hate* seeing Steph sad.

'Next time I hope you douse his whole mattress,' I said.

Steph guffawed. 'Like a period-blood water-pistol.'

We both laughed. And looked at each other for a moment. Suddenly it was like my insides were stretching out into a massive grin and sunshine was pouring in, because Steph was smiling at me and we were just talking and joking about something stupid. Did she still want to be my friend? Did she still care?!

Then Steph looked back down at her destroyed fishcake. And I looked back down at the table. Faith looked between us like she wanted to bang our heads together.

posted by EditingEmma 16.48
The Most Awkward Afternoon Ever
Got to the gates today and, lo and behold, Weird Adam was there *again*. Gracie turned to me in fear.

'Emma,' she began, 'I'm sorry, I can't...'

'Hide with me by the gates every day for the rest of our lives? Yes, I know.'

She grimaced. 'I could maybe stay five minutes.'

'It's OK, Gracie,' I said. 'It's time to be bold. Brave. It's time to face up.'

'What do you mean?'

'I think I should talk to him.'

Gracie started shaking her head. 'No, no I don't think that's a good idea.'

'It's the only way.'

'But what will you *say*?!'

'Um, leave me alone...but nicer.'

'What about...I don't know...all the horror movies and stuff?'

'Eh?'

'I mean, no one goes up to *talk* to the murderer.'

I shrugged. 'I don't know. Maybe if they did that in the beginning, no one would wind up dead.'

She shook her head again. 'All right…I'll wait for you behind that tree. What's our signal? You know, if he's about to murder you?'

'How about, "HELP! I'M BEING MURDERED, HELP!!!"'

Gracie crossed her arms and blinked at me three times.

'Are you going to murder me first?' I asked.

She rolled her eyes. 'I'll be over there.'

Inner monologue of the next ten minutes·

OK. Deep breaths. Deeeeeep breaths. You can do this. YOU CAN DO THIS.

Heading over to him. Inching closer. He's leaning against the gate, shuffling from side to side and looking around him every now and then. Thankfully, he's not wearing his *Matrix* coat or I don't think I'd be able to keep a straight face throughout this.

Oh God. He's spotted me. Now we have to do that thing where you've seen someone from really, really far away so you can't greet them yet, and you have to just sort of awkwardly watch each other get closer…and closer…

He looks very solemn. *Is* he here to kill me?

Closer and closer…closer and closer… Pretending to be really interested in that tree over there, so I don't have to keep maintaining eye contact…

And I've arrived. Hmm. Gracie was right, what *am* I going to say? How does one greet their stalker?

We both just stood there awkwardly. He brushed a stray hair out of his eye. Given how much time this guy has spent trying to get me to talk to him, you would think he'd have been better prepared for the talking part.

'Hi,' I ventured.

'Why hello.' He smiled nervously. 'MayIwalkyouhome?'

'Aha,' I laughed. 'Well, you do know where it is.'

He nodded. 'So, then?'

Hmm. He didn't seem to pick up on the undertone of what I was saying.

'Look, Adam, I, uh… Did Holly speak to you?'

'Holly speaks of a great many things,' he replied. 'I believe our most recent conversation was about abstract drumsticks.'

'I…yeah. What *are* those?'

'Well that depends on how you're looking.' He raised his eyebrows up and down, like Holly does.

I can really see why these guys are friends.

'Look, I actually meant, did Holly speak to you about me?'

'She mentioned I might want to stop sending gifts. So here I am instead.' He gestured to himself.

Dear Lord.

'Uh, the thing is, I just… I really meant what I said before.'

He frowned. 'That you can't understand why anyone would put peanut butter with jelly?'

'Uh, no, although, it's true.'

'That ham and pineapple is clearly the best pizza topping?'

'Uh…Wow, we really got into…'

'That you love your friend Steph more than anyone in the world?'

Owch. That one slammed me in the ribs. So much had changed since the night I met Adam.

But that was still true.

After a moment of feeling like all the breath had been taken out of my body, I snapped back to the moment.

'Look, Adam, I meant the bit that I said to Holly, about not wanting to go out with you. I, er…er…' I floundered. 'I, um, I would have LOVED to. But I actually have a boyfriend.'

'Oh, right,' he said, frowning.

I smiled, feeling a bit bad but happy to make my escape, but just as I was about to run off he said, 'Holly said you're single.'

Crap.

'Er, you're right,' I sighed. 'OK… The truth is… Um, I really just want to take a bit of *me-time*.'

'Me time?' He wrinkled his nose. 'What does that mean?'

Suddenly…I felt quite irritated by his tone. He was standing there looking all accusing, as if me not wanting to go out with him required some detailed essay of explanation. Because how could I *possibly* not want to, if I'm single?

I sighed. Lying to this guy wasn't really confronting the problem, either.

'You know what, Adam,' I said. 'I'm sorry. I'm sorry I said I have a boyfriend when I don't, because that implied the only reason I might not want to get with you is because I'm already owned or something. I'm sorry I said the thing about *me-time* which yes, does sound like bullshit because it is. I am having me-time, but if I met someone I really liked then I could probably still make time for them... We've only just met and I don't really owe you any explanation, but the actual reason I don't want to go out with you is... I just don't.'

'But you can't know you don't want to go out with me, we've only met once.'

'I, um, I still don't really want to. And I've had enough of going out with guys I don't really want to go out with, just for the sake of it.'

His face changed a bit, then. It's like he was finally, actually catching on.

'Oh,' he said.

'Look, I...'

He put up his hand. 'Don't worry. I see. Treat 'em mean, keep 'em keen.'

'No,' I said. 'It's really, *really* not...'

'Treat 'em like dirt and they stick like mud.'

'No, really...'

'No, please, it's fine. Bye, Emma,' he said, and started to walk off in a huff.

Well, that went well.

Gracie's head popped out from behind a tree. She sidled over to me.

'He looks *grumpy*,' she said.

'I know, I... Oh God. He's turning around!!'

Adam started marching back to us. Gracie gripped my arm in terror.

'Oh, and I want my squirrel chair back!' he said, pointing his finger at me, face deadly serious.

'That's fine,' I squeaked.

We watched him recede into the distance, waited until he was a good few metres away, and both BURST out laughing.

Then, believe it or not, is when things got even more awkward.

Me and Gracie were still hugging each other, falling about laughing and spluttering.

'How could....how...' Gracie started.

'How could anyone look so serious...' I continued, '...about a *squirrel chair...*'

When suddenly, Charlie and Leon came up behind us.

'What's so funny?' asked Charlie. 'I need a good laugh after Philosophy with Susan. Mr Allen made her recite Kant. As if Kant isn't boring enough already.'

Leon could barely hide his surprise; he clearly didn't know that me and Charlie spoke. He was looking between us all wide-eyed and flustered.

'I...' I was laughing so hard I couldn't even take a breath.

'Squirrel chair,' Gracie squeaked.

We kept laughing. Charlie was grinning and Leon looked ridiculously uncomfortable. He pulled at Charlie's arm, but Charlie ignored him.

'Ohhhh,' he said, 'Was that him?! The guy sending you all that stuff?!' He pointed at the very distant figure, reaching the end of the road.

'Yes, it was…he wants his squirrel chair back.'

I managed to say it calmly until I got to 'chair' and it came out more like 'chhaaiirrnnghh'.

'What happened?!' asked Charlie.

'Yeah, lovers' tiff?' interjected Leon.

He was trying to sound jokey, but it came out all cold and flat. The comment landed on the floor like a dead fish and we all pretended not to notice the change in atmosphere. Leon went bright red.

This time a few months ago, I would have been so excited that it clearly bothered him. I would have rushed to make sure he knew that me and Adam weren't a thing. But today I just said, 'Something like that.'

'Which way are you two going?' Charlie asked.

I pointed.

'Us too,' said Charlie.

Dear God. Does Charlie not have an awkwardness radar? The four of us started walking down the road. Leon was completely silent, and I tried to join in with Charlie and Gracie's babble as much as possible by saying 'mm, yeah,' and 'oh, I know,' a lot. Which wasn't at all convincing, because they were talking about their mutually discovered love of fishing.

'Have you tried jigging?' asked Gracie.

'Oh yes.' Charlie nodded sincerely.

'What do you use as your lure?' Gracie asked, all interested.

'Mm-hmm,' I said. Which didn't even make any sense.

Thanks to Gracie and Charlie, I have now discovered that walking dynamics, when certain people in the group are completely OBLIVIOUS to them, are incredibly difficult. Charlie and Gracie were having this great conversation (bully for them) and so were naturally walking closer together and a bit in front. Every so often I'd drop back, and Leon would drop back, and instead of doing the NORMAL thing and dropping back to talk to each other, like two other people would do, we both just sort of jogged to keep up with Gracie and Charlie.

Then, we'd accidentally get a bit ahead of them, spot each other and jog backwards again.

It really was a very strange oscillating formation and people on the street kept getting annoyed because obviously, four people walking in a line is completely ridiculous.

Eventually, we broke off and THANK GOODNESS, no one tried to hug anyone goodbye.

It's been a really, *really* tiring day.

posted by EditingEmma 21.08
Message from Holly:

> So when do you want to drop off the squirrel chair? 21.01
> We probs need to think about the logistics here 21.01

AGHHHH.

Thursday, 11 December

posted by EditingEmma 08.07

At breakfast, I made the mistake of telling Mum about Adam turning up at school. For some reason this really, *really* bothered her. She froze and turned on the spot like she'd been possessed by the devil.

'*Why* didn't you tell me about this?!' she boomed.

'I am telling you,' I said.

'Why didn't you tell me *sooner*?!'

'Sorry.' I shrugged. 'I didn't think it was a big deal.'

'Not a big deal?! NOT a big deal?!'

I really never know what she wants me to say, when she repeats my own words back at me like that, so I just shrugged again. That clearly wasn't the right thing to do.

'DON'T YOU SHRUG AT ME!' she yelled, pointing her spoon in my face. 'This is serious! The gifts were one thing, Emma, but *following you around*?!'

'He wasn't really "following me around"…'

But it was too late. I'd lost her. She went haring off to her bedroom. I could hear her printing something. Five minutes later, she came storming back into the room and threw some papers at me.

'We're going to this,' she said.

I looked down at the sheet of paper. It read:

'WHAM-BAM-SAM'S SUPER-DUPER SELF-DEFENCE CLASSES'.

'Er, no we're not,' I said.

'Er, yes we are. This weekend.'

'What if I had plans this weekend?!'

She snorted.

'All right, fine,' I continued. 'But why *Wham Bam Sam*?! Can't we go somewhere more normal sounding?'

She looked sheepish. 'I already booked it.'

'Oh, Mum. WHY.'

'He was the first search result on Google so it must be fine.'

Yes, that's reassuring.

posted by EditingEmma 13.19
More Friendship Drama

Got a message from Charlie:

Can we talk? 13.03

Um sure, I'm with Gracie in the SFC? 13.03

So he came over to us, waving awkwardly at Gracie. She waved back, then did a stupid raised-wiggle-eyebrow at me behind his back. When will she get into her head that we're just friends?

'Can we go for a walk?' he asked.

'Sure,' I said. 'Is something wrong?'

'Um, kinda.'

Mysterious…

We started walking out of the sixth form centre. I could see Gracie inside watching us all goggle-eyed. She really needs to start watching some good TV, if she finds *this* entertaining. Too much Maths homework has gone to her head.

'What's up, Charlie?' I asked.

'It's Leon,' he said.

I internal sighed. What was it this time?

'He's not speaking to me,' he carried on.

'Oh? Really?'

'Yeah. Really.'

'Weird. Why?'

'Well, that's what I wanted to ask you… Have you…said anything to him?'

'Er, I don't know if you'd noticed, Charlie. But he's not speaking to me either.'

'So you haven't said anything at all?'

I shook my head.

He sighed. 'For God's sake, Leon.'

'What?'

'I think he's not speaking to me, because of you.'

'What?!' I exclaimed. '*Why*?!'

'I don't know. He got all weird about the fact I hadn't told him we knew each other. I said, I'm sorry, I speak to lots of people. I didn't realize I had to update you on every new acquaintance.'

'And what did he say?'

'He just went all stroppy and red and he's been ignoring me

since. Like, really blatant ignoring. Aggressive scowling and pass agg comments about me to other people. *Whilst I'm still standing there.*'

'Jeez.'

'It's just ludicrous on so many levels. Firstly, what happened to bros first?! I'm sorry, I feel so offended that he's actually wrecking our friendship because he thinks we like the same girl.'

'Yes, that's—'

'And secondly,' Charlie cut me off. 'If he likes you so bloody much, why has he been going out with Anna this whole time?'

My heart plunged.

'Er, good question Charlie. You might actually know more than me about that.'

He shrugged. 'I don't, I'm sorry. He's so cagey about it. I get snippets...'

I raised my eyebrows, encouraging him to carry on.

'I guess... I guess it might have something to do with that blog that went up last term. You really touched a nerve.'

I winced. 'Yeah, I know.'

'But people make mistakes,' Charlie went on. 'Including *him*. He should have forgiven you and gotten over it. God, I've always kind of known he's stubborn and pig-headed... but...never usually to me!'

Charlie sniffed. I saw how much this was affecting him.

'I'm sorry, Charlie,' I said.

He shrugged.

Just as we were circling back towards the sixth form centre, Leon came out of it. He was with a big group of boys and dropped behind them to stare at us for a moment. Then he went all red and shuffled off with them.

'Arrrghhhhhhhh!' Charlie moaned, putting his head in his hands. 'Now it's going to be ten times worse!'

'It's OK,' I said, patting him on the shoulder.

'Where am I going to sit at lunch?!' he wailed.

'Um, you can sit with us,' I said.

I feel really bad. I feel like in making friends with me, Charlie's lost Leon. Just like how I made better friends with Gracie and lost Steph. I genuinely thought 'focusing on my friendships' would give me such an easy term, but now that I think about it, there's so much more room for complication. I mean, when you're dating someone, you're dating them and that's it. The loyalty is pretty clear. With a group of friends you've got loyalties in all different places. Loyalties that can potentially conflict.

Evidence: Navigating friendships is sometimes harder than navigating romantic relationships.

posted by EditingEmma 13.51
At Lunch
Really, really wish I *hadn't* invited Charlie to lunch with us. Gracie has gone all silent and weird and keeps giving me what I imagine she thinks are 'meaningful glances' but actually just make her look like she really needs the toilet. In between her scrutinizing gaze, and Leon's glares from across the room, I'm beginning to feel just a little bit persecuted.

Sacré-bleu! I can't wait to go home.

posted by EditingEmma 20.34

Methods of Stopping Excessive Social Media Use

So, since discovering my 'problem', I have been testing several methods to stop myself obsessing over social media.

1) Hide Phone From Self

Doesn't work for obvious reasons.

2) Ask Mum To Hide Phone

Doesn't work because she gives in when beaten with a pillow.

3) Use an App Blocker

Does work but then I just go on my laptop.

4) Block Sites on Laptop Too

Does work but then I steal Mum's phone, which leads to her beating *me* with a pillow.

Evidence: Clearly, destroying my phone and laptop is the only answer.

posted by EditingEmma 23.39

The Other Method Of Stopping Self-Stalking

Unfortunately, I think I've found a method that works and I really, really wish I hadn't.

I want to cry.

It was on the picture of the dress I made for Battle of the Bands (the one I never actually wore, because no one else liked it).

I was half watching TV, half refreshing my notifications, when a comment popped up from some user I've never seen in my life.

'So desperate for attention what a slag.'

So desperate for attention?!

WHAT A SLAG????!!!

SLAG??!?!?

I feel so, so upset. I've deleted the picture. I don't even want to look at it. I feel so intruded upon, like they're sitting here in my bedroom watching me. But also really publicly humiliated – like I've been put in the stocks or something. Who else saw the comment before I deleted the picture?!?!

I clicked on the person, but they had no picture and just a load of numbers as their name. Staring at their faceless profile was making me feel worse, I got so upset I just turned my laptop off.

I thought, what with all the Leon and Charlie drama, that this day couldn't get any worse. That almost feels like a happy memory now. Instinctively, I reached for my phone to call Steph and then remembered I couldn't. Now I feel twice as awful and five times as lonely.

Put my phone and my laptop at the bottom of my wardrobe. Going to bed.

Friday, 12 December

posted by EditingEmma 11.18

We were all sitting around at break and Gracie said, 'Are you OK, Emma? You seem a bit down.'

'Oh. I'm... Well, yeah. I am a bit.'

'What's wrong?'

'Nothing,' I said.

'Did you see that picture that Abby Matthews uploaded of her new eyelash extensions? I wish my parents would let me get eyelash extensions,' she huffed.

'Um, no, I didn't see.'

Because I never want to go online again. Ever.

posted by EditingEmma 13.20

The Difficulty of *Les Orgasmes*

At lunchtime, Faith slumped down next to me and Gracie. I was incredibly relieved by her presence, because Gracie kept asking me if I was OK and I really, *really* don't want to talk about it.

'I'm having a problem,' she said.

'Queef?' I asked.

'No, not that,' Faith answered.

'What is it?'

She took a breath, then stopped. 'I can't say.'

'Ooookay,' I said.

'Don't pressurize me!' she growled.

'I'm not pressurizing you! *You* brought it up!'

She folded her arms. 'I wasn't going to say anything, because some things are private. But…'

Silence.

'Well. When we…you know…I can't…'

Gracie and I looked at each other.

'Can't…?' I encouraged.

Faith sighed. 'When we're doing stuff, I can't… I mean… It's not ending the way I want it to.'

'Ohhhhh,' me and Gracie said together.

'But that's fine!' I said. 'Don't freak out. It will happen.'

'It's all right for *you*,' she snapped. 'You could probably have an orgasm if you accidentally sat on a remote control.'

'*Woah!*' I sat back, out of the firing line. 'Please don't take this out on me and my vagina.'

'I'm sorry.' She sighed. 'I'm just jealous. It seems easier for some people. It's so unfair.'

'I think it's definitely easier for guys,' said Gracie. 'And Emma, obvs. But I think it's normal for girls. Some can't at all.'

'Really?' asked Faith.

Gracie nodded. 'And you can, right?'

'I definitely *can*. But why not with Claudia?'

'What do you think, Emma? What's the secret?' asked Gracie.

'WHY does everyone think it's so easy for me?!' I gaped.

They just looked at me.

'Six in half an hour?' Faith said.

'Yeah, all right, on my own maybe!! But not with Greg!'

'*I* think it's to do with being relaxed,' said Gracie. 'Emma's very relaxed.'

'Relaxed?!' I exclaimed. 'Because all relaxed people keep a collection of a boy's Chewit wrappers under their bed and sit around crying over them.'

Thank God Mum accidentally threw those away.

She bit her lip. 'All right, well, not relaxed about Leon. But generally. I mean, you shrug things off pretty quick. You're kind of confident.'

'*Confident?!*' I shrieked. 'I'm incredibly awkward, the ENTIRE time.'

'Yes, but you're um…confident in your awkwardness.'

I shook my head. 'Faith's confident too. I'm not sure that has anything to do with it. I think it's just physical.'

'Maybe it's a mixture of things,' said Gracie.

Normally, I'd be quite pleased if someone called me 'confident'. But I feel like a fraud. This whole time I've been sitting here half listening to my friends and half thinking about what other mean comments might have popped up on my blog or if anyone else is looking at me thinking horrible things and judging my pictures.

I'm not confident at all.

posted by EditingEmma 21.05
I'm Scared Of My Blog
So, not this blog, obviously, because it's private. But my other blog. The one with *the comment* on it. I haven't looked at it since *the comment*. And I keep reminding myself that it's probably just one comment and I deleted it, and now I can probably just forget about it.

So why am I still so terrified of logging on?

posted by EditingEmma 21.59
That's Why
I don't believe it. I finally just worked myself up to log on again, telling myself I was being stupid, and there, sitting on a different photograph, is another comment from the same user.

So fake, slut

So fake, slut. The words are echoing round and round my blog that only ever made me feel safe. Round and round in my head. Round and round in my bedroom. Round and round my wardrobe, full of the clothes that up until now only made me feel good about myself.

Who is this person?! Why are they doing this? I don't even want to know. I don't want to think about it. I blocked the account, snapped the laptop shut and pushed it away from me. I'm never, *ever* going back on there. I never want to look there again.

Suddenly my homey little corner of the internet, which I made to express myself and feel happy, has become a snake pit. My laptop and my phone are glinting at me from the corner of the room, and suddenly they don't feel like tools to build myself up, they feel like a portal for people to come and tear me down.

posted by EditingEmma 23.28

I've had a little cry but I feel a little calmer, now. I'm never, ever going online again. All I've been doing is obsessing over myself on there anyway comparing myself to people…measuring how much attention I'm getting…and for what? For me to make myself feel like crap, and for random people to make me feel like crap? This was never what it was supposed to be for, and clearly, the only solution is to never go on there again.

I'm clinging to my bed, to my real, solid bed, where no one can ever hurt me and no one's words can reach me.

Saturday, 13 December

posted by EditingEmma 14.07

Feeling a bit better today. Instead of using my time online or making more 'slaggy' outfits, I've been spending it wisely doing extra French homework. Also, because Mum's friend Heather is here, and it's hard to keep feeling gloomy around Heather. They're going to Graham's exhibition tonight and she's ridiculously excitable.

'Oh, but do you think what I'm wearing is all right? I was going for "leek" but I'm not sure I pull it off.'

'Um...' said Mum.

'I've been studying miscategorized vegetables in preparation. Did you know that a tomato is actually a fruit?'

'Um...'

I could genuinely listen to this all day.

posted by EditingEmma 15.25

Hurluberlu Holly

It strikes me, learning all this French, just how limiting the English language really is. I have just discovered the world *'hurluberlu'* which can be used to describe an eccentric, scatterbrained person. This fits Holly much better than 'crazy' which has many different meanings.

Like, why do we only have one word for love? The way I loved Leon, for instance, is very different to the way I love Faith or Gracie.

Not that I *loved* Leon. Stop right there, brain.

posted by EditingEmma 17.03

Mum and Heather came back from their walk. Apparently, a crow swooped down and 'attacked' Heather outside the café. For the past twenty minutes, Heather's been sitting by the window, glancing furtively outside, as if it might be out there waiting for her.

'I just can't believe it,' she kept saying. 'Did you see its eyes, Allie?'

Mum ignored her.

'What film shall we watch?' she asked.

'*The Birds*?' I suggested.

Mum threw me a terrible glare.

'Oh, by the way, I rang up Steph's mum and she thought it was a good idea too. So Steph's going to come along.'

'You did WHAT?!' I bellowed.

'I'm sorry, Emma. Personal safety is more important than your silly little fight,' she said smugly. 'And Steph's mum agrees.'

Oh this is unbelievable.

'Mum, are you serious?! I'm *sixteen*, not six. I don't need you to get involved with my friends. Oh my God... I can't *believe* you called Steph's mum!!!'

'As I said, it's about personal safety, not you.'

'Oh whatever!' I snapped. 'Why don't you just stick us in a sandpit and tell us to play nicely!'

Mum just smiled.

I don't believe this.

Apparently, as a result of Heather's 'traumatic experience', she's decided to join us for self-defence tomorrow as well. Huzzah.

Sunday, 14 December

posted by EditingEmma 08.01

Wham Bam Sam Is Not Sam

Ugh. It's so EARLY. And I'm expected to be ACTIVE. I probably wouldn't even be properly active if you put me on a racetrack, rose the guy from *Saw*, told him I was fair game if he caught me and then said 'GO.' I'd probably just accept my fate and have a Yorkie bar.

It's been quite awkward with Steph so far. She smiled at me when she got in the car but then went straight on her phone, so I've obviously been obsessing over whether she's sending messages to Andy like 'omg I'm so bored' or 'wish I was with you instead'. Thankfully the drive wasn't that long.

When we walked in, we were greeted by a very enthusiastic man. He shouted, 'WELCOME' so loudly and so close to my ear, I wondered if it was part of the class and if I was supposed to elbow him in the stomach, or something. Thankfully I didn't. Mum said,

'Hello, are you Sam?'

He shook his head. 'No, my name's Gary. But that doesn't rhyme with Wham Bam.'

posted by EditingEmma 08.10

I really, really wish I *had* elbowed Scarily Intense Gary. He made us sit in a circle and go round introducing ourselves so that we feel 'comfortable'. I'm pretty sure this tactic has made approximately zero people feel comfortable, ever, in all the time it's been used by sadistic or clueless teachers.

First was a guy so unimaginably large, you wondered who would ever dare start a fight with him. He even called himself 'Big Dave'.

Mum whispered, 'I don't want to stereotype or anything, but... *Why is he here?* His hand is the size of my head.'

I was about to answer when Gary landed on me.

'And what's your name?' he asked, looking deep into my eyes.

'Um, Emma.'

'And why are you here today, Emma?'

'Um, because pepper spray is illegal,' I said, and he ROARED with laughter.

I honestly wasn't trying to be funny.

He moved on to Heather, next.

'And what brings you here today, Heather?'

'I had quite a nasty attack, actually,' she answered.

'I'm so sorry to hear that,' said Gary, full of concern.

'Thank you,' said Heather. 'Yes, it was quite traumatic.'

Gary nodded.

'I can't get it out of my mind, you know. I just keep going over it.'

Mum started waving her arms behind Gary's back, mouthing, 'STOP, STOP,' at Heather, but she didn't seem to get it.

'And I'd like to prepare myself, you know, for the future.'

'I can only imagine what that experience must have been like, and how it must have impacted you,' said Gary, gravely. 'But you've come to the right place, and we can begin to help you feel safer and more able to protect yourself, should the situation arise again. If you ever need to talk, we have a variety of leaflets in reception and can help you find the right place to turn to.'

'Thank you,' said Heather, tears in her eyes.

Mum put her head in her hands.

The next person in the group was a guy called Liam, and he had *genuinely* been attacked, and as he was talking Heather kept nodding at him like she really understood what he was going through.

Seven hours and fifty minutes left of this.

posted by EditingEmma 11.05

And now the fun really begins. After three hours of 'security theory and the study of victim/prey mentality and body language', which I think basically amounted to 'don't walk around with both your headphones in', we've come outside to begin training.

I don't know if I can do this. Potentially it would be safer for me to break into Mum's car and attempt to drive it home, without one single driving lesson, than to be matched against Big Dave.

posted by EditingEmma 11.47

As it turns out, I CAN do this. It's just a lot of shouting 'NO' and then taking a step back, which I'm very, *very* good at. Also, and I wouldn't tell Mum this because she'd be all smug, but doing an activity together has momentarily made things seem *almost* normal with me and Steph...

'I thought we'd be, like, learning to karate chop people or something,' she said, huffing and folding her arms.

'Me too!' I said gleefully. 'Come on, Steph, advance towards me please.'

She sighed. 'You're enjoying this way too much.'

'Oh, I'm sorry. Sad we've found a sport I'm better at than you?'

She snorted. 'Whatever this is, it isn't a sport.'

She reluctantly took a step forwards.

I sprung back. 'GET AWAYYYYYYYYY!' I screamed, startling Heather, who had been beside us quietly hissing 'No! Noo!' at Mum.

'Very nice work!' Gary strode over to us.

'Now look what you've done,' said Steph, 'you've attracted Scary Intense Gary.'

'Jealous?' I asked.

Gary approached, and patted me on the back. 'A star for effort,' he said to me.

Steph rolled her eyes. God I miss her eye-rolling. It felt so, so good to hang out together that even when she accidentally kicked me I laughed with joy. Disgusting.

posted by EditingEmma 16.39
Driving Home
The rest of the day was FAR less easy and Steph obviously excelled where I kept falling over, so all was right with the world again.

'Right, team,' Gary said, rubbing his hands together. 'Now I'm going to show you how to safely bring an attacker to the floor, without causing physical harm. So, volunteers?'

Big Dave raised his hand.

'And another?'

Everyone else looked resolutely at the floor. Heather whimpered.

'OK, hmm, how about…'

Not me not me not me not me.

'Emma.'

Crap.

'You were so enthusiastic during phase one: voice commands. Let's see what you've got.'

Oh God.

I looked desperately at Mum, my most darling and dearest parent. She brought me into this world, so she must surely care about whether I stay in it, right? I felt certain she'd call out, 'I VOLUNTEER AS TRIBUTE,' and I would graciously allow her to take my place, whilst also pretending to be distraught. I would salute her and wish her luck. 'May the odds be ever in your favour' etc., etc. BUT NO. She kept her eyes firmly on the ground.

At least now I know where I stand, should there ever be an apocalypse.

I approached Big Dave, who really did look bigger than ever close up. He smiled down at me in what I imagine he thought was a reassuring way, but with his head blocking out the sun and his entire face in shadow, looked vaguely demonic.

'OK, Emma,' said Gary, reaching one arm out. 'When Dave comes towards you, like so, I want you to take this arm, and move under it, like so, putting one leg here so you won't topple over, then put this arm around Dave's neck, like so.'

He very quickly did a series of complicated moves way beyond my comprehension, where he was somehow able to lower me to the floor. The group cheered.

'Right, now, you try it with Dave.'

My heart fluttered. I cleared my throat awkwardly. Dave, equally awkward and still smiling, started slowly coming towards me with one arm out. I managed to take his arm and move under it, no trouble, but when it came to putting my arm around his neck, I was just sort of feebly reaching up to him on tiptoe, as if I was trying to get something down off a very high shelf.

'That's it!' said Gary. 'Now lower him, lower him!'

Big Dave obliged and I felt myself being crushed under his weight. *If I could just...* No. I couldn't. We both fell over in a heap.

Me on the bottom. Obviously.

I could hear Mum snorting with laughter. *Traitor*. I thought that must surely be the end to my humiliation, but no, Gary made us keep going until we sort of got it right. Then, when we *did* get it right, he said, 'OK, great. Now Emma, you have to lie like so, with one leg here, to keep your attacker in position.'

Essentially, the position he was demonstrating was just spooning someone, with their arm twisted behind their back.

Then he LEFT US THERE, whilst he went and demonstrated with other people.

This is really not how I pictured my day going, I thought. Lying in the middle of a field, the sun setting, spooning a very large, friendly bald man called Dave.

posted by EditingEmma 18.15
Back Home

In bed. Thank God. I was just dropping Steph off at her house when Charlie called.

'Hey, question. WHY are you lying in a field spooning the biggest man I've ever seen in my life?' He laughed.

'Oh my God...' I turned to Steph. 'Steph, you put that on THE INTERNET?!'

She smirked. And despite her complete and total disregard for my humiliation, I felt wildly, unreasonably happy. Were we still friends?

'Long story,' I said to Charlie.

'Well, I want to hear it.'

'Can we talk later?' I glanced at Steph. 'Bit busy right now.'

'Yeah, sure. Message me.'

'Bye, Charlie.'

I hung up and she said, 'Charlie who?'

'Oh, Charlie. You know? Dark precned hair, doing the fashion show.'

'Right,' said Steph.

I opened my mouth. All the other things I wanted to tell her were on the tip of my tongue. Like how I thought I was over

Leon but how he kept creeping back into my thoughts. Like how stupid I felt for speaking to Dev. Like how nervous I was about the show. Like how I thought I'd freed myself from social media but seemed to have ended up in its clutches again. Like how someone was targeting me online. Like how much I missed her.

But then she just turned around and went into the house. 'See ya,' she said.

I guess we weren't still friends.

posted by EditingEmma 20.19
Do I Even Exist?
I've deleted literally every single social media account. Rash, you might say. Thoughtless, even. Cowardly.

I say…BOLD.

I feel so…anonymous. *Sleuthy*. If a tree crashes in a forest with no one to hear it, does it make a sound? That is me. Emma. I am that silent tree. If I have a funny thought, is it still funny with no one to tell it to? If I take a nice picture, is it still nice with no one to see it?

I tell you what I have done, too, I've thrown that 'slag' dress in the bin.

Now assessing all the other outfits I've made for the show. Are they slaggy, too? *Am* I a slag? What is a slag, really? I used to feel so sure about them, but now all I can see is what other people might think about them. I can't remember how I ever loved making them so much.

Monday, 15 December

posted by EditingEmma 13.59

Friends Are Too Nosy

Am doing more French homework in the tech room. Well, actually, I ran out of homework quite a while ago so I'm learning more random French words.

After lunch, Charlie and Gracie followed me out.

'Hey, you never messaged me last night,' he said. 'I want to know who you're spooning in fields!'

I smiled. 'Sorry, I got distracted.'

'Are you OK?' he asked.

I nodded, hoping he would go away.

'Are you coming to the design room today?'

'Um, no.'

'Right...' he said. 'Except the show's on Saturday?'

'I'm aware,' I said, my heart stopping. I did not want to think about it right now. People looking at things I'd designed. People judging me, just like those comments.

'So, where *are* you going?' he carried on.

'French in the tech room,' I said.

'Riiiiiight.' Charlie and Gracie looked at each other.

'What?!' I said. 'French is important!'

'So is the show,' said Charlie.

God, why did I want to make more friends again?! It's just even more people to have an opinion on you. I'm going to stay here where it's nice and quiet…without any of the usual *blablater* (whiffle whaffle) of my nagging *amies*.

posted by EditingEmma 22.05
Neuroses Increase with Age
Mum came into my room.

'I have presents for you,' she said.

'Presents?!' I said, clapping my hands together. 'Yay!'

She sat down on the edge of my bed.

'This,' she said, reaching into a bag, 'is a rape alarm.'

…………

'Oh,' I said.

'Why? What did you think I was giving you? A Barbie?' she snapped.

I sniffed. 'Well, a Barbie's not looking so bad right now.'

'I'm giving you the gift of protection. Be grateful.'

She reached into her bag, and pulled out a can.

'Is that…is that *pepper spray*?!' I squealed. 'You know that's *illegal*.'

'I know. This is fake pepper spray. So your attacker will *think* you have it.'

I shook my head. 'Mum, seriously…'

'Ah, ah, ah.' She waggled her finger. 'I don't want to hear any more. They're going in your bag.'

Resistance was futile.

'And remember,' she warned darkly as she retreated from the room, 'you've always got your keys.'

What does *that* mean?

It's ironic, isn't it, that my mum's spending all this time trying to prepare me for 'outside attacks', and where I feel the most threatened right now is sitting in my bedroom. I glance over at my laptop, still banished in a corner, and turn out the light.

Tuesday, 16 December

posted by EditingEmma 16.34

In The Design Room

I'm in here pretending to make clothes, but actually doing more homework. Gracie and Charlie kept nagging me about why I wasn't designing and at least this way they're off my back. Anyway, it's juuuuuuust me in here. All by myself in my nice, peaceful bubble. Social media less. Human contact less. Alone.

Oh. Alone except Leon. Who just walked in. Great.

Well, this is awkward.

posted by EditingEmma 16.42

Ughhh. Why doesn't he just *leave*?! He looked like he was about to leave, when he first walked in...in fact, he sort of shuffled backwards and forwards a few times, clearly not knowing what to do. But then he sat down and carried on his work, and every now and then he looks up and we catch each other's eye and AGHHH. I swear, he *must* think I'm staring at him. Which I'm definitely not. It's just every time I look up, he happens to look up as well.

Unless he's staring at me?

UGHHHI IH. WHY did he have to come in here?! This was supposed to be my peaceful time!

GO AWAY, LEON.

posted by EditingEmma 17.05
Should I Say Something?

In the half an hour he's been in here, I've done nothing. Actually *nothing*. I can't concentrate. I am literally just sitting here, feeling awkward and weird and upset and going over everything that's happened between us, which feels like it's too big for this room. Everything that's happened is piling up around me, around the desks, across the floor, up to the ceiling until it's blocked my view and I can't see anything else.

I've thought about leaving lots of times, too. But it's like I can't do that either. Because all the *stuff* is getting in my way. I'm trapped in my chair, with him, in this tiny little enclosed space, getting smaller and smaller as it fills up with all our history. I know he's thinking about it, too. I can feel his brain working through the memories. I can feel his discomfort radiating off him in waves. He's been painting the same bit of wood for twenty minutes.

Should I go over? Should I do it? Should I try to talk to him, like my mum said?

I stood up.

And sat back down.

Stood up.

Aaaaand back down again.

AGHHHH. This is ridiculous!!!

posted by EditingEmma 19.07
Saying The Things You Want To Say Is Very, Very Hard
Walking home now. Eventually, I did it.

I stood up. My chair fell to the floor with a sudden clatter. Leon leapt back like I might be about to stab him, which was quite amusing.

I walked over to him quickly. Boldly. I did not once stumble.

I stood before him…everything I wanted to say on the tip of my tongue.

I opened my mouth.

And nothing came out.

… NOTHING came out.

Leon stared at me. I stared at Leon. At first, there was fear in his eyes, which started slowly turning to general amusement. The sides of his eyes crinkled in a warm, open smile and I started melting, because I realized just how much I've been missing him. Then I started to feel indignant, because when he smiles at me like that it always feels vaguely like he's playfully mocking me. Then I started to feel my body reacting to him because DAMN I FORGOT HOW CUTE HE IS. Then I started to feel angry at my body for reacting like that, against my will.

It sounds like we stood staring at each other for quite a long time, but really this was probably all happening within a second.

'You look like a goldfish,' he said.

I closed my mouth.

'Stand up,' I ordered.

He stood up. We were standing quite close together, now, and stared each other in the eye. I opened my mouth again. But instead of speaking, which I promise, was absolutely my aim when this started... I leaned forward and kissed him.

It was so incredibly familiar, in a way, and the memories of kissing him a million times before came flooding back in, like a strange kaleidoscope of fragmented Emma and Leons throughout time. The way his lips pressed again mine in the same patterns and pressures as they did before awoke all these old sensations in my body...it was like my lips were finding their way home and taking the rest of my body with them. But it also felt new, strange, alien...like kissing him was opening up all these new spaces I didn't even know I had inside me. And they were just getting bigger and bigger and emptier and emptier the more I kissed him, like I could never get enough, and it would never be enough to fill me. I was...*hungry* for kissing him, like I hadn't been before.

It wasn't just kissing like all the other times we kissed when we were actually going out. I mean...it was *kissing* kissing. Sort of...um, rabid kissing. Fierce kissing. Messy kissing. Sinking into each other kissing. Grabbing parts of each other kissing like you're trying to grab as much of the other person as you can...sort of like if you stop, they might disappear.

We kissed harder, and fell back against the set. I was pressing on top of him and my hands were in his hair and then on his chest and then round his waist and...

Then there was a cracking sound. Something split underneath us and we went tumbling to the ground. We both sat on the floor for a moment, looking a bit stunned. I'm not sure if it was the kissing or the fall.

'Um, sorry about your set,' I said.

'It doesn't matter,' he said, looking at me. A strand of hair had fallen in one eye, and he looked a bit hot and bothered.

And then, suddenly, everything felt very overwhelming. And I got up.

And I ran.

Then I remembered I had left my bag, so I ran back in to get it, and ran back out again.

'Bye, Leon!' I called over my shoulder. 'Go home! It's late.'

He just sat on the floor staring after me, all bewildered in confused. *Ha*. WELCOME TO MY WORLD, MATE.

Oh God. Oh God. Oh God oh God oh God. What have I done? Or is it a good thing? Or a bad thing? I don't know. I don't know what came over me. I just had the strongest urge to kiss him and I was about to walk away when I thought… why?! If you want to kiss him…just *kiss him*. Ugh, I'm pretty sure when my mum said 'sort stuff out with Leon' she meant verbally. This was definitely…the *opposite* of verbally. And we didn't sort ANYTHING out.

posted by EditingEmma 19.37

Something Bad Has Happened

On the walk home I got my phone out; just to send a message to Gracie, because I really needed to talk to someone about what had just happened, NOT to go on any form of social media. Instead of turning on my data I wrote her a text. It felt practically Shakespearean. Anyway, I wrote, 'I JUST KISSED LEON. WHAT DO YOU THINK IT MEANS? His lips are as soft as a baby rabbit.'

And just as I hit 'send' I realized something awful.

I hadn't sent it to Gracie.

...

...

...

... I sent it to Leon.

I SENT IT TO LEON.

'No! No! No!' I screamed, stopping in the middle of the street. This old couple turned around in fear, as if I might eat them.

'Oh my God! I take it back!! I take it back!! Unsend!! UNSEND!!'

I looked up at the old couple, who were still staring at me.

'Do you know how to unsend a text message?!' I asked in desperation.

They looked a bit baffled and started walking away.

ARGHHHHHHHHH.

HIDE ME AWAY IN A HOLE. FOREVER. OR AT LEAST UNTIL I AM EIGHTY AND EVERYONE I KNOW IS DEAD AND THEN MAYBE I CAN COME OUT AND LIVE TWO HAPPY BLISSFUL YEARS OF LIFE BEFORE I DIE TOO.

Aghhhhhhhhasfnnbnbngfjoirtuhthdaknscnvn.

Oh God. Maybe he hasn't seen it yet. *Is* there any way to get it back?! Can I ring O2 and ask them to recall it? Can I break into his house and steal the phone?!

'Delivered.'

NO NO NO NO this isn't happening!!!! THIS ISN'T HAP-
PENING.

posted by EditingEmma 20.30
Why hasn't he replied yet?

posted by EditingEmma 20.33
No seriously, why?

posted by EditingEmma 21.05
I've Been Discovered

I was still staring at my phone, willing it to buzz, when Mum
came in holding something made out of burgundy fabric in
her hands. For a moment I thought, *Oh, that's nice fabric.*
Then I realized.

It was the dress.

'Emma,' Mum said, sitting on the edge of the bed. 'What's
this?'

'Um, a dress,' I said.

'Why was it in the bin?' she asked. Her eyes were boring
into me.

'I... I decided I didn't like it any more.' I glanced down, and
then back up at her. She looked really confused.

'Emma, what's wrong?' she carried on. 'This isn't like you.
You spent ages on this. Is something the matter?'

'No,' I lied.

'And why have you deleted your Instagram account?'

Crap. I forgot she had Instagram now.

'Is this about Leon again?' she asked.

I rolled my eyes. 'Not everything is about Leon.'

'Well, what is it?' She sounded strained. 'I'm worried about you.'

I took a breath, still considering whether to tell her… And then I didn't. It was like saying it out loud made it real. And saying things to a parent always makes things this massive deal. I thought of the way she reacted about Adam turning up at school, and somehow I just couldn't face this yet. I wanted to keep it at a distance.

'I just need a bit of a social media break,' I said. 'And I really just didn't like that dress.'

'Well, OK.' She shrugged. 'But next time give it to charity.'

Then she kissed my forehead and went back to her own room. I kind of wanted to call for her to come back. I wanted to ask her for a hug.

But then she'd definitely know something was up.

posted by EditingEmma 22.40

Message from Leon. Finally.

> I don't know, Emma, what do you think it means ;) rabbit kisser 22.38

Oh this is so embarrassing.

posted by EditingEmma 00.07
Still Awake. Still Thinking About The Kiss
It felt so different than it did before. Like, all the same feelings were there and stuff, but it felt less...PG. It felt like I could have taken all my clothes off then and there, whereas in the old days with Leon it used to be more innocent. Potentially, this is my long and enduring sexual frustration talking. Or, I don't know… maybe in all this time I've become less nervous? Maybe...I've taken him down off his pedestal a bit?

Do I want to be with him, now?

Does he want to be with me?

What does this mean?

At least this has distracted me from the comments on my blog. And the way Steph turned around and went back inside her house, leaving me behind without a second glance.

Wednesday, 17 December

posted by EditingEmma 11.18
Dissecting The Meaning of 'The Kiss' At Break
Talking to Faith and Gracie about my kissing Leon. When I told them, Gracie clapped her hands dramatically to her cheeks and Faith raised one eyebrow as if to say, *Knew it.*

'What do you think it *means*?' I asked.

'For God's sake, Emma.' Faith shook her head. 'You initiated it. Surely that means you don't have to ask.'

'You would think that, Faith,' I replied. 'But apparently my own actions are just about as mysterious to me as someone else's.'

Faith sighed.

'Well let's try and figure it out,' said Gracie helpfully. 'What were you thinking when you did it?'

'Um. His lips look nice.'

'Right. And how was the kiss?'

'Good.'

'And how did you feel afterwards?'

'Umm...Good.'

'I've got it!' said Faith. 'I know what it all means!'

She leaned in to us. I waited with baited breath for her pearl of wisdom.

'It means…you wanted to kiss Leon,' she said.

Then I got my fake pepper spray out of my bag and threatened her with it.

posted by EditingEmma 12.31
CAN Girls And Boys Be Friends?
I don't believe it. After all my objections and eye-rolling and total, complete confidence in Gracie's breathtaking wrongness…she has actually managed to seed doubt in my mind. A tiny, tiny seed…barely visible…but still in existence. An amoeba seed.

'Emma,' she started cautiously, as we were walking to class. 'Feelings about Leon aside. How do you think Charlie's going to react to this?'

I groaned. 'Gracie. Charlie. Does. Not. Like. Me.'

'Are you sure about that?' she asked.

'Yes, I'm *sure*,' I said. 'I know in my bones that we are just friends, in the way I know in my bones that you and I are just friends.'

'OK,' she said. 'But he seems to really care about you. You know, constantly asking why you're not going to the design room, which I would also like to know, by the way, and letting you dress him in those stupid graph paper hats.'

'Hey! He *likes* those hats!'

She wrinkled her nose. 'If you say so,' she said. 'But I think you should talk to him about the Leon thing.'

And suddenly, there it was…the seed. It formed. And now I can't *un*-form it.

Is it possible he likes me? Am I really that blind?

posted by EditingEmma 14.27
Faith Is WAY Too Honest

'Claudia's coming on Saturday, by the way, Emma,' said Faith on the way to Art. 'She's excited to see your stuff.'

The thought of the show sent me into mild panic, so I changed the subject.

'Is she sleeping over at yours after?' I asked.

She raised her eyebrows. 'What do you think?'

'But *really*, you could have her over for sleepovers. My mum would put up a penis-repellant force field around my bedroom if she could. But I mean…your parents wouldn't know she was anything more than a friend, right?'

'If I *lied*, you mean, then yes.'

'But…given that you've had to sort of lie this whole time and it's been so rubbish for you…might as well use it to your advantage now?'

'That's Emma logic. I'm not interested in Emma logic.'

'*Fine, fine*. I was mainly joking anyway.'

'Sure you were.'

I thought for a moment.

'Seriously though, is having a relationship making it harder for you? You know, to omit the truth? Do they know about Claudia at all?'

Faith paused.

'They've heard of her. Did you finish your textiles piece?'

And that's all I was getting…

posted by EditingEmma 16.59

The Mythical 'Slag'

After school I tried slipping off to the tech room instead of walking home with Faith and Gracie like normal, but Gracie caught up with me.

'All right, that's it,' she said. 'Emma, what are you doing?!'

'My homework,' I said.

'I can see that,' she said.

'Then why did you ask?'

'I meant it like, *what are you doing?*'

'I thought you loved homework, Ms Cambridge Immerse.'

'*I* love homework,' she said. 'But *you* don't.'

'Well, people change. Isn't this a positive improvement?'

She made a face. 'Yeah, it would be, if you were actually doing it because you wanted to do your homework.'

'Why else would I be doing it?!' I rounded on her.

'Because you're avoiding your phone.'

I opened my mouth. I closed my mouth.

'You haven't posted anything in days,' she carried on. 'You aren't replying to anyone's messages. You just sit around burying yourself in French verbs… and… and…secretly kissing Leon!!'

'*Je yaourte,*' I said.

'What?'

'It means, literally, *I yoghurt.* It describes the act of singing in a language one doesn't know very well or is making up.'

Gracie folded her arms.

'Don't try to cute your way out of this. I'm not dropping it.'

'But if I hadn't studied so much, how would we ever know about yoghurting?!'

'I...'

Then Faith came over. 'Why are you shouting about yoghurt?'

'I'm trying to get Emma to tell us what's up,' Gracie said.

They both looked at me. I sighed.

'All right, fine,' I said, and told them about what happened.

For a moment they both said nothing.

'Oh, Emma!' said Gracie. 'Why didn't you say something?'

'That's horrible!' said Faith.

'Can I see the picture?' asked Gracie.

I showed her.

'You don't look like a slag at all!' she cried.

'Ugh, SO not the point,' said Faith.

'What do you mean?' asked Gracie.

'A "slag" is not a thing.'

'What?' repeated Gracie.

'It's a term that perpetuates the ideal of a virginal, virtuous woman and shames her for her sexual enjoyment and choice of clothing.'

Gracie blinked. 'Well, maybe, but it still exists.'

'No. It doesn't. Because if you call someone a slag, thus perpetuating this ideal, you're implying something negative about anyone who doesn't conform to it, and FACT: enjoyment of sexuality and...*daring* clothing...are not negative things. Therefore the word refers to something that doesn't exist.'

Gracie blinked again. 'Well, whatever, but the *word* still exists.'

'Ugh, fine, OK,' said Faith, 'the word exists but it's a gross word and refers to something that doesn't exist so *shouldn't* be a word that exists.'

'How are you doing at Philosophy, Faith?' I asked.

'Got ninety per cent on my last essay, thanks.'

'So what about a girl who slept with ten men in one night? Would you call her a slag?' continued Gracie.

'Ugh!! And there's my main problem!! You said "girl"! You would never call a man a *slag*.'

'I would,' said Gracie, 'I would call him a man-slag.'

'Exactly!!!' cried Faith. 'Man-slag already implies something different. Makes it like a joke. As if a guy can't really be a slag but a girl can.'

Gracie considered. 'I've never thought of it like that before...'

'A slag is not a thing,' continued Faith. 'Emma, that outfit is sexy, and daring, and you can dress however you want to dress. Come on, let's go home.'

I agree with her *logically*. I really do. But whilst my logical brain is telling me she's right, I think about that comment and I get this knot in the pit of my stomach, made up of shame and insecurity, and then my illogical brain thinks maybe it would be easier to stop designing clothes and stay offline.

I think I'm glad I told someone and I appreciate them trying to help, but neither of them seemed to quite get it. Gracie sort of missed the point, and Faith's intellectual responses don't always work for me at solving feelings. I keep thinking about what Steph would have said.

Thursday, 18 December

posted by EditingEmma 12.05
I'm A Hallway Creep

It happened again!!! I don't believe it... My lips have a life of their own!!

I was just heading to English after break and I moved too quickly and spilled lots of stuff out of my bag. Leon was coming in the other direction and he bent down to help me.

'Here,' he said. 'You forgot your, er...pepper spray?' He looked at the object in his hand, totally bemused, and then just started laughing. Like really, *really* laughing. And then I started laughing. And we just stood there laughing and laughing in the corridor when everyone else had gone to lessons, and our laughter was echoing round the empty hallway which made us laugh even more. Then I got out my rape alarm in one hand, pepper spray in the other, and started swinging them around, and we laughed harder.

'I've missed you,' Leon half snorted.

We were looking at each other, still laughing, and suddenly it just wasn't funny any more. Suddenly I just had to grab him and kiss him again. I pulled him in and put my lips on his and it was just so…easy. So unbelievably easy. And then there we were, making out in the corridor, when everyone else had gone for lessons.

WHAT IS HAPPENING?!?!?

Eventually, I managed to break off. I pulled away and yelled, 'I'm late for English!'

'So what's new?' he said, and kissed me again.

And now I am super, super late. So late that Ms Parker told me to go away again. So late that I'm just sitting back outside in the empty corridor, feeling dazed and weird and thinking about everything. Thinking about Leon. Thinking about Steph. Thinking about my stupid lips that keep kissing when I didn't instruct them to. Thinking about how I never ever want to go back onto social media. It's funny…normally I wouldn't mind being kicked out of lessons so much, but today I could really, *really* use the distraction.

Leon messaged me.

> You know, you looked quite intimidating striding towards me swinging your rape alarm and wielding your pepper spray.x 11.59
> Still thinking about it, eh? x 12.00
> I don't expect that mental image will ever go away. x 12.00

Aghghghghgh. What is this craziness?! So I guess we're talking again, then? Or just kissing again? Yargghhhhhhhhhhhhhhh-hhhhhh.

What should I be feeling about this?

posted by EditingEmma 13.50
Sitting In The Tech Lab

You know what, for once I am not going to analyse how I feel about this. There is no 'should be feeling about this'. I kissed Leon. Twice.

So what?

Really, we're all just animals, aren't we? We like to think we're above being animals, but we're not. Animals don't have to think about or justify what they're doing. And who am I to argue with the circle of life?

No, I shall not think about *le baiser* any more. I will just sit here and learn more French. So I can communicate with some other animals, just like me, over in France.

posted by EditingEmma 13.56
Gracie Turns Detective

Gracie came into the sixth form centre and sat down next to me, unfolding a little piece of paper.

It read:

Gracie's List of Suspects
Hannah Condom
Cyber-bullying you in return?

Kayleigh Spencer
Getting you back for lying?
Pet grief sent her over the edge?

Anna
Could still be upset about the Leon thing?

Greg
Could still be upset about being dumped? Felt angry again after seeing you at BOB?

'That's all I have, so far,' she said. 'But I think we should try and find out who's doing this.'

'Hannah Condom?!' I scoffed. 'Come on!'

'She did seem pretty upset…'

'I explained to her friends it was a big misunderstanding. Cross her off. And Kayleigh, she was too nice.'

'What about Anna?'

'Anna is way over this,' I said. 'She seems so calm.'

'Maybe she's only calm because she's getting her revenge behind your back.'

I pressed my lips together. 'And Greg?'

'He's clearly not over you,' said Gracie.

'Yeah, but… I don't know. I just really don't think it's anyone I know. It's just some random person,' I said.

'But why would a random person do this?'

'I don't know. There are lots of strange people on the internet,' I said.

'True. But it seems so unlikely. Who even looks at your blog except your friends?'

I shrugged. 'It's just some random person who thinks I'm a *slag*.'

'Could you think of anyone else it might be?' she asked.

'No,' I mumbled.

I had this nagging feeling, then. Because I wasn't being *totally* honest with her. But I stayed quiet.

'Well, last time... It *was* someone who knew you.'

She looked down at her shoes.

'Yeah, but... That was different. You would never go online and call me names.'

'I am still really, really sorry you know,' she said quietly.

'Oh my God, Gracie, we're so past this,' I hugged her. 'But I'm sorry too. I'm so happy we're not there any more.'

'Me too. I smug hhoooo,' she said into her coat.

'What?'

'I love you,' she said.

'I love you too,' I said.

Then I wanted to cry. But I didn't, because I have enough things that make me want to cry, without adding things that actually make me happy to the list.

posted by EditingEmma 15.01
Staring At Gracie's List Of Suspects
In Maths. Could Gracie be right? *Could* it be someone I know?

That sort of makes it worse, somehow...

Ugh. I can't believe I'm back here. Thinking about who might have done something horrible to me on the internet. I think this time is actually worse. Messaged Gracie.

Can I come over after school? X 14.49

Yeah sure x 14.50

'Are you all right?' asked Charlie, who was wearing his graph paper capotain.

'I'm OK,' I said quickly. What Gracie said about him has been playing on my mind.

'OK,' he said, touching my shoulder.

I repeat: he *touched my shoulder*.

DOES he like me?

I really, really don't have time or head space for this right now.

posted by EditingEmma 16.25
Back at Gracie's

'All right, so I lied to you earlier. There is one other person I can think of,' I said.

'Who?!' Gracie opened a Dairy Milk bar and stared at me.

'Give me the list.'

She fumbled in her coat pocket and handed it over. I wrote:

Dev
Because I had random…um…sexy chat with him online?

'Which would be completely unfair because he was there too, but hey, that's the sexist world we live in,' I added, putting the lid back on my pen.

Gracie was open-mouthed, Dairy Milk bar forgotten.

'WHO is DEV?!' she yelped.

'Ugh, keep your voice down, all right!!! He's this…' I buried my head in my hands. 'Ugh, he's friends with Steph's cousin. Me and Steph both used to, um, *talk* to him…'

'And what did you "talk" to him about?!'

'Um…venting our frustrations.'

'EMMA!!!' Gracie screeched. 'I can't believe you had *cyber sex*!!'

'OK, whatever it was, it was NOT cyber sex.'

'Why didn't you tell me?!'

'Agh, because it's EMBARRASSING all right. I'm basically still a thirteen-year-old.'

Gracie put her hand on my shoulder, then. 'Emma, why did you feel embarrassed?! I thought we'd moved on from that.'

'We have. It's not you,' I said. 'I was just ashamed. I don't know.'

'Why?'

'I'm so horny, Gracie.' I put my head on her shoulder.

'I'm so horny, too!!' she giggled.

'I thought you don't even masturbate,' I said.

She bit her lip.

'All right, I'm only telling you this because you're really, really down.'

'What?' I said.

She looked around her, as though we weren't alone in her bedroom.

'…*I do masturbate*,' she said, wincing.

There was silence as she waited for my response to this giant revelation.

'I figured,' I said.

'Ugh, you're so rude!' she exclaimed.

'What?! Why?!'

'Because that was a big thing for me to admit.'

'All right, all right, sorry! OMG!' I slapped my hands to my cheeks in mock horror.

Gracie pursed her lips.

'If I actually didn't masturbate, that would be OK too, you know, Emma.'

'Yeah, of course, but I *knew* you were lying!' I laughed.

'Well, anyway, there you go. So now you know I'm the same.'

'No no,' I said. 'I'm sorry. Admitting that you masturbate is not the same as going to some creepy boy who refers to himself as "Godlike Dev" for internet sexy chat.'

'You didn't mention the "Godlike" part.'

'Well, now you know.'

She pursed her lips even tighter.

'All right. *Fine*. I'll tell you something else. But you have to swear, *swear* you'll never tell anyone!'

'I swear.'

'Swear on Amy Sherman-Palladino.'

'I swear! What did you *do*?!'

She buried her head in her hands.

'I bet it's not that bad,' I said.

'It's bad.'

'I bet it's not.'

'It's bad!'

'Prove it, then. Go on.'

She sighed. 'Oh my God, it's so, so bad. The other day...
everyone was out of the house.'

'Yes?'

'And I was...um, well, using my hairbrush.'

'Interesting,' I said.

'What?!' she squealed. 'Don't you use objects?!'

'No,' I said. 'Just my hand.'

'Oh my God! I *am* weird!'

'Gracie,' I said. 'There are many different ways to masturbate and, not that I'm exactly an expert, but probably many
different ways to have sex. We all enjoy different things and
you are not weird. Continue.'

'Well. I've been thinking recently that it's...well, it's too thin
for my needs. And um, well, wondering what else there might
be to use. So I, um, explored the house.'

'Yes...' I encouraged her.

'And, well, um. My brother's Wii remote...well...it vibrates.'

'Oh my God!' I started laughing.

'But then, ugh, but then I heard him come back in with his
friend. And he started yelling, "GRACIE! GRACIE! Have you
seen my Wii control?"'

I was laughing so much by this point.

'And he stormed up to my room and I stuffed it under my
pillow, and was all like, no, no, I haven't seen it. But then he
started yelling about how Mum must have taken it, so that
he'd do more homework, and how it was bang out of order.'

'What did you *do*?!' I wheezed.

'Well, I was going to, um, clean it and put it back. But he was so angry I didn't want to risk getting caught. So I threw it out the window.' Gracie winced. 'And it landed in the neighbour's garden. And Andy and Mum are still fighting about it.'

'Oh my God! You *thief*!!' I guffawed.

Gracie took a deep breath. 'So now,' she said, 'Do you accept that you're not alone?'

'I accept,' I said, still laughing. 'You're a dirty Wii-humping scoundrel, Gracie Morton.'

posted by EditingEmma 18.01
The Plan
We have spent the past two hours coming up with a brilliant, mastermind plan, complete with equally brilliant mastermind Plan B... NOT.

Plan A
Make friends with a computer genius and get them to trace the location of the commenter.

Plan B
Try and surreptitiously look over the suspects' shoulders for clues.

'Is this *it?!*' I cried. 'Is this the best we can come up with?!'

Gracie shrugged. 'I guess.'

'Well,' I said, 'you'd better not put *plan-making* skills on your future application to Cambridge, Gracie. Because if you do, I'll send them these.'

'Yeah, well, if you do that, I'll send whatever fashion school you're applying to pictures of you in that disgusting green jumpsuit.'

I really need to take those pictures down.

'The computer genius one isn't so bad,' she carried on. 'If only making friendships didn't take so damn long... Would you be happy to figure out the mystery in a couple of years?'

'I'm really, really hoping to have moved on with my life by then.'

'We could *bribe* a computer genius?'

'Hmm. Not bad. Do either of us have any money?'

'Um, I have two hundred pounds that I got for my birthday,' she said.

'Ooh!'

'But I'm definitely not spending it on this. What about you?'

'Er, I have eighteen pounds fifty and a Dairy Milk bar.'

'The Dairy Milk bar is mine, actually.'

'All right, all right! So much for sharing is caring!'

'Clearly, we need a new plan.' Gracie sighed.

'Ooh! Ooh! I know!' I said. 'We could comment on the next comment, with things that *only* the suspect would know. If it is them, that would definitely scare them off!!'

'Like what?'

'Like...say it *was* Dev...and say he called me a slut, or something. I could write... I don't know about that but I have been told I'm rather GODLIKE.'

Gracie paused.

'If it's not Dev, though, won't they think you're really strange?'

'Yes,' I said. 'But funnily enough, I'm not that worried about whether the person trolling me thinks I'm strange or not. I just want them to go away.'

'I don't know, though. I'm not sure about actually interacting with the troll. Isn't all the advice to ignore it and stuff?'

I nodded. 'You're right. I really don't want to get into any online spats. I think that will just make me feel worse.'

'Yeah, don't rise to the bait.' Gracie sucked in her cheeks. 'You could hope they get bored and go away, then start up your blog again?'

'I don't know. That feels like giving them what they want. Next?'

She shrugged. 'I'm out.'

Sigh. I went home no closer to figuring anything out.

As I was leaving, I looked out Gracie's window and saw the sullied Wii control, lying in the neighbour's bush. At least I have that hilarious image to hold on to, in dark times.

Friday, 19 December

posted by EditingEmma 10.16

I Don't Know What I'm Doing

I passed Leon in the hallway earlier.

'Hey,' he said, and offered me a Chewit.

And suddenly, I'm not sure why, but I felt irrationally angry. What, did he think everything was just going to go back to the way it was?! Maybe last term that would have been the case... But I wasn't that girl any more.

'What are we doing?' I asked.

'Um, eating Chewits?'

'You know what I mean,' I said.

'I know what you meant.' He looked at me questioningly.

'Well, then?'

'I don't know, Emma. Why don't you tell me?'

'You know, Leon,' I said. 'You can't just start...offering me Chewits...every time you and Anna break up. It doesn't work like that.'

He opened his mouth like a round 'O'. I had the most annoying urge to put my finger in it. *Stop it, brain.*

'*You* kissed *me*!' he exclaimed. 'TWICE!'

'Yeah, well,' I said.

'Yeah, well, what?'

'Yeah, well… That doesn't stop me being hella mad.'

He smiled then. 'You can't pull off *hella mad*,' he said.

I tried really, really hard not to smile back.

'I'm still upset with you,' I said. 'You upset Charlie, too.'

He put a hand through his hair. 'Yeah, yeah, I've upset everyone.'

He did look really frazzled and distressed then. I felt a flash of pity against my will.

'All right, bye then,' he said, and walked off.

I know I've been kissing *him*, but for some reason him coming over to *me* felt different. It made me feel out of control. AGHHHHHHHHHHH. Is that fair?! I don't know!!!

posted by EditingEmma 10.21

I really wish I'd taken a Chewit and *then* told him to go away.

posted by EditingEmma 13.05
Rest Of The Day's Events

1) Analysed Charlie's Every Move

Charlie sat with us at lunch again today and I decided to look closer for signs of love. He did offer me his pudding. Is Gracie right?!

2) Suspected Something Is Up With Faith

'I'm not sure Claudia is coming on Saturday any more, Emma. She says to tell you sorry.'

'Oh, that's fine,' I said. One less person to worry about. 'Why?' I asked.

Then Faith went all cagey and started talking about her new paintbrush.

3) Was Accidentally Mean to Crazy Holly?

I was doing homework in the design room. Holly was in the corner, octopussing away. Then she said,

'Can't wait to break this out on Saturday!'

I stopped.

I turned.

'What do you mean, *on Saturday*?' I asked through gritted teeth.

'Y'know, wapping out ma moves at the big showdown.' She flailed an arm.

'No,' I said. 'You can't do that.'

She just winked.

And in the moment, all I could think about was how awful I already felt about hundreds of people judging my outfits. Judging *me*. Let alone with Holly and her weird dancing making things worse. People would definitely mock her. And by proxy, people would basically be laughing at *me*. I've had enough of other people's nasty comments.

'Holly, I mean it! You'll ruin it! Why can't you just be normal for once?' I yelled.

It was meant to come out jokey, but it didn't. We both knew I wasn't joking. Holly stopped dancing and stared at me. Charlie looked up from his table and frowned. I put everything down and left.

Holly's not upset, right? Crazy Holly is never upset... She doesn't live in reality. Real things don't touch her. Right?

Again, we're all animals. Just animals. Animals don't have time to think about any of this. They just think about what's for lunch.

And *I* am having pie.

posted by EditingEmma 13.45
The Mission

I can't believe I'm saying this but...the pie didn't make things better.

I'm in the tech lab, still thinking about what I said to Holly. I feel *awful*. I think of Holly's shocked, hurt face and I just start crying.

I'm not myself. I know I'm not myself. I would never, *ever* have snapped at Holly like that if I wasn't so worried about what people thought of me. And I'm worried about what people think of me because I've allowed this stupid, horrible person to rule everything. I've given them so much power over me.

I unfurl Gracie's list of suspects.

~~Hannah Condom~~
~~Kayleigh Spencer~~
Anna
Dev
Greg

I know what I have to do. If I'm ever going to figure this out, I'm going to have to actually talk to these people.

And I'm starting at the top.

Anna.

posted by EditingEmma 13.50
Operation Get Anna Alone – Take Two

Back lurking around corners spying on Anna. FFS. But this time I will show no mercy, *Patricia*.

What counts, legally, as a kidnapping? If I leap on Patricia and tie her to a chair somewhere, with tape over her mouth, just to get her away from Anna for a bit…will I do time?

posted by EditingEmma 13.59
SUCCESS

That was far easier than last time. Anna broke off to go to the toilet whilst Patricia was having her hair plaited and couldn't move. I followed her. Unfortunately, I came in after she'd already gone to the loo and I had to stand listening to the sound of her weeing for quite a long time. When she eventually came out, I sidled up to her.

'Anna,' I said.

'Emma,' she replied, looking vaguely creeped out. As you might, by someone lurking around listening to you wee.

The status quo was much as it ever was.

'I'm doing some research for a class project. Do you mind if I get your opinion on a poll?'

'Um, sure,' said Anna.

'Great! OK, so the question is...um... How do you feel about the word *slag*?'

I waited. She blinked.

'Ah, what are the options?'

Of course. A poll normally had options.

'Um, a) great word, accurately describes the, uh, thing it's describing and er... B) like Swiss cheese – neutral, baby, or C) it's a horrible word, no one should ever use...unless it's women reclaiming the word and making it mean something else.'

'Er, well...C. Obviously.'

'OK, C...Interesting, interesting.' I scribbled down her answer on an imaginary bit of paper. Then realized I was just writing in thin air which looked a bit bonkers, so I stopped. Anna stared.

'Right, thanks a lot!'

I retreated back into the shadows of the corridor.

And now I'm analysing her answer. It *definitely* wasn't her. Not because she actually said C) – which, of course, is exactly what a person secretly calling someone a slag online *would* say – but because she looked so entirely baffled by the whole encounter. Not even a hint of recognition around the eyes. If it was her, she probably would've twigged why I was asking...but nope. Pure, solid confusion, with a side of unadulterated fear.

posted by EditingEmma. 14.39
On my way to afternoon lessons I passed Kayleigh Spencer, who (of course) avoided eye contact. I started to wonder, was I

too quick to strike her off the list? Is her super nice, cat-loving exterior actually masking an ice-cold, calculating villain? What if her and Hannah Condom are in it together…? Maybe she's even planning to recruit Anika Khatri?! WILL SHE STOP AT NOTHING on her campaign of hate?!?!

Then Kayleigh stopped to help a Year 7 kid tie their shoelace and I exhaled. I really, really don't think she's an ice cold supervillain.

All this is making me INCREDIBLY PARANOID.

posted by EditingEmma 16.44
A Revelation
Was walking home with Gracie when A THING happened.

'So, did you speak to Charlie yet?' she asked.

'Uh, no,' I said.

She sighed.

'All right, sorry!!' I said. 'I will!'

Then she went kind of…moody?

'All right, well, you should do it soon,' she said. 'Because if he does like you, it's not very fair that you're running around kissing Leon in hallways. And it's not very fair, you know, on the people who might want to kiss Charlie in hallways.'

Then I glimpsed her face. She looked sort of…vulnerable.

I suddenly twigged what might, *maybe*, be going on here.

'Gracie… What are we really talking about?'

'Charlie liking you.'

'Are we…talking about anything else?'

'Like what?'

'I don't know...maybe someone liking Charlie...'

She looked away, then. Her eyes fluttered and she went all pink.

'OH MY GOD!' I screamed.

'Shhhhhhhh!' she whispered urgently.

'It's hardly like I'm announcing it on a tannoy!' I yelled. 'What do you think is going to happen?'

'Someone might hear you!!!' She looked around her, all shady-like.

'What?' I said. 'You mean like that old man feeding the ducks? No offence, Gracie, but I'm pretty sure he has zero interest in your love life.'

'You never know!!' she hissed. 'He might be Charlie's grand-dad or something!!'

I massaged my temples. Gracie having a crush was going to make my life very, very long. She gets embarrassed about dropping something on the floor.

'I don't believe it!!' I said. 'All this time. Is this why you've been so obsessed with me and Charlie??'

She bit her lip. 'Maybe,' she said.

'When did you realize??' I asked.

'I think I've known a little bit, for a while now. But properly the other day in the sixth form centre. I dropped my sausage roll on the floor, which was SO EMBARRASSING...' (see) '...and he picked it up and started eating it, and gave me his.'

'True romance,' I said.

'It was very chivalrous.' She blushed.

'So, does he meet all your *criteria*?' I grinned.

314

'Hmm, about eighty per cent,' she said. 'I mean, he's only a Grade 5 Violin.'

'*What?!*' I slapped my hands to my cheeks in mock horror. 'How are you guys going to function?'

She grimaced. 'It's not ideal.'

FFS.

'Anyway, *now* will you stop going on about me and Charlie?' I continued.

She shrugged. 'I believe you don't like him. But what if he likes you?! And I like him?! That would be so...'

'Embarrassing?' I said, sarcastically.

'Yes!' she said.

I actually don't see how that would be embarrassing at all, but whatever.

'All right, all right, I'll talk to him,' I said.

'Thank you,' she breathed.

Oh God. Now I'm even more nervous about speaking to him...

posted by EditingEmma 19.50
Back To Investigations
I was just settling in for a quiet evening of learning, when Mum burst into my room.

'All right,' she said. 'WHY is your phone in the blender?'

'Um, safekeeping?'

She raised one eyebrow.

'It's not like we ever use the blender,' I said.

'We do sometimes.' Mum frowned.

'No, we used it *once* to make that misguided kale smoothie. Then we poured it down the sink. Then it clogged our drains. And THEN we had to call Fit Plumber.'

Mum paused, lost in memories. 'Maybe we should use the blender more... Well anyway, here's your phone.'

'I don't want it. Put it back in the blender, please.'

'Emma, what on earth is the matter?!'

I sighed. 'Just leave it on the bed.'

When she'd finally gone, I tried to carry on, but I could feel the phone *staring* at me. My old friend. So many happy times spent together... I could almost hear it asking, *Why are you doing this, Emma?! What did I do wrong?!*

I picked it up.

All right, seeing as I'd already had one awkward conversation today...I might as well have another. At least this one didn't have to be face to face.

Emma: Dev, did you call me a slag on my blog?

The reply was instant.

Dev: ?!? Why would I do that, sexy mama?!
Emma: Because of our 'chat'
Dev: Anything you say here is free of judgement, Emma.
And the same for what I say to you? It's a safe space.

Silence.

Dev: And on that note...

I turned off my phone. *Ugh,* no. Not again.

I do actually believe him, though. The times we met he seemed super harmless. His whole vibe is not really like that... I really don't think it was him. Still, though, I won't be having any more 'chats' with him. I don't know...even if he is harmless, I feel kind of weird about it. Anything you say online is immortalized and out there for other people to share as they choose. I don't think I'm going to be having any more 'chats' with anyone other than someone who, maybe far, far away in the future, I am a hundred per cent sure I trust...

At least I didn't send him any pictures. I certainly wouldn't do *that* for anyone that I wouldn't also trust with my life.

Like Steph.

Although why I'd be sending Steph naked pictures of me, I don't know.

I miss Steph.

posted by EditingEmma 21.09
Keep getting the most irritating messages from Gracie.

> Please don't tell Charlie what I said 19.17
> I know you're friends but I'm your friend too 19.18
> Emma please, swear to me 19.20
> For God's sake, I swear! 19.20
> On Lauren Graham? 19.20
> I swear on Lauren Graham 19.21

I just don't believe you 19.21
You're going to tell him 19.21
Actually I was going to get little Gracie <3 Charlie t-shirts printed, and make everyone at school wear them 19.21
?????????????? 19.21
What?! Emma please!! 19.21

People in love have absolutely no sense of humour. Still, if nothing else, Gracie's deranged messages have been distracting me (a bit) from how nervous I am about tomorrow.

I can't *believe* it's tomorrow.

Saturday, 20 December

posted by EditingEmma 11.31
Just Another Day Any Other Day

But it is not any other day. It is the day of the fashion show.
   I feel sick.

posted by EditingEmma 15.45
Getting Ready For The Show

I don't know what's happening to me. I usually *love* getting ready, and putting an outfit together and thinking about what make-up and hairstyle will complement it in the right way etc., etc. ... But I'm just not enjoying it. In fact, I would go so far as to say I'm actively *hating* it.

   Everything I put on looks wrong. I feel like I detest every single item I own. I've started my make-up and scrubbed it off again three times, and now my face looks a bit red and raw.

   What is *the matter* with me?!?!

   This is really the one and only area of my life where I *don't* feel insecure. The bit before going out and actually talking to people, where you and your choice of clothes and make-up and self-expression are the only things that matter. I'm used to feeling awkward and bumbling on the inside, and then masking it with a great outfit. But it's like all my self-consciousness has finally made its way out of me. It's *showing* in my clothes.

posted by EditingEmma 16.32
I Have Three Hours To Redo EVERYTHING

Oh my God. Oh my God. OhmyGod ohmyGod ohmyGod ohmyGod.

Oh. My. God.

I just got to school and suddenly, looking at the outfits I've spent hours and hours carefully planning and many more hours lovingly crafting, that I've poured my heart and soul into, that I've been so excited to show the world and thought about basically solidly for nearly two months... Suddenly, I'm wondering...

Why on earth I bothered.

They're rubbish. Obviously. Total crap. Everyone's going to hate them. Why did I put that button there? Why did I choose that shade of blue? Why did I think that dress looked good when it was so obviously exceedingly ugly? Why did I think I could do this? Why why why why why why why.

WHY.

It's OK. Breathe. Breathe. You have three hours. You can remake everything. Fine. Let's just start pulling everything apart. It will be fine. It has to be fine because it's clearly the only way.

posted by EditingEmma 16.59

I Don't Believe This

I sensed someone hovering beside me as I tore apart my outfits. I don't really know what on earth I'm doing to them, now, but just touching them and pulling stuff off arbitrarily seems to make me feel a lot better. Anyway, it was Charlie.

'So…nervous?' he asked.

'Aha, ahahahahha,' I replied. 'Whatwouldmakeyouthinkthat?!'

'Hmm. Glazed eyes. Maniacal grin. Clawing frantically at your outfits.'

'Idon'tknowwhatyou'retalkingabout.'

He took my arms then. 'Emma, seriously, stop. Stop touching the clothes.'

'But…'

'Put the shirt down.'

'But I…'

'Emma, NO.'

Then I used my self-defence move on him, and tackled him to the floor.

'Hahaaaaa!' I shouted, spooning/holding him on the ground.

'How the HELL did you do that?!' His shout was muffled, because I was holding his arm in front of his face.

'Thank you, Wham Bam Sam!' I called triumphantly.

'Look, you shreally need to caghhhlm daawghn, is all I'm sagghhying,' said Charlie.

'I'm perfectly calm, thanks,' I said, as he started wriggling. 'It seems as though it is YOU who is not calm.'

'Becaushhh I'm beinnngh held caahhptive!'

Eventually I consented to release him. We were both still on the floor, and burst out laughing. I was laughing so much I was too weak to get up.

'This is what they mean when they say, ROFL,' said Charlie. We both lay there for a bit, looking at the ceiling. 'Maybe I can't physically restrain you, but I can distract you instead?' he went on.

'Go on then,' I said.

'So I, um, I have this problem.'

'I always thought you had the eyes of a bed-wetter,' I said.

We started laughing again. I was so hysterical by this point, I was basically just wheezing.

'No really,' I said, eventually. 'What is it?'

'Ughhhhh,' he said. 'I like someone.'

I froze. Oh God. Here was the moment. Was Gracie right all along? Was my radar for these things completely broken? I didn't know what I was more worried about; breaking it to her that her crush didn't feel the same, or having her be totally smug and continuing to believe that boys and girls can't really be friends.

Oh God. I closed my eyes, preparing myself for the inevitable. Wondering how to let him down gently. It was going to be hard.

'Who?' I asked, bracing myself.

He was silent for a moment, and then… 'Ghrmmsaaachhiiie,' he said into his hands.

I unfroze. And started breathing a massive, massive sigh of relief.

'Did you just say *Gracie?*!' I squealed. 'GRACIE?!'

He kept his head in his hands and nodded. I stared at him for a moment, processing this new information.

'Oh thank GOD!' I yelled laughing. 'I was right! I *knew* I was right!!'

Charlie looked up. 'Right about what?'

'You fancying me!!!'

'Errr...what?!?!' Charlie made a vomit face.

'All right,' I said. 'No need to look *quite* so repulsed.'

'Sorry, but God, no. No, we're not like that. Ugh No offence.'

'We're not! We're not like that! I knew we weren't!' I kept laughing and threw my arms around him. 'Charlie, this Gracie thing, it's so great. I...'

Then I paused. Did the not-telling rule still apply here? Or was it OK to tell now?

'Please, please don't tell her Emma.' Charlie looked up. 'I know she's your friend, but I'm your friend too.'

Where have I heard that before?

'I think she likes Pete Wheeler in the year above. I saw the way she was looking at his arms the other day.' He shook his fist. 'Damnit, how is Pete so BURLY? I'm going to have to start working out.'

'Charlie, I...'

'Please don't tell her. It would be so embarrassing.'

Really, when you think about it, two single people liking each other should be the easiest thing in the world, but I can see that getting these two together is going to be like lugging a dead horse up a mountain.

I have no idea why I'd be doing that, obviously, but I imagine it would be very difficult.

I think I'm still hysterical. CHARLIE DOESN'T LIKE ME. I KNEW IT.

posted by EditingEmma 18.15
People With Eyes

I keep peeking outside and people are here. People with eyes. Eyes that are going to be looking at things that I've designed.

It's early days but seats are filling up. I should be happy that loads of people have come, but I'd rather they all just went home and took the pressure off.

posted by EditingEmma 18.27
Oh Lord

I was still peeking through the curtains when Charlie came up behind me.

'Oh my God, is that…?' He gasped.

'What? Who?!' I asked. Had a celebrity shown up?

'Keanu Reeves?' he said.

I looked in the direction he was pointing and caught the glimpse of a *Matrix* coat, reflecting the stage lights.

'Haha, very funny,' I said.

'He's here to blind us all,' Charlie said, shielding his eyes.

'All right, stop now.'

'He's here to steal the limelight with his unique style.'

'You're not…'

'Damn him, showing us all how it's done! He's probably got Gucci begging to give him a job.'

'You're not funny,' I said.

'I am quite funny,' he replied. 'Aren't you worried the fashion courses you apply to are going to learn of your dalliance with that man and refuse your place?'

'Shut up,' I said. 'That won't happen.'

Will it?

Then I spotted another familiar face.

Greg.

'Oh God,' I groaned.

'What?' Charlie asked. 'Another creepy ex-boyfriend?'

'All right, first things first, Adam is NOT an ex-boyfriend. That, over there—' I pointed '—is my actual ex-boyfriend.'

Charlie peered over. 'Which one?!'

'The one in the dark blue shirt.'

Charlie furrowed his eyebrows.

'What?' I asked.

'Well, I'm just confused… He's not wearing a cape or dark glasses. I'm surprised you were ever attracted to him.'

I shoved him.

'I have to go,' I said.

'Where are you going?' Charlie asked.

'I need to speak to him.'

'About what?'

'Be back in a second!' I shouted, running off.

And now I'm loitering in the hall. If I don't take this oppor-tunity to speak to Greg now, I might never do it. At least being nervous about this is distracting me from being nervous about the show.

posted by EditingEmma 18.40
I Am An Idiot

After standing in the doorway waving for about a million years, Greg finally saw me. He looked faintly alarmed and shrugged at me, as if to say, *What do you want?* I beckoned him over and then he began clambering over various parents to come talk to me. On the way he accidentally fell and sat on some middle-aged woman's lap, skewing her glasses. Then after apologizing profusely, he stood up and it happened again.

I was bright red with laughter by the time he got to me.

'I'm glad you found that funny,' he huffed.

I was still wheezing. 'And that's the reason we got on so well,' I said.

There was an awkward silence. I cleared my throat.

'Um, anyway...' I said.

'Yes?' He looked at me expectantly.

I know I say this every time, but he really does have a very kind face.

Just at that moment, Charlie loomed behind Greg mouthing, 'STOP! NO! NO!' and waving his arms about.

'What is it?' Greg repeated.

'I...'

Charlie was still behind Greg, now hopping around from

foot to foot and dragging his arm across his neck, as if to say, *Kill this conversation.* He really did look quite bonkers.

'I, um… You have a nice shirt,' I said.

'You wanted to tell me that I have a nice shirt?' Greg blinked.

'Precisely,' I said. 'Blue always suited you.'

'Riiiiight.' Greg frowned.

'Trust me, I do fashion,' I said, putting my hand on his arm and then walking away, leaving him standing there a bit bemused.

'*What?*' I hissed at Charlie, once I'd got him alone. 'What is it?'

'I know what you were going to talk to him about.'

'I doubt that,' I said.

'You were going to ask him if he'd posted stuff about you online.'

I blinked. 'Oh. How did you…?'

Charlie took a deep breath. 'Because I think I know who it was.'

My heart stopped, then started thudding. 'What are you talking about?'

'I really didn't want to tell you this *tonight*. Can we talk about it after?' Charlie looked pleading.

'No,' I said. 'Now.'

He shuffled from foot to foot.

'Charlie!' I demanded.

'All right.' He sighed. 'I came up behind Leon and…'

'Leon? You think it was *Leon*?' I scoffed.

'I know it sounds a bit far-fetched. But I know him really

well. He was on your blog, and…well, he looked like he'd been caught out doing something awful.'

'Well, you probably caught him stalking me,' I said.

'Yeah, I mean, that's what I thought. But he went…weirder than normal. I don't know. I can't explain it. Then I saw that you'd deleted all your social media accounts and I said something about it, and he went all funny again. I don't know. It wasn't until later when Gracie mentioned about the comments that I even put two and two together.'

'Gracie told you?'

'Don't be mad at her. She's worried about you.'

My heart stopped thudding and went deathly still. Could it really be him? Was he getting me back for last term? Oh my God… The comments did come up *before* we started getting with each other again…

All this time, have I been secretly making out with the person abusing me online?

'Emma…' Charlie began.

I put a hand up to stop him.

'You were right, Charlie,' I said: 'Let's talk about this later. The show's about to start.'

He nodded and took my arm, and I suddenly felt a rush of warmth for the support. I felt like I might burst into tears. But I didn't. I had more important things to get on with right now than worrying about the person trying to tear me down. Whoever that person was.

posted by EditingEmma 19.16

The Drama Continues

I was just heading back into the green room with Charlie, when someone yelled, 'WHY is no one appreciating how DRUNK I am?!'

I turned around and, when I saw who it was, you could have knocked me over with a feather. Faith was sprawled in a corner, rolling about on the floor. I stood for a moment, staring but not really believing my eyes. I was quite alarmed. I'd NEVER seen Faith like this. I had absolutely no idea what to do. Selfishly, just for a second, I panicked and stood completely still. Ugh.

I'mahorriblepersonI'mahorriblepersonI'mahorribleperson. I know it's awful but I was already so nervous and still a bit in shock from what Charlie had said and…just for a moment… I felt angry with her. *She's* meant to be the together one. She's my rock. My calming paper bag to breathe into. What am I supposed to do if she falls apart?! Especially RIGHT NOW.

Could I just walk past and pretend I hadn't seen her…?

'UGGHH,' she wailed and started sobbing into the wall.

Probably not.

I rushed over to her.

'Faith! FAITH! What are you doing?!'

She looked at me blankly, as if I was a long lost cousin twice removed from Alabama who she'd only met once before in her life.

'Emma,' she said, finally.

'Yes, yes, it's me. Faith, what's wrong?!'

'What's wrong?! What's *wrong*?!?!' she cried, and started unzipping her shoe.

I watched bemusedly as she took the shoe off and threw it across the other side of the hallway.

'That's what's wrong!' she declared.

'Your shoe?' I asked gently.

She nodded.

I backed away slowly, reached out for the shoe and handed it back to her.

'Here you go,' I said.

She looked at it for a few seconds, before pushing it away.

'You've made me a fool,' she said.

I stood there for a few more moments, clutching her shoe as she sobbed. More and more people were turning up and I was supposed to be backstage now. I rang Gracie and Steph but their phones were both turned off. Damn them for being such diligent audience members! Who actually turns their phone all the way off?! Why couldn't they just put it on silent like *normal* people?!

'Faith,' I said, leaning down to her. 'Faith, what is it?'

'She doesn't understand,' she sobbed.

'Who doesn't understand?'

'YOU KNOW,' she said.

'I don't,' I said carefully. 'I'm sorry. Hope? Your mum?'

'Claudia,' she said, blowing her nose on her sleeve.

'What doesn't she understand?'

'I'm not like her. She...she doesn't understand. I'm not like her.'

'What aren't you like?'

'I'm not strong. I can't. I'm not like her.'

'Oh, Faith, you *are* strong.'

'Ughhh,' she wailed. 'You're just the same!!! *You're so together, Faith, you're so STRONG, Faith.* Why does everyone expect me to be STRONG all the time?! What if I'm not?!'

I thought guiltily back to a minute ago when I saw her crying and felt annoyed.

'I lied to her, Emma. I told her my parents knew about us.'

'Oh,' I said.

'I didn't want her to think I was ashamed of her. But now... now she's so upset that I lied.' Faith sobbed.

'Oh Faith,' I said. 'It will be OK.'

'Will it?' she asked.

Just then, Charlie appeared at the door.

'Emma! Emma, it's nearly starting!' he called, then saw Faith. 'Oh,' he said.

'Help me, would you?' I called back.

Together, we picked her up, one of us under each arm, and sort of carried/dragged her backstage. We laid her on a table and she patted Charlie on the arm and said, 'Good boy.'

'How much has she had to drink?' said Charlie. 'And where did she get it? I could use some.'

'I don't know,' I said, stroking Faith's hair.

'Come on, we have to go.'

'Do you think we can just leave her here?' I asked.

'I think it's better that she sleep it off,' he said.

'All right, everyone, we're on in five minutes!' Ms Parker

called out, interrupting us. Everyone started scuttling around. Abby Matthews (one of the models) started pouting even more vigorously than usual. Crazy Holly flung a pair of furry shorts in the air (I wonder which model agreed to wear those?).

I kissed Faith's head and left her on the table. She was curled up into a ball, still clutching her shoe. And now I'm sitting behind the curtains in the dark, linking arms with Charlie. I'm typing in one hand and eating Haribo in the other.

THE MUSIC IS STARTING. IT'S STARTING.

posted by EditingEmma 01.35
Back Home. In Bed.
I'm back home now and So. Much. Has. Happened.

The show started and it was really weird… The models (and by 'models' I really mean Abby Matthews and her pals prancing around) started walking up and down the catwalk (and by 'catwalk' I mean planks of wood badly cobbled together by Crazy Holly) and then the funny thing happened. Abby Matthews was at the end of the catwalk doing some very questionable hip movements and my outfit was in the spotlight. Suddenly something inside me lifted, just for a moment, and it was sort of like everything else, including everyone in the room, disappeared. I could only see the dress that I'd so lovingly created, with the light bouncing off of it. Even Abby Matthews's strange gyrating couldn't distract me. It was just me and the dress and nothing else mattered.

It was a little bit like the end of a rom com and me and the outfit were getting married, or something. But anyway, I felt *proud.* So insanely proud I thought I might cry. Which I know is stupid because I make outfits all the time and at the end of the day we were only in my school hall, not Fashion Week. But still. I did that. *Me.* And *I* like it. It's mine and I like it. Why have I been so ridiculously worried this whole time about whether other people like it?

'Charlie,' I whispered into the darkness.

'Mmghmm,' he whispered through a mouthful of Haribo.

'I'm just going to do something,' I said.

He nodded and I ran off.

In the dressing room, Holly was just zipping up her furry shorts on some girl I recognized from Maths class.

'It's just, I mean…' The girl was saying. 'They weren't furry a couple of days ago.'

'Things change,' said Holly. 'Roll with it.'

'Holly?' I asked, approaching.

Holly stood up.

'I'm sorry I denied you freedom in your creative expression,' I said.

'Huh?' She frowned.

'I'm sorry I said you couldn't dance like an octopus. You *must*. You must dance like an octopus. You must dance like no octopus has ever danced before.'

Holly paused for a second. I thought she might say something incredibly profound and we'd discover new depths to our friendship. But she patted my shoulder and said, 'Octopuses can't really dance.'

When I sat down next to Charlie again I was still nervous,

but it was like my nerves put on a brave face. I just sat back and took it all in, every now and again taking soothing bites of Haribo. And I think… I think I maybe, possibly, just *a little bit*, began to enjoy myself.

Holly came out right at the end. She emerged in my 'show-stopper' dress (it really is quite something – long sleeves, gold sequins and beads, cut out at the back) and walked quite normally to the end of the runway. I wondered, for a while, whether she was going to octopus it up at all. But then the familiar sounds of Hotley Crew started through the sound system and I knew what was coming. Holly stopped dead and put her head down. The entire room went deathly still. No one made a sound and listened only to the soft, resounding vibrations of the didgeridoo.

Charlie gripped my arm. 'Sorry,' he whispered.

'No, I'm excited,' I said.

'Good,' he said, beaming. 'Me too.'

And then the didgeridoo stopped. The lights went dead. One girl squealed and I heard Ms Parker hissing, 'What's going on?! What's going on?!' But quick as a flash a single spotlight came back on, shining just on Holly's right arm, which was waving back and forth like a glorious, sedated sea creature.

'Spectacular,' whispered Charlie. 'Entrancing. Magnificent.'

Slowly, Holly came back into view and kept dancing. There was no music any more. Literally just Holly rocking out in silence in her strange, bizarre way.

'*That's* why she wanted to be involved in literally every single team,' I said. 'She was staging a takeover.'

Charlie nodded in awe. 'That girl's going to be famous one day,' he replied.

'What for?' I mused.

'Literally anything. Inventing some kind of strange contraption. Breaking the world record for most lemons eaten by a human being. Voyaging to unknown territories. Being president.'

'You're right.' I nodded, as Holly finished. 'No possibility seems ruled out.'

There was a slow, confused clapping as the lights came back on. Ms Parker came on stage and said, 'Thank you, Holly,' through gritted teeth. Holly gave a little bow, with a flourish of her hand.

Then Ms Parker invited us all up on stage. Charlie and I stood up, gripping each other in fear, and staggered out like moles coming blinking out into the sunlight. I was *convinced* I was going to fall over. Really, with someone as poorly coordinated as I am, the possibility of not falling over seems infinitesimally small. I am far more likely to fall than not, on an average day, and definitely more likely in front of an audience. But for once I actually didn't.

Me and Charlie propped each other up and walked into the spotlight to take our bows with the others. People were clapping and I could see my mum in the front row pretending to throw roses at my feet. Gracie was sitting next to her clapping in her usual demure, sophisticated manner and patting my mum on the shoulder, sort of like she was also my parent or something. Even Faith had roused from her drunken stupor and was perched at the edge of the stage looking sickly and green, but also proud and wise…like my very own drunk Yoda.

I looked around for Steph and my heart did a little dance. Even though we were fighting there she was, yelling, 'A HUN-DRED POINTS TO HUFFLEPUFF! A HUNDRED POINTS TO HUFFLEPUFF!'

I'm obviously *not* a Hufflepuff, but whatever.

I felt so, so, SO happy and proud and loved. I felt like I might burst. I didn't want anything to ruin it… but…ugh… I'm ashamed to admit it…but I couldn't help noticing that Leon wasn't anywhere to be seen. It wasn't like I was *trying* to look for him, or anything, especially given what Charlie said earlier. But my eyes were just scanning for him anyway. Against my orders. STUPID EYES. You're a part of *me*, eyes! Stop wandering off on your own!!! But anyway…he wasn't in the room. Not on stage with the other set people. Not in the audience. Not anywhere.

I think I might *almost* have let it ruin the moment. It might have done, if I hadn't remembered what Steph said at the very beginning of term, about this being something I was doing just for me and not letting Leon ruin it. And thinking about Steph and what she said made me feel all warm and glowing. She was right. I shouldn't let *anything* ruin this for me. Obviously if anyone who was important to me hadn't shown up it would have been hurtful, whoever they were…Mum, friends…but this still would have been my thing. My moment.

It's not like I'm not upset by Leon not coming. Obviously, it sucks. But separating that out into something I'm upset about on its own, without letting it take down the entire evening with it, was like a breath of fresh air.

After we were done on stage we came back in to start packing stuff away. And by 'packing stuff away' I mean taking turns to try on Holly's furry shorts.

Just as it was my turn, Greg appeared in the doorway.

'Hey, just wanted to say well…' He faltered, looking at the shorts. 'Done.'

'Thanks,' I said, trying to sound casual. Like someone who wasn't wearing a pair of furry shorts might sound.

'Look.' He ran his hand through his hair. 'I just wanted to say sorry for the last time I saw you.'

'*You*? Say sorry?' I stuttered.

'Yeah, I shouldn't have done that at Battle of the Bands. Made you feel awkward again. It's history.'

'Greg,' I laughed. 'You don't have to be sorry. *I'm* sorry.'

'Yeah, well.' He paused, then took a breath. 'It's great to see you.'

'Really?' I asked.

'Really.' He smiled. 'I hope you're happy, Emma.'

'I hope you're happy too,' I said.

He gave me a hug. And then I felt something shift. Here he was, still standing in front of me and being everything that Leon wasn't, yet again… But I didn't actually feel tempted or needy or like I wanted him to make me feel OK. I just…felt OK.

'Thanks,' I said, releasing him from my furry grip.

'No problem,' he said. And that was that.

'So what happened there?' asked Charlie as Greg walked away.

'It was just…'

Then he interrupted me with laughter.

'No, sorry, I take it back. I can't take you seriously when you're dressed like that.'

Just as Greg left the room, Leon entered. With Anna.

Because *that's* where he'd been…of course.

He looked at me across the room and started trying to come over to me. I pointedly turned my back on him. Because I literally don't care any more. At all. I had a lot of feelings for him. A LOT. So many feelings that it's incredible someone could have squished every single last ounce of them out of me. Quite masterful, actually. But they are officially gone now. As if it wasn't enough to swap me in and out of ridiculous, boring, immature benching cycles and then bully me online, he misses the one thing that actually meant something to me.

Every single last feeling. Gone.

'Emma?' he said from behind me.

'I saw you,' I said. 'And that's why I'm facing *this way*.'

'What's wrong?' he asked quietly. 'Me and Anna aren't back together or anything. She just wanted to talk about things. I thought I owed her an…'

'God, Leon, you're *so desperate for attention, slag*.'

'What?!' He turned me round to face him.

'Oh don't pretend you don't know. Charlie told me.'

'Charlie,' he repeated.

'Yes. Now, if you don't mind.'

And then I turned back to the wall again.

I heard him walk away. Charlie came up to me and said, 'Damn, Emma. Cold.'

I shrugged and let him feel the breeze of my icy glare, too.

'You know,' he said, 'I've said it once and I've said it again, it would be a lot easier to take you seriously if you weren't wearing furry shorts.'

After I'd removed any item of clothing that made me look like a bison and passed them back to Holly, we finished packing up. I was about to head home, thinking I had well and truly had enough drama for one day. Seriously, enough. And I like *Pretty Little Liars*. If a PLL fan has had enough drama then you KNOW it's been enough drama. But that's when I noticed Andy lingering awkwardly by the dressing room door.

Great.

I went over to him.

'Uh, hi, Andy,' I said. 'I think Steph's already gone.'

He looked *incredibly* uncomfortable, and kept shuffling his feet. 'Actually, I wanted to speak to you,' he mumbled.

'Oh,' I said.

'It was a great show,' he said. 'How much did you raise in the end?'

'About £2000, which is pretty amazing,' I answered.

'Oh, awesome!' he cheered...then tightened his lips again. 'And did you...have fun?'

If Andy was anything like Gracie, this was going to take all night, so I cut straight to the chase.

CHLOE SEAGER

'Oodles of fun,' I said. 'What's up, Andy?'

It came out a bit sassier than I intended. I think, and I don't *like* this about myself, because I recognize it isn't anything he has actually done...but I think I have come to maybe, just a tiny, tiny, weeny, *only a little bit*...loathe Andy's existence.

He sighed. 'I think... I think maybe I owe you an apology.'

I blinked. 'For what?'

His lip started twitching in that really annoying way that Gracie's does, and I *reeaaaallly* had to stop myself from reaching out and pinching it.

'I... It's hard to say.' He shrugged. 'I've not done anything wrong, I guess. But I just wanted to say, I'm really sorry for not doing anything right either.'

'What do you mean?'

'This whole thing with you and Steph.'

My heart jumped into my throat. He sighed.

'I think...' He carried on. 'I don't know. It's not like, it's not like I encouraged her to be annoyed at you... But I didn't exactly discourage it, either, do you know what I mean?'

'No, not really.' I could feel adrenaline flooding my body. Andy was still looking at his shoes, but he looked up at me then.

'I didn't do the right thing,' he said, straight to my face. 'Whenever you guys had a stupid argument. I could always see both sides of it, but I just... I just let her be mad at you.'

Steph was mad at me?! Steph was MAD AT ME?! This was music to my ears. To be mad, you have to actually care.

'Mad?' I asked, trying to sound casual. 'About...?'

'You know, about you missing her birthday. She kept saying

you'd moved on and made new friends. I tried my best to cheer her up, but she was sad the whole time.' Andy ran his hand through his hair. 'Sometimes you need the people close to you to actually point out the other side of things. And I didn't.'

'...Why?' I asked.

He looked down at his shoes again. 'I was jealous,' he mumbled. His hair flopped down in front of his face, but I could see that his skin was basically the same colour as his auburn locks.

I wanted to laugh out loud.

'Jealous?!' I screamed.

'So, so jealous.' He kept looking down. 'And when she was mad at you, I guess she was kind of all mine.'

My mind flashed back to periodbloodgate, when I was totally secretly enjoying Steph being annoyed at Andy. I knew how he felt.

'God, it's so stupid!' Andy yelled. 'I got so jealous, I was even jealous that she was *mad* at you!! I kept inventing scenarios in which *I* could possibly make her that mad... And I couldn't think of any! You know, I think even if I cheated on Steph, she'd be hurt but she'd shrug and get over it.'

And then I really did laugh out loud. 'OK, you know if you cheated on Steph, she wouldn't just *shrug*. But I know what you mean. She's independent.'

'Not from you,' Andy said. 'You're her number one.'

I beamed. With all these compliments, I suppose Andy's existence was becoming a *little* less loathsome to me.

'Anyway, I'm being irrational, I know that now,' said Andy.

I shrugged. 'I guess I'm no stranger to irrational behaviour, either,' I conceded.

'Yeah, well, we all saw the beheaded bear.'

'That was *my mum*,' I protested.

'The apple doesn't fall too far from the tree.' He smiled. 'So, can we please pretend to Steph, and to each other, that this conversation never happened?'

'Works for me,' I said.

'But next time you and Steph have a fight, I promise not to just sit there smugly.'

'Me too,' I said. 'Unless you react like a dick about a spot of blood on your bed again. In which case I *will* slip you laxatives and then humiliate you when you poo yourself.'

He looked mildly terrified then.

I don't think I undid all of our good bonding...

Definitely not *all* of it.

posted by EditingEmma 00.01
Friends and Number Ones
In bed, still thinking about everything. Thinking about how anticlimactic it feels to have got so worked up about something I should have been enjoying. Thinking about Leon. And mainly thinking about what Andy said. The phrase 'you're her number one' keeps going round and round in my head, making me glow with pride and happiness, and then have a mild panic. Glow. Panic. Glow. Panic. It's completely exhausting... In a way, I feel *so* relieved. I'm still Steph's number one.

But I can't always be.

I think all this time I've been convincing myself Steph doesn't care any more, or that her boyfriend is more important than me...is because it would be so much easier if that *were* the case. But I know it's just not that simple. I know that I am still her best friend, but that her relationship is a private, separate part of her life and I can't know everything about it. I can't be number one *all* the time. And somehow that's scarier than being mad at her, or upset with her.

And...and my mind is racing forward to the day she's going to go out into the world and make other friends, and have an actual, *real-life job*, a partner who she wants to stay with... and maybe some children if she wants, and...and all these things are going to take priority. They're going to take priority OVER ME. If not all the time at least some of the time... And I'm FREAKING OUT.

I know, now, part of the reason we've been fighting isn't because Steph's outgrown me, but because I've not wanted to accept us growing up.

Sunday, 21 December

posted by EditingEmma 09.37

A Letter (Yes, A Letter)

This morning I was still in bed when Mum came in and shoved a letter at me.

A letter.

'This better not be *your stalker* again,' she barked.

We both stared in fear at the envelope lying on my bed.

'Hand delivered,' she added. '*Hand delivered.*'

'Oh God,' I groaned into the pillow.

'Open it,' she snapped. 'Go on!'

I sat up and rubbed my eyes. I don't think I've ever received a letter before in my life. Unless you count all the fast food leaflets I get since me and Steph ordered that 6-4-5 cheesy bread deal from Domino's. (I never thought I'd say this, but it really was too much cheesy bread.)

Anyway, I opened the letter. It said:

Dear Emma,

I write to you in the hope that you will forgive me for what I'm about to relay, and with the fervent wish that our friendship may continue to flourish. I have made a discovery that causes me much sorrow and anguish, which it pains me to share with you. But alas, I must.

I'm grieved to report my friend, whom I once thought kind and gracious, has turned out to be a wicked sort of man after all.

I'm sorry to say that last night I chanced upon Adam's mobile communication device and was met with a grave sight indeed. The slanderous comments by which you have been plagued I now believe were of his doing.

Please accept my sincerest apologies for having acquainted you with such a man and my promise that I shall cut off all communications with him henceforth.

Much obliged,
Holly Ignatius Barnet

P.S. if you didn't get any of that – Adam's the one who's been commenting on your blog and I'm not speaking to him any more. I'm really sorry.

Mum stared over my shoulder at the letter.

'Emma,' she said, sitting down next to me. 'Is this why you've been offline?'

I sort of wanted to bat her away and pretend like everything was fine. But I crumpled. I nodded and started sniffling into her shoulder.

'You really should have told me,' she said.

'I know.' I nodded.

'If something like that happens again you *must* tell me, do you understand?' she said.

I nodded again.

'I just wanted to pretend it wasn't happening,' I said.

Mum nodded.

'I feel like such an idiot,' I went on. 'I didn't even think about *Adam*. I barely know him. And I thought he liked me... Why would he do that?'

Mum shrugged. 'People can be awful when they feel rejected.'

I had a little cry, but I actually feel better now. Knowing who it is and why they did it makes it nastier and more targeted... But also like it's less about me, too. This was obviously all about him. And the more I think about it, the more I think that most things like this are. Even if this person hadn't known me... targeting me online would still mean more about them than about me. You really have to think that anyone doing that sort of thing has their own motives, whatever those motives are.

On her way out of the room Mum said,

'Is Holly's middle name really Ignatius?'

posted by EditingEmma 10.01
Oh God

Oh God. Oh God oh God oh God oh God. And then I had a thought...if it was Adam, then...it wasn't Leon.

It wasn't Leon.

Zut alors! What did he think I was banging on about yesterday?!

Oh my God. I have zero idea what to think or do about this,

or what it means, but right now I'm going to stop thinking about me and think about someone else.

posted by EditingEmma 11.38
Faith Came Out (For Real This Time)

Just left Faith's house. I went round to check she was OK, after last night. Faith's mum, Lillian, let me in.

'Hi, Emma,' she said. 'Faith's upstairs.'

'Great, thanks,' I said, and bounded to Faith's room.

Faith was lying on her bed sketching a lychee.

'Hello,' I said, sitting on the floor, so that my head was just behind the lychee. (Maybe I could photobomb her sketch, too? She might start drawing me without even realizing. That would be MEGA-PHOTOBOMB.)

'Hiya,' she said, not looking up from her lychee.

'How are you?'

'I'm all right, thanks,' she said coolly.

I sensed that she was withdrawing on me, after her unusual display of emotion last night.

'So, all OK after yesterday?'

'Yes, thank you.' She kept sketching.

'Right. Um, spoken to Claudia?'

'Yes.'

God, this was like drawing blood from a stone.

'What did you say?'

'I told her that I was sorry I lied about being out to my parents. I told her that I planned on being honest with her in the future, and that I'm out to my parents now.'

'Well, that's good that you… Wait, *what*?! You told your parents?!'

'Yes.'

'WHEN?!'

'This morning.' She kept staring at her stupid little lychee. Suddenly I picked it up and put it on my head.

'Hey! Emma!' she cried indignantly.

'What? You mean you can't keep drawing it like this?'

'No.' She folded her arms.

'What about like this?' I put it in my mouth.

And then regretted it INSTANTLY, because it was really large and spiky.

I started choking.

'God, Emma!' Faith jumped down off the bed and started patting me on the back. Once we'd got the whole lychee out of my mouth, we finally talked properly.

'Thanks for ruining my art project,' said Faith, staring at the slightly mangled, spit-covered fruit.

'No problem. What *happened*?!' I asked. 'How did it go?! Your mum seemed completely normal when she opened the door.'

Faith sighed. 'Yeah, it was… Fine. But I always knew it would be fine.'

I gaped at her. 'What do you mean?!'

She shrugged. 'What I just said.'

'… Then…why…'

Faith paused. 'I mean, I always knew it would be fine but not fine, if you see what I mean.'

'Uh, no, not really.'

She thought for a moment. 'I never thought they'd like...you know, kick me out of the house, or anything. I never thought they'd be openly upset. It was more like...'

I waited.

'... It was more like... I mean, they were just being so overly polite, trying so hard to be OK with it, which I knew they would... But, it's like, it kind of hurts just as much, because it shouldn't be something that anyone has to *try to be OK with.*'

I nodded.

'I could feel them reconciling themselves to it, you know? And that's the thing. My relationships will always be ones they reconcile themselves to, not ones they're just unquestioningly happy about. I mean, I'm sure they *will* be happy for me, but it will never be quite the same as with Hope and Simon, you know? Not exactly.'

'I'm sorry, Faith.'

'It's OK.' She shook her head. 'It's done now. I think partially I've resented the idea of coming out for a long time, because I hate that I even have to "come out", you know? Like, everyone should be like Claudia's family. No assumptions made. But a lot of people aren't like that.' She shrugged.

'Do you feel any better now?' I asked.

'Kind of. Except they reacted exactly how I thought they would. Like...before I did it, I could always pretend that they *might* react differently, you know?'

'Ugh, I'm so sorry.'

'And it's not like coming out really means that you have this one awkward moment, and then it's all fine from there. All I've really done is set myself up for a thousand more tiny awkward moments.'

'Oh God.'

'The first time they meet Claudia, AWKWARD. The first time Claudia holds my hand or something in front of them, AWKWARD.'

'I'm sorry, Faith.'

'It's OK. I do feel better that I've done it. And it's fine. It will be fine. I needed to do it.'

'Yeah.'

'I don't want there to be a part of my life Claudia can't be involved in.' She smiled. 'And now there isn't.'

'Apart from like…going to the toilet,' I said.

Faith laughed. 'Yes, apart from going to the toilet.'

posted by EditingEmma 12.01

Orgasmo!

Before I was about to leave, Faith put a hand on my shoulder and said, 'By the way Emma, *I did.*' She raised her eyebrows.

'You did?!'

'I did!'

I laughed out loud and yelled, 'ORGASMOO!!'

'Emma,' she hissed. '*Shut up.*'

'I'm sorry,' I laughed. 'I'm just happy.'

'It's both lovely and slightly creepy that you're so invested in my sex life.'

'No problem, pal,' I said, punching her in the shoulder. 'So, what changed?'

Faith shrugged. 'Well… it's quite simple really. Last night, once we talked about all this, and I told her the truth about my parents, we started talking everything else too. Including *that*.'

'Bold,' I said.

'As soon as I said it,' Faith carried on, 'it just got so much better. Like I'd actually included her in the activity, instead of thinking I was in it alone. I think I'd been forgetting that it's something two people do *together*. I asked Steph about it before and she said it's all about communication. Like, her and Andy don't speak about things, as such, but they *let each other know*. Hints. Non-verbals. I'm not really a non-verbal person so I just told her.'

'See, I'm clearly never going to have a functional relationship,' I said. 'I'm too awkward to give non-verbals *or* talk directly about things.'

'Nah, you'll get there,' said Faith.

'Well, anyway, I'm very happy for both of you and all your orgasms,' I said.

I sort of am. *Sort of.*

But it also seems like something so ridiculously far away, for me. Me, who makes out with my ex-boyfriend randomly in corridors and then says nothing, with no idea of what we are or what it means or what we're doing. Yes, truly WONDERFUL communication skills. Top notch.

It was time to be brave. I knew what I had to do.

posted by EditingEmma 12.47

Step One Of Being Brave: I'm Back!!!

I've officially turned all my social media back on. The online world is such an easy way for people to be awful and vent everything that's going on for them because it's anonymous. But being online is also a way for people to be kind to each other and support each other. I've been making it this massive thing in my head like 'social media is evil' or something, when it's really just a method of communication and it's how people are using it that's important. And that includes me, too. I know now it wasn't just those comments that made me have this complete freakout. It was obsessing over it. Defining myself by it. Of course these comments were going to send me completely over the edge... If all I'm thinking about is my social media accounts and someone's being nasty to me on social media, I felt like my entire self and identity had been totally ripped to shreds. But taking myself off it completely isn't going to do any good, either.

I just have to learn how to stop letting it take over my life.

And also, block Adam on every single outlet possible, and remember to talk to someone *immediately* if something like that ever happens again.

posted by EditingEmma 13.05

Step Two Of Being Brave: On My Way To Leon's

Yes, you did hear me correctly. I am on my way to Leon's house. Because we need to have a conversation. An actual conversation, where we don't start kissing. I'm not entirely sure whether this is a good idea or quite how it's going to go but...anyway, my feet are still moving. So. Can't argue with that.

It's snowing. Actual snowing. Which is making what I am about to do a lot harder because it feels all romantic and movie-like. I have to keep reminding myself that tomorrow, when the snow is gone and I don't feel all gross and sentimental, I will know I've done the right thing and didn't throw away ALL MY SELF-WORTH for a kiss in the snow.

A kiss in the snow...

I have always really, really wanted a kiss in the snow...

With Leon...

STOP IT.

posted by EditingEmma 13.37
Lingering Outside Leon's House

Oh God. OhGodohGodohGodohGodohGod. WHY did I think I could do this?! Face to face?! Why didn't I just send an awkward email like a normal person?! Or come to think of it, say absolutely nothing about this ever again, like he did to me last summer?

And just as I'm about to turn away, I hear the door open. And I crouch down behind a bin.

'Hello?' I hear him call.

I carry on crouching.

'Emma, I know you're there. My mum heard you yelling "CRAP" to yourself about half an hour ago.'

The jig was up.

I stood up and waved to his mum, who was standing in an upstairs window looking a bit bewildered. She disappeared behind a curtain.

'I, um, took a picture of myself and my nose was surprisingly red,' I said. 'It's REALLY cold.'

'Well, maybe don't stand around outside in the freezing cold taking pictures of yourself...' he said.

'I don't have a mirror on me.' I shrugged.

'Yes, that explains everything.'

Silence.

'If you knew I was here, why didn't you come out?'

'I assumed you'd eventually come in, but you never did, so...'

Silence.

'So,' I said.

He came closer. And leaned in towards me. For one moment it was just me and him and *the snow* and I stopped thinking anything. Just for a moment.

'Your nose really *is* surprisingly red,' he said.

'Yes,' I said, remembering myself. Remembering why I came. *Remember why you came, Emma.*

'I'm here because.'

'Because...' He looked amused. One eyebrow was perfectly raised over his stupid perfect eye, that had that mischievous glint in it that always, without fail, makes me kind of annoyed at how *smug* he is but also kind of want to grab him and kiss him at the same time.

I took a deep breath.

'What did you think I was talking about yesterday?'

Leon was silent and looked down.

'Leon?' I prodded.

'God, Emma, it's all right,' he said to his shoes. 'You like Charlie. I get it.'

I laughed. 'Seriously?! Is that what you think?! Seriously?!'

He shrugged.

Oh my God. Is the entire world completely bonkers?

'Leon, for God's sake. I don't like Charlie!! I like YOU! I've liked you since before hitting puberty! Since before dinosaurs walked the Earth! Since before the old Taylor Swift died!' I yelled.

It came out a bit threatening. He looked quite startled. I ploughed on.

'Yesterday Charlie said he saw you on my blog writing something. That's what I was talking about. I don't know if you've noticed but, um… Well, I've been offline recently. Someone was posting really horrible things about me. I thought it was you.'

Leon looked up at me. 'Oh,' he said.

'Yeah, oh.'

We were silent again.

'Anyway,' I carried on, 'I just wanted to tell you that I know it wasn't you and I'm sorry for saying those things yesterday.'

'It's OK,' he said. 'I can see why Charlie thought that. I, umm… Well. I was writing something on your blog. But not that.'

I frowned. 'What? What were you writing?!'

He paused. 'Emma, I already knew you'd been offline because of that. I was writing back to them.'

'You were *what*?!' I screeched.

'I know, I know,' he said. 'It was stupid. All that happened was me getting into stupid, immature online fights and then making it worse. But it just made me so *angry*.'

'Why would you get involved?! How could you possibly think that was a good idea?'

He took a deep breath. 'Because I like you, Emma. Since before hitting puberty. Since before dinosaurs walked the Earth. Since before the old Taylor Swift died.'

We both fell silent. The words hung in the air.

It sounded a lot more romantic when he said it.

He started moving towards me. His familiar smell of soap and bubbles and Chewits filled the air.

No, no no, I thought. This is exactly what I didn't want to happen.

DON'T GET TAKEN IN BY THE CHEWITS.

'Leon,' I said, holding out a hand to stop him. 'I don't need you to fight my battles for me. And I'm really glad it wasn't you, but this doesn't erase everything. You've still hurt me. A lot.'

'I know,' he said, backing away.

I took a deep breath.

'So yeah, what I really came to say is… We can't go out again,' I babbled. 'I mean, I know you hadn't, um, actually asked me to, so maybe this is kind of presumptuous, but when someone tells you they really like you it's usually because they *do* want to go out with you. Anyway, so yeah, I like you a lot actually, *still*, despite my best efforts not to. And so…yes. We both like each other. Confirmed.'

I nodded. He nodded back, still smiling.

'And that would usually mean the going out of those two people. Who like each other. But I just... I don't think... I don't think we should.'

He didn't look amused any more.

'I, um, I... Wow, this is hard. I don't want to make it sound like I'm having a go at you or anything, because I'm not. I just... OK, last night. You weren't calling me a slag online. Now I know you're not a total asshole. But... You missed the show I've been working really hard on since the beginning of term.'

'I told you,' he said, 'Anna really wanted to talk, and I felt like I owed her that.'

'YES, you did, totally, completely. But—'

'I thought you'd get that,' he interrupted me. 'I thought you'd get that I did that to you before, and I'm trying to be better now.'

'I *do* get it. I do. But... I mean... Did it really have to be *during the show*? I mean, I guess what I'm asking is, did you think maybe it might have been OK to say, "Anna, can we talk in an hour instead of right now?"'

'Kind of sounds like you're having a go at me,' he said.

'No, I'm not... But did you?'

He shrugged. 'I guess I didn't think about it. She wanted to talk, so I went.'

I nodded. 'Just like she told you that you still like me, and you went with it.'

'What does *that* mean?' he snapped.

He looked pretty mad. I took a deep breath.

'It means, if Anna hadn't realised you still liked me, and broken up with you, would you have broken up with her? Would we be here now?'

He stopped looking at me, and looked down at the floor.

'I'm really not having a go. I'm asking a genuine question.'

Silence.

'The thing is, Leon... I'm sure about you. But I don't want to be with someone who isn't sure about me. I don't want to wonder if me and my boyfriend would even be together if the decision weren't made for him by someone else. I don't want to feel uncertain of his feelings. I don't want to doubt whether I can rely on him. I want to be with someone where I feel safe, and I can trust them, and talk to them about everything, or... I don't know. It just isn't worth it.'

He looked up at me then. 'How long have you been practising that?'

'About as long as you've been practising deflection.'

He smiled. 'Well, it sounds like you've got this all worked out, so.'

I so badly wanted him to contradict me. To prove me wrong. But he didn't.

'Bye, then,' I said.

'Bye,' he said, and stood there.

I turned away first. I could still feel him standing behind me as I walked down his garden path and along the road.

It was all very solemn and dignified, until, completely predictably, I stumbled on a bit of ice and reached out to steady myself, accidentally putting my hand on the tail of a cat on a nearby wall, who hissed and bit me.

Cats really are the worst. I'm glad I never became friends with Kayleigh Spencer.

I turned back, nursing my hand and hoping Leon had gone back inside. But nope. He was still there. Watching me go. The cat thing doesn't lessen my dignity in this situation, right?

posted by EditingEmma 14.17
Step Three of Being Brave: On My Way To Steph's House
Tralalala, lalalalalala. Trying to keep my spirits up on the way to my next stop. Because if this goes as badly as it did with Leon, I think I may as well just throw myself into a pile of snow and freeze to death in it.

This *has* to go OK. Things *have* to be OK with us.

posted by EditingEmma 14.35
Steph's House
Well, that was a fail. Jess answered the door and said Steph's been out all morning. Where on earth is she?! Surely she's not playing football in these Arctic temperatures?! Can you even kick a ball across snow?

'Thanks anyway,' I said to Jess.

'Sure,' she said. 'What happened to your nose, by the way? It's extraordinarily red.'

Going home, feeling lonely as Lonesome George.

posted by EditingEmma 15.21

My House

I got to my street, wondering how I could try to pass the rest of the day without crying, when there, in front of my house, I saw a black, high-heeled ankle boot sticking out into the snow.

I know that ankle boot.

'Steph?' I said, approaching the door. She was crouching on the step, hugging herself and shivering in her inappropriately thin winter jacket.

'You're here!' she yelped.

'Have you been waiting there all morning?!'

'Yes,' she said.

'Oh my God,' I said. 'That's beautiful.'

'Well,' she said, 'actually it was bloody freezing so your mum let me in and we had tea and watched *EastEnders*. But we kept an eye out for you, and when we saw you on the street I ran out to pretend I'd been waiting here all morning.'

'That's even more beautiful,' I said.

'Where have you been?!' she demanded.

'At yours,' I said.

'*Awwww*,' she said, 'we're like a really terrible rom-com.'

We laughed, and then an awkward silence fell.

'Emma, I'm so sorry,' she said.

'*You're* sorry?! I'm sorry!!!' I replied. 'I'm so so so so so so sorry.'

'I'm so so so so so so so SO sorry.'

'I'm really, very, incredibly, enormously, gargantuanly, whoppingly, elephantinely sorry.'

'I'M SORRY!' Steph shouted.

'What has *happened* with us?!' I asked.

'I don't know,' said Steph.

'I've wanted to say something for AGES. But then…'

'You didn't?'

I nodded.

'Me too,' said Steph.

'I think I just found it easier to ignore it,' I said. 'Because then I could sort of pretend I was OK and that was better than admitting it.'

Steph nodded vigorously. 'I didn't even tell Jess about it or anything. I just got all moody and acted out, and then pretended it was actually because she'd used my mug, or something.'

'I thought you didn't care if I was at your birthday!' I said.

'I thought you didn't care about being at my birthday!' she said.

'I got really paranoid you were replacing me with Andy!'

'I got really paranoid you were replacing me with Gracie and Charlie! … And Hannah Condom, of course, my biggest threat.'

I launched myself at her, toppling her over a bit, and buried myself in her Steph smell.

'I missed you,' I said.

'I missed you too.'

posted by EditingEmma 20.47

Still With Steph

Still with Steph, discussing how everything could have possibly gone so wrong and talking about how we're never, ever going to let it happen again.

'I'm sorry I didn't ask you why you went offline,' said Steph. 'I knew it must have been something bad and I just convinced myself you'd rather talk to Gracie about it.'

'Gracie really helped,' I said. 'But I wanted to talk to you too. I wanted you so so badly.' I nuzzled her jumper.

'I know, I'm sorry,' she said. 'I guess I just got all sensitive because you guys were clearly talking about stuff that I couldn't be involved in.'

I sighed. 'Look, it's just because…'

'I'm dating her brother, I know,' Steph said.

'You knew?!' I asked.

'Yeah, it was pretty obvious,' said Steph. 'And I guess…UGH, it's stupid…but I guess I felt kind of betrayed you didn't tell me. Which is stupid. Obviously Gracie is entitled to not want to speak to me about that, and you were just being a good friend. I'm sorry.'

My lip wobbled.

'I did want to tell you about it, but I couldn't,' I said.

'I know,' she said. 'I know. I was being unreasonable. And I'm sorry about the way I left you after that self-defence class.'

'Why did you?!' I asked. 'We were having fun!'

'Well, exactly,' said Steph. 'We were having so much fun and it was like everything was back to normal. Then Charlie phoned you and I didn't even know about him…and…I don't know. I've never *not* known things about you before.'

I nodded. That was exactly how I'd felt.

'And then I remembered that it wasn't even you who'd invited me. Your mum invited me.'

'Only because I thought you didn't want to speak to me!!'

'I know *now*, but in that moment I really felt like your mum had pushed me on you and you'd rather have been there with Charlie.'

'That's not true!'

'I just kept thinking about how many times you'd bailed on me.'

'I wanted to give you space!'

'Yes, but you didn't tell ME that. You just kept cancelling!'

'Oh God.' I put my head in my hands, thinking about how it must have looked. 'I'm such an idiot.'

'You gave me so much space, Emma. So much space you stopped telling me anything. And this absurd saga to find a new friend…I mean…You're allowed to make new friends, obvs.' She bit into a mini-bite. 'But you kind of made me feel like I'd moved to Australia!'

She sprayed chocolate bits all over my shirt and didn't notice in her normal, nonchalant way, and I didn't even care. I could have licked the little pieces of chocolate off me. She could literally have spat in my mouth and I'd have loved it.

'And when you weren't completely absent, you were crossing boundaries,' Steph added gently.

'Ughhh. I know,' I said. 'I find balance hard. I'm sorry I went through your messages.'

'I'm sorry I overreacted to it,' said Steph. 'It just felt like another thing that made us more distant. Like you couldn't just ask me.'

'I just…Ugh. It seems SO stupid now. But I got really scared you'd had sex and hadn't told me.'

Steph laughed.

'Which, anyway, is *completely* your prerogative!!' I said. 'That's personal. I mean, just because I share everything, doesn't mean you have to.'

'I...'

'And when we're older and you go to uni or get a job or whatever...I'm not going to know everything, am I?!' I said. 'Unless I literally move down the corridor.'

Thinking about it, that might not be such a bad idea.

'And when you like, maybe have some babies, I can't always be there...can I? Unless you give me a room in exchange for free babysitting.'

Again, another GREAT idea if I do say so myself...

'Emma, Emma.' Steph held up her hands. 'You know I'm seventeen, not *thirty*.'

'I know.' I breathed a sigh of relief, coming back a couple of decades.

'So back to being our actual age.' She chomped through more chocolate. 'I haven't had sex yet.'

'I knew it!!!' I yelled. 'HAHA, Gracie!!!'

Steph stared at me.

'Sorry,' I said. 'Please continue.'

'I'm not ready.' She shrugged. 'Andy's not ready. We're not ready. But I've been really, really wanting to talk to you about whether I might be.'

Relief flooded my veins. She *did* want to talk to me about it. She didn't have to, but she wanted to.

'What do you think?' I asked.

'I don't know. Maybe I'm approaching being on the verge of almost-ready. But then again…I'm in no rush,' she said.

'No,' I agreed. 'There is absolutely no rush to do ANY-THING EVER. In fact, I think you should just stay here on this sofa. I'll bring you all the snacks and love you could ever want. You'll start to smell but the only person who'll see you is me and I won't care. One day you'll want to leave but you'll have lost the use of your legs and you'll have no qualifications, and then you'll legit have to stay for ever.'

I hugged her.

'That sounds nice, Emma.' Steph patted me.

'Oh, but you might need to move for this,' I said, reaching in my pocket.

I brought out the tickets. FINALLY.

I watched her unwrap them, and seeing her face light up was the best thing in the whole, entire world.

'Oh my God!! But you hate football!!!' she screeched.

'But I love you,' I said.

'I love you too,' she said. And we stared at each other for a moment.

It was so, so nice to have Steph back. I don't think I even realized how truly miserable I've been. I mean, apart from all the whinging I did about it. But I mean the *truly* miserable feelings, as if something in your life is missing and empty. We spent the rest of the afternoon hugging and telling each other about all the things that have happened in the past few months, in the kind of absurd, minute detail that would drive Faith up the wall.

posted by EditingEmma 22.01

FFS

Charlie just rang me.

'Emma?' he said. His voice sounded kind of weird.

'What's up?' I asked.

'I, um, I just wanted to ring you because I thought you should know something.'

'...What?! What happened?' My heart started pounding.

'It's Leon. He's moving.'

'OK...' I said. 'Why did you want to tell me that?'

'I mean really moving,' he replied. 'Like, to Scotland.'

And then my heart stopped pounding. It slowed completely, to a dead stop.

'Emma?' Charlie said, but he sounded really hazy and far-away.

'Uhuh,' I said.

'Are you all right?'

'Why is he moving?' I squeaked.

'His mum got a research grant up there.'

I nodded slowly.

'Emma, are you still there?' said Charlie.

I nodded again.

'EMMA?!'

'Sorry, sorry,' I said. 'I forgot you can't see me nodding.'

'Are you OK?'

'I'm fine.' I cleared my throat. 'I already told him it wasn't going to happen anyway.'

'Yeah, that's kind of what I wanted to talk to you about.'

Charlie paused. 'He told me what you said. And um...Well. I just thought you should know, I think the reason he didn't fight you on it was because he's going away.'

'Oh,' I said.

'I just. ARGH. I've been in two minds about whether to tell you or not. Because he has been a total prick to you in the past, and to Anna. And to *me*. But I feel like he has genuinely been trying to change, and... Ugh, I don't want to defend him, but I kind of do. He knew he had to break up with Anna, she just got there first. He really messed up by missing your show, but he was just trying not to let history repeat itself and to treat her better than he treated you...'

I was still nodding along. I caught sight of myself in a mirror and I looked totally bonkers.

'...I just felt like you should have all the facts on this,' he finished. 'It felt kind of wrong, him leaving and you not knowing.'

I can't really remember how we ended the conversation, but somehow we'd hung up and I was on the other side of the room, lying on my bed.

This shouldn't make a difference. I'd already made my mind up.

But if it shouldn't make a difference, then how come I feel like the ground underneath my feet has suddenly disappeared?

Monday, 22 December

posted by EditingEmma 18.07
ORGASMO PARTY

I'm still feeling incredibly dazed and weird and like I have no idea what's going on right now. But I do not have time to think about this. Right this minute, I will not sit around thinking about what I may or may not be feeling about Leon. Because now, I must focus on throwing Faith her 'orgasmo' party. Steph and Gracie are here, setting up the games.

It turns out it's a lot harder to have a 'sexy themed' party than you might think.

'How do we make the party hats sexy?' asked Gracie.

'Um, draw little naked people on them?' I said.

'I'm not doing that.' She sniffed. 'You do it.'

'Give them here.'

I started to draw, but they just looked like weird stick people. Some with third legs. We all frowned at the hats.

'So sexy,' said Steph.

'All right, all right. Just leave them. There's no way of making party hats sexy anyway.'

'What about the cake?' asked Steph.

'Cake is always sexy.' I nodded.

'And *Articulate*?' Gracie asked. 'Are we only allowed to use dirty words?'

'Umm…yes.'

'And what about the pin the tail on the donkey?'

'Um. Don't use the donkey. Draw a naked person instead.'

'Not again!' whined Gracie.

'All right,' said Steph. 'So we've got some party hats with stick people on them, a pervy version of *Articulate*, and a *sexy cake* which, in actual fact, is just a regular cake.'

Silence.

'Yes,' I said. 'But we can all yell "ORGASMO" when she gets here.'

'Don't ever go into party planning, Emma,' said Steph, shaking her head.

Then the doorbell rang.

'Is that Faith?! We're not ready!!' Gracie looked around her in distress.

'It's as good as it's going to get, Gracie.' Steph patted her on the shoulder.

'It's not Faith,' I said, getting up.

When I swung open the door, I was greeted by a giant owl.

'I'm so glad you wrote me back,' said Holly, flapping her fake wings.

'Why are you dressed as an owl?' I asked.

'An owl is the ultimate enemy of the squirrel. Adam would go BESERK if he thought I was dressed as an owl. But I've chosen my side.' She rubbed her hands together.

'Right... Thanks. I think,' I said, wondering what I was letting myself in for.

When Holly came in, dressed as a giant owl, she looked around at all the sexy party stuff and said, 'You guys are strange.'

posted by EditingEmma 19.51

Faith arrived and we all lurked in the dark. As planned, we all yelled 'ORGASMO!!!' when she came in.

Not as planned, her father was actually dropping her off at the door.

'Er, I'll just, er...bye,' he said, and ran off down the driveway.

Now we're just lying around, chatting rubbish and shoving our faces full of sexy cake. When I stood up to get a drink, Faith looked at me and said, 'By the way, nice dress, Slag.'

I smiled and looked in the mirror. I'm so glad Mum got it out of the bin and kept it.

posted by EditingEmma 23.01
All Alone

Everyone just left. I'm having that kind of high you get after just sitting around laughing with your best mates for hours, and also still feeling like I'm flying through the clouds because me and Steph made up. I can still hardly believe it. As she was putting her shoes on, I was looking at her features, which seem like a face to me again now, and I reached out to touch her ear.

'What are you doing, weirdo,' she said, batting away my hand.

I could've cried with joy. You can only really insult the people you love the most to their face like that.

But I'm also feeling kind of weird and lonely, now. I tried desperately to get someone to stay over, but they all have to get up early in the morning. Faith has a family friends outing and Steph's going along to a Morton family thing with Gracie and Andy. Holly had 'business to attend to'.

Sigh.

Now I have to be alone and I'm definitely going to be thinking about the thing I was avoiding thinking about. But I think I've reached a conclusion.

My conclusion is…that I don't really have a conclusion. I'm not sure how I feel about this, but that's OK. I'm not going to know how I feel about it tonight. But what I do know is that he's leaving. Whatever I may or may not feel about Leon now, he's been a huge part of my life. And behind everything…I mean, behind all the hormones and horniness and confusion and messiness… Behind all that I do believe we have cared about each other. That we've been, dare I say it…friends. That's how we started, anyway. And I'm determined that whatever else is going on, that's how we're going to end.

> Hi, it's me. I just wanted to say that I know you weren't trying to hurt me and that I'm sorry things got messed up, and that there are no hard feelings here. I'll always be your friend. 22.40

He started typing something, then stopped, then started typing again.

You know, Emma, you don't have to say 'it's me' because my phone tells me it's you. 22.45

...It just felt more dramatic that way. 22.46

I'll always care about you too. Bye, Emma. x 22.49

Bye, Leon.

posted by EditingEmma 00.07
New Realizations and Resolutions

So, I've been thinking about everything I've learnt this term instead and, once again, redesigning my blog. Because it's been a bit of a roller coaster, and I think I'm in need of yet another fresh start.

There's SO MUCH to be happy about. I started out the term on the hunt to make new friends and, even though it didn't totally go to plan, I did make two new ones. OK, so, Charlie and Holly were sort of happy accidents and I may have made a few casual enemies along the way too...but I'm sure one day Anika Khatri will unblock me and Hannah Condom will get married, change her name and forget her grudge.

My friendship with Gracie is totally transformed and OK, so I may have had a huge fight with my best friend which was mainly my fault, but my heart was in the right place... And I actually think our friendship is going to be stronger for it.

And so I did get a little bit obsessed with my, erm, online presence. Which rapidly led me down rabbit holes of comparing myself to others and defining myself by what I'm uploading. But I've stopped that now, and lots of good stuff, like doing the fashion show, came out of this resolution too.

New Realizations

I stopped obsessing over boys and started focusing on myself, which would have been great, except I started focusing on my IMAGE which is categorically not the same as 'myself'. Obsessing over how many likes you're getting on things and how you're coming off on social media is really no more healthy than internet stalking. It's just internet stalking yourself.

Whilst I stopped comparing myself to Leon's girlfriend, I started comparing myself to everyone else on the planet. YOU CAN ONLY BE YOU. (Even if you haven't exactly worked out who that is, yet...)

Focusing on your friendships is amazing and worthwhile, but they cannot be the sum total of your existence either. Everything is a balance and getting it right can be really hard.

New Resolutions

1) Carry on focusing on my friendships but, like romantic-type-relationships, don't obsess over them either.

I will do this by:

A) Not internet stalking my friends if I miss them. I will make *actual* contact.

B) Accepting that my friends have other things going on in

their lives, too, and whilst expecting a decent amount of attention from them, I won't try to hog them unreasonably.

2) Continue to use my blog for self-expression, but don't become fixated on it or let it define me:

I will do this by:

A) Never again feeling bad about nasty comments left by sad people who have nothing better to do with their lives than try to bring other people down. And remembering that those people often have their own motives/reasons/circumstances making them do what they do, that aren't about you. And for every bad comment that I am focusing on, I will remember the TEN GOOD ONES that I am most definitely forgetting.

B) Trying not to forget the 'me-behind-the-blog', and making more time for that version of me.

C) Stopping comparing myself to other people PERIOD, and by remembering that everyone else has a themselves-behind-the-internet, too.

Once again, behold my new blog.

Acknowledgements

Thank you as always to my Mum, the Lorelai to my Rory, for everything you do.

Lots and lots of love to Nell, Catie, Sarah and Rachel whose friendship endures despite all our many 'fails' over the years.

Thank you to Patrick for being unwaveringly supportive as I continue to lock myself in my room writing and neglect housework. I don't know what I'd do without you (or your little hoover. But mainly you).

Thanks to Lauren Gardner for being a fab agent, pal, general babe and supplier of Chewits. (Eight months and I still haven't worked through that pile).

Thanks to Anna Baggaley for putting so much thought into this book - I will miss working with you – and to Hannah Smith for stepping in and being Superwoman in her absence! And a big thank you to the one and only Lucy Richardson for being a superstar publicist.

I'm also very grateful to the people I never get to meet, but who do so much work behind the scenes - Sandra, Anna, Kate, Steph and Aisling and to everyone else at HQ for continuing to cheer Emma on. The same goes for Tashya Wilson and the US team for doing brilliant things with Emma across the pond.

Massive shout out to the whole blogging community. One person who deserves a special mention is the lovely and awesome Jim Dean. (How many copies is it now?!) You're the best unofficial publicist a gal could ask for.

Also a big HEY to my fellow funny YA writers whose chats/drinks/tweets mean so much in the middle of the isolating writing process.

Last but not least, my cat Edie. You really are very fluffy.

ONE PLACE. MANY STORIES

Bold, innovative and
empowering publishing.

FOLLOW US ON:

@HQStories